THE GOLDEN AGE OF THE MISSISSIPPI
THE DAWN OF A BOLD NEW ERA

In the turbulent years before the Civil War, steamboats ruled the Mississippi—carrying the wealth of a nation along the great river at its heart. These mighty ships were the lifeblood of America, and the hopes and dreams of the people who rode them united North and South at a time when history was trying to tear them apart.

But many wished to see the Union torn apart. On both sides of the Mason-Dixon line, honorable patriots stood ready to die defending their way of life. And dishonorable profiteers called for war, seeking only to add to their political and financial prestige. America teetered on the brink of civil war, a giant powder keg waiting for a match to ignite the bloodshed. . . .

ASSASSINATION

Turn the page and meet the passengers and crew of the *Tempest Queen* . . .

All Aboard the *Tempest Queen!*

THE CAPTAIN: William Hamilton was a veteran of thirty years on the Mississippi—the mighty river flowed through his veins as sure as his own blood. But the time was near when he would sell his beloved *Tempest Queen.*

THE LANDOWNER: When he saved the ship from pirates, Clifton Stewart proved he was no longer the pampered, arrogant landowner's son who arrived on the *Queen.* But one thing would never change—his undying love for the beautiful mulatto chambermaid Mystie.

THE CANDIDATE: Stephen Douglas was an honest man, a politician sworn to serve his country rather than to profit personally. And he was the nation's only hope to prevent a bloody civil war. . . .

THE PLOTTER: Robert St. James believed in slavery and secession—he was a good Southerner. But he was an even better businessman, and the two had a way of conflicting. . . .

THE ASSASSIN: Genevieve St. James was beautiful, charming, and dignified. But underneath the polished exterior was a ruthless woman who would do *anything* to get what she wanted.

THE CHAMBERMAID: Mystie Waters knew she still had feelings for Clifton. But after what he had said to her on that fateful night, she didn't think she could ever forgive him. . . .

THE FIANCÉ: Barnabas Antone was captain of the *Guiding Star*. After that ship's horrible explosion, he was happy to ride the *Tempest Queen* up to Illinois with his bride-to-be, Mystie Waters.

THE FREEMAN: Zachary was one of the former slaves who worked below to keep the *Queen* running. The last thing he expected was to become friends with a former slave-owner.

THE DETECTIVE: Allan Gill had a habit of always being around when something dangerous was about to happen. And the plot he tracked aboard the *Queen* was as dangerous as they came. . . .

THE AGENT: Alex Strider was reliable—he could be trusted with money and didn't ask questions. And if people crossed him, he could take care of himself—and them—to his satisfaction. . . .

PRELUDE

She nuzzled deeper into his arms, listening to his even heartbeat, his contented breathing, feeling the warmth of his slightly moist body against her, his strong, smooth hand resting lightly upon the swell of her hip beneath the covers. They both smelled of lovemaking, and now, exhausted and satisfied, Genevieve St. James shut her eyes against Robert's chest. For a long while she drifted in and out of a restless slumber.

Beyond the closed window, Gen could hear the far-off hoot of an owl somewhere out among the oaks of Carleton Manor. The hour was early—how early, she did not know. Robert seemed to have fallen immediately asleep, but try as she might, the worries of the day yet to come kept her brain whirling.

How far she had come in so short a time! Last year it was billiard rooms, saloons, and wharf boats. Then Robert had come into her life and now all this: Carleton Manor, a house so large she still had not explored every nook and cranny . . . and more servants than she knew what to do with. It was all perfect except . . . Then she remembered, and a shiver went through her body. What Robert was planning was impossibly daring, and although it gave her pause, the sheer excitement of it was better than anything she and Banning had ever contrived back in the old days.

A chill wind through the leaky window stirred the chintz drapes. The low, full moon was bright in the sky. Its pallid light fell through the French doors and painted the room a ghostly gray, sketching the lines of her wardrobe and chiffonier where they sat in deep shadows. On the back of a chair by the bed was her crumpled dressing gown, exactly where Robert had flung it after tearing it off her in his passionate haste. In the moonlight it appeared to be an animal lurking, preparing to spring at them.

That was silly. Yet Gen remembered the fears she used to have as a little girl; the night monsters that shadows would conjure up from the grain of the woodwork or a lump of clothing cast carelessly aside or a hat left atop the chimney of a lamp . . .

A dog barked somewhere outside.

Gen stirred, no longer finding comfort in Robert's warm body. The coals still glowed in the fireplace and she considered rising.

"Can't sleep, Gen?"

His voice surprised her. "No," she said softly into his chest. "I thought you were asleep."

He gave a soft laugh that she heard rumble deep through

his body, but his eyes remained shut, his breathing calm, steady. "I have been thinking."

"About today?"

Robert opened one eye and looked at her. "That . . . and other things."

"Other things?"

"You are a superb lover, Gen."

"Oh." She poked him gently in the ribs. "Be serious, Robert."

He turned toward her. "I am."

"No. I mean about *today*."

"Today is going to be all right."

She was aware of his hand slipping slowly off her hip caressingly.

"How can you say that with such conviction?" she whispered.

"We have gone through it all—over and over again. Nothing will go wrong. Believe me, if I thought for one instant you might get hurt . . ." He didn't finish his sentence. He didn't have to. Gen knew how much Robert loved her.

"Yes, I know. But what if—? And this friend of yours, this Mr. Strider. How can you trust him with so much money?"

"Strider is a good fellow. He has done work for my father in the past. He's never let us down."

"Still, one hundred thousand dollars. . . ."

"Are you having second thoughts, Gen?"

"No, of course not." That wasn't quite true, of course. "I know what we are doing is necessary. But telling myself that doesn't make it any easier."

"I know. The part you have to play now is the most difficult of all, Gen. If there was any other way . . . but there isn't. Besides, it is not only for us. It is for the country. For the South!"

The South.

Gen felt a surge of pride that momentarily submerged her trepidations; the notion passed quickly. The South was one thing, but the fortune Robert intended to make off of her was something else entirely. Then Robert's hand began to roam. Teasing. She felt a delicious, intoxicating wave sweep over her.

"I know," she breathed, letting a soft moan of pleasure escape her lips.

Robert rolled over, smothering her again.

Emma pressed her ear against the door, listening to the sounds coming from beyond it, all the while keeping her eyes fixed upon the stairs at the far end of the hallway. When their talk ceased, her black brow wrinkled and a frown deepened upon her face.

Then she heard footsteps. Emma stepped back from the door an instant before Jackson's gray head appeared at the top of the stairs. He had come up them stooped over, and now he paused, straightening himself, tugging the ends of his short, black jacket back in place. Jackson was the oldest slave on Carleton Manor. He had been with Carleton St. James when the family patriarch had built the place in 1808.

Jackson spied Emma by the doorway and a faint scowl appeared, but it fled as he came toward her in an unhurried stroll, standing painfully erect, displaying with dignity his position above the other house slaves.

"Dey is awake, Jackson."

The tall, gaunt black man eyed the door.

Emma went on, "I's gonna draw de missus bath now." She started toward the stairs, then stopped and turned back and said sternly in a low voice. "Yo' don't go a knockin' upon dat door jes' yet, Jackson. Yo' gib dem two a few minutes, hear?"

Jackson nodded his head as if he understood the meaning behind that, and Emma hurried down the stairs. In the foyer she glanced quickly around. It was deserted at this early hour. Emma peeked into the ladies' parlor. None of the house servants were there, either. The furniture sat upon the stenciled carpet, gray in the faint light that filtered past the oak trees beyond the windows and through the curtains. She listened. Voices came from outside the house, from the kitchen out back. That was all. Emma wheeled abruptly on her heel and hurried through the dark gentlemen's parlor and across Robert St. James's study to where Jobie was asleep on a pad by the library fireplace.

"Jobie," she said shaking the boy awake. "Jobie, yo' wake up dis minute."

The boy blinked, then yawned and sat up, rubbing his eyes. "What is it, Mama?"

Emma hustled him to his feet, straightened his shirt around, and combed back his wiry hair with her fingers. "It is time, Jobie."

All at once the boy was wide awake.

She hustled him through the dark rooms. At the doorway to the foyer she stopped and peeked around to make sure all was clear, then hurried him out the front door. Outside on the dark portico, Emma dropped to one knee, leveling her eyes with the boy's while fussing with his tattered clothing and wrapping her shawl about his shoulders.

"Don't tarry none, 'cause yo' got t' be quick. An' beside, I's gonna be worryin' 'bout 'yo. Now yo' know what t' do?"

"Yes. I's t' go t' de Johnsons' place and talk t' a white man named All'n." His words were accompanied with white puffs of steam in the chilly predawn air.

"And what is it yo' are gonna say t' dis white man?"

"I's gonna tell him dat de missus is leavin' dis mornin'."

"Dat's right, honey." Emma gave the boy a hug and didn't try to hide her concern; it showed on her face and sounded in her tight, quick words. "Yo' be almighty careful, darlin'."

"I will."

"An' keep a eye out for dem pattyrollers, hear? An' don't let no one see yo'."

"Yes, Mama."

"Now, off wid yo'."

Jobie skipped down the dark steps to the broad, gravel driveway, gray beneath the waning moon. Emma watched him run off into the shadows of the oaks, and in a moment he was gone.

Shaking, Emma got control of herself. She had never before done anything against the St. James family in the twenty years she had been with them. But ever since that woman had come to live here . . . She calmed herself. Master Robert's business was none of hers, she reminded herself. Remembering her duties, she went back inside. Ruby was lighting the lamps with a long hickory wick when Emma came through the house.

"Mornin', Emma," the young Negro girl said.

"Where is Hilda and Hester?" Emma asked sharply.

"Out t' de kitchen." Ruby stretched for the chandelier and put the wick to only one of the lamps there.

Emma went down the corridor to the back door and out, taking the short stone path back to the brick building that was already bustling with Negro servants carrying out their predawn tasks. A steaming kettle on the huge hearth had turned the kitchen into a sweat house in spite of the morning chill. At the far end of the building two black women were starting the day's laundry. On this side a third woman was rolling out biscuit dough, and already had one batch put aside to rise. A fourth woman was tending the fire beneath the great kettle. Emma said, "It is time t' draw de missus bath. Hilda and Hester, come fetch de water upstairs."

The two laundresses abandoned their washboards, took up oak buckets, filled them from the kettle, and carried them into the house. Emma said to the cook, "De marster and his missus will be takin' breakfast early dis morning. See dat yo' got it ready."

"Don't yo' worry 'bout me, Emma. I will have it fixed fer dem on time."

Emma narrowed an eye at her, then went back inside the great house. She stepped aside as Hilda and Hester came hustling down the stairs, empty oaken buckets banging together. Emma climbed the stairs. Jackson was waiting patiently at the door. Emma went into the room next to the bed chamber and tested the water in the copper tub. Hester and Hilda came in with four more buckets of hot water, and then immediately went rushing back for more. In five minutes the tub was filled and Emma had tempered the bath with cold water and had stirred in the soap flakes and perfume.

Once everything was prepared to her satisfaction, Emma stuck her head out the door into the hallway and gave Jackson a nod.

The knock at the bedchamber door broke their embrace. Robert rolled to his side and said, "Yes?"

Gen squirmed beneath the sheets as the door opened and a wedge of yellow lamplight from the hallway slashed into the room. Jackson's tall silhouette stopped just inside the doorway.

"It is four-thirty, suh."

"Thank you, Jackson."

"Emma has got the missus bath drawn."

"Thank you, Jackson," Gen said.

"Anything else, suh?"

"No. I'll be out in a few minutes."

"Very well." Jackson closed the heavy door and the room was once again dark, except for the pale light of the colorless moon.

"I ought to go before the water cools. You know how fussy Emma is about that."

Robert drew her gently to himself, kissed her lightly upon the chin. "How shall I survive this next week until you return, my darling?"

Gen smiled and disengaged herself from his arms. "I am sure you will be just fine, my love. You have your friends, your whiskey, your club, your cards, and all those mysterious meetings that keep you awake into the early hours. I suspect you shan't miss me at all while I am away." Gen gave him a staged pout.

"None of those things will ever take your place."

She slipped out of the bed and in the shaft of moonlight paused and turned back. Gen knew Robert enjoyed seeing her this way: Tall, naked, young, and healthy. She gave him a parting smile that held promise, then took up her dressing gown, slowly slipped it over her shoulders, and passed through the doorway at the back of the room, into the chamber where Emma had her bath waiting.

The gray sky was filled with the sounds of birds awakening. The house and grounds were coming alive as well, with the bustle of black servants and the smell of cooking breakfast. Outside, smoking chimneys had left a dirty smudge above the house while inside, lamps were being extinguished and curtains and shutters were being opened. To the east, the sky looked as if someone had sprinkled pink rose petals across it. It promised to be a beautiful day. Still, Gen was not happy. She was saddened to be leaving, and she was worried as well. Gen could never remember being truly worried when Banning devised a scheme. But then, his schemes had never been as bold or as daring as Robert's. One of the slaves passed by her, carrying her luggage out to the waiting carriage.

Robert appeared at the door. He looked dashing, she thought, in his tall, black riding boots and his chestnut frock coat over the starched white shirt. She adjusted the shawl about her shoulders. He took her by the arm down the wide brick stairway out front of Carleton Manor. She was wearing a rust sateen traveling dress, trimmed in velvet, and shoes that took most of ten minutes for Emma to button up. What would she do, she wondered, without a servant along to tend to such things? In the few short months since she had come to Carleton Manor, she had grown dependent upon them. Who would have ever guessed she would have come to this? Well, she would just have to cope.

A Negro boy, perhaps no older than fifteen, was holding the horses.

Robert brought her around to the carriage step. "Now, promise me you will be careful," he said, staring deep into her eyes.

"I promise," Gen said softly, struggling for a smile. "I will be careful. In the meantime, my love, take good care of this." She removed the gold band from the finger of her left hand and placed it in his palm. His fingers folded, grasping it, and her hand with it. He kissed her discreetly upon the cheek. On the driver's seat, Jackson kept his eyes ahead, but the other servants were looking on curiously.

"I hope you have thought of a good story to tell them," she said softly, indicating the line of black faces up on the portico.

"I have. The same story you will use on your trip. You are merely visiting your sister in Alton," Robert said confidently, grinning. But she knew he was as concerned as she was. The grin was for her sake.

"My sister in Alton, hm? Certainly we could have come up with something more convincing than that."

"It is not important. They will believe anything you tell them." His hand dipped into his pocket and came up with a small, brown-paper packet. He pressed it quickly into her palm and she immediately put it into her reticule. "You know what to do with it?"

"Of course." Now it was her turn to sound confident. Gen stepped up into the carriage. "Until I return," she said, suddenly gay. She arranged her skirts and sat down. Robert stepped back and gave Jackson a nod. The old Negro got the horses moving and the carriage rattled away, down the long driveway.

As soon as the carriage passed under the stone arch at the end of the drive, the oak trees immediately engulfed the roadway, closing in on it, forming a tunnel of interlocking branches.

A figure emerged from the shadow of the trees lining the road and peered after the receding carriage. The man stepped back where his horse was tied. He lifted the young Negro boy off his saddle and set him on the ground.

"Dere she goes," Jobie said.

"Aye, there she goes, laddie. You did good, Jobie. Tell your mama I will not be forgetting this."

"Yes, suh. I will tell her."

The man mounted the horse and looked down at the boy. "Now, back with ye to the house, and be careful ye are not seen. Tell your mama I will do what I can to help her, but I canna promise anything. In the meantime, give her this." He reached into the pocket of his shabby coat and flipped a gold coin to the boy.

Jobie looked at it, hardly believing his eyes. "Yes, suh, thank you, suh."

The man turned his horse away, then looked back. "Now, be gone with ye."

Jobie ran off into the woods. When he had gone, the man urged his horse out onto the road, careful not to follow too closely, and as he rode he sang softly to himself:

> She sent him o the red gowd,
> Another o the white monie;
> She sent him a pistol for each hand,
> And bad him shoot when he gat free.

CHAPTER ONE

In the predawn chill, Captain William Hamilton climbed the stairs to the texas deck and lingered near the edge, viewing the dark river around him, the toes of his boots but a foot from the painted gingerbread scrollwork that encircled the deck. It has been said that a riverboat was nothing more than an engine on a raft with eleven thousand dollars worth of jigsaw work around it. Hamilton grinned at the thought. The *Tempest Queen* was considerably more than that to him.

He inhaled deeply at the night air. Looking aft, the waning moonlight danced off the wake of the *Tempest Queen*'s twin paddles as if some giant had cast out a million fragments of broken mirrors. Hypnotic, almost. He tugged thoughtfully at his gray, carefully trimmed imperial beard and then buttoned his blue wool coat against the chill. The *Tempest Queen* was running downriver under a full head of steam, and the wind up on the deck was brisk.

From his vantage point, Hamilton could not see the eight furnaces below, but he knew that Chief Mate Lansing would have them glowing cherry red, and the firemen would be heaving cordwood into them at a furious rate. It was necessary. When traveling downriver you had to keep ahead of the current or you would loose your rudder.

Ahead, the red, smoldering torch baskets cast their light on the black water unfolding before the bow. Here and there the lights of riverboats moving up the Mississippi glided past. Off to the larboard side of the boat Hamilton saw the single lamp of a raft. It seemed to be standing still as the *Tempest Queen* steamed past, but he knew it was moving along with the current at a good seven knots. Upon the dark levees, the cane planters were burning their great piles of bagasse, which smoldered for days, smoked as the devil's own hell, and smelled worse—even this far out in the middle of the river.

Far ahead, just coming into view around one dark bend in the river, were the lights of Baton Rouge, the *Tempest Queen*'s home port.

Captain Hamilton stepped away from the edge of the deck and continued on his way to the pilothouse. Overhead, the sparks from the two billowing chimneys were like Fourth of July fountains, lighting up the night sky. He went into the darkened pilothouse and closed the door behind him. There was a fire burning in the stove to keep the night chill at bay, and the little glass-walled room was comfortable.

"Good morning, Mr. Grimes."

"Morning, Captain," Absalom Grimes replied in an easy

voice. His fist gripped the tall helm, and his eyes remained focused on the black water unfolding ahead.

It had been over a year now, but still Hamilton would sometimes come up to the pilothouse expecting to find his old pilot, Patton Sinclair, behind the helm. But Sinclair was dead, murdered at the hands of river pirates. It hardly seemed a whole year could have passed, yet as he thought back on that ill-fated excursion up the muddy Missouri River, Hamilton found it difficult to reconstruct the events that led to Sinclair's murder.

"Baton Rouge ahead," the captain said.

"That she is."

Grimes was a good pilot. He knew the river as well as any man on the Mississippi, and he would be the first to boast that he could take a steamer from the Gulf clear up to Saint Louis in a fog bank with his eyes shut. All in all, Grimes was typical of the breed of men who plied their trade behind the helm of a riverboat. Hamilton had looked up Grimes after Sinclair's death. The two pilots had been long-time friends; they had been partners aboard the *G. W. Delany* for a season back in '57, and Grimes had spent a fair amount of time on the high bench in the *Tempest Queen*'s pilothouse riding the river between berths. At the time Hamilton found him, Grimes was between berths—which seemed to comprise much of that riverboat pilot's employment—and he agreed to take his friend's place at the helm of the *Tempest Queen,* and there he had been ever since.

"We should be pulling in ahead of schedule," Hamilton said, turning the enameled face of his silver watch to the moonlight coming through the wall of windows encircling him. The old captain looked out into the blackness where here and there pricks of lights marked the location of riverfront plantations or those infernal smoldering piles of the season's stalks. Somewhere nearby, his plantation used to sit, elegant and fashionable; an old house built at the end of the last century—but the fickle Mississippi had reclaimed the land one stormy night more than two decades ago. Hamilton's wife and children had perished in that single cataclysmic event as well. All that remained of the old place was a small plot of land high up on a hill, and someday—someday soon—Captain Hamilton was going to sell the *Tempest Queen* and build himself a modest retreat up on that hilltop.

He heaved in a sigh, let it out slowly. He was weary. It was time to hand over the reins of the *Tempest Queen* to a younger man. Or, as it more likely would turn out, to one of the many new corporations springing up and taking the boats out of private ownership. Hamilton shook his head. The river was changing, he thought wryly. Then he grinned. Change was the only predictable thing there was about the Mississippi.

"I'll leave the docking in your capable hands, Mr. Grimes. I shall be down on the main deck checking in with Mr. Seegar and Mr. Lansing, if you should need me." Hamilton knew it would be a frozen day in Hades when a riverboat pilot would admit to needing anybody's help, especially that of the boat's master.

Grimes grunted his reply as he kept his view ahead and reached for a bell cord overhead to signal the engine room that they were coming into port.

Hamilton went back out into the chill air and took the narrow stairway down to the hurricane deck. He was aware of the big packet altering her course, angling now to larboard, bucking the current as she left the center of the stream. Her paddles were thrashing the water, straining to line the *Tempest Queen* up with the approach Grimes would be taking. Overhead, the escape pipes were chuffing rhythmically, and beneath his feet, Hamilton felt the pulsing heartbeat of his boat's mighty steam engines as she drove on through the darkness.

He descended a ladder to the promenade that encircled the cabins on the boiler deck. As his feet touched the planks, the great bronze bell up on the hurricane deck pealed three times, its deep, mellow voice drifting far out over the river, summoning the leadsmen to their posts on the guards. In a few moments, the leadsmen began shouting out the river's depth to the pilot overhead.

"M-a-r-k three! M-a-r-k three! Quarter less three . . ."

Hamilton made his way forward to the formal stairway at the head of the promenade, then down to the main deck and through the shadowy shapes of fifty tons of farm implements, five hundred sacks of Northern potatoes, two hundred twenty-five barrels of Northern butter, and one hundred forty crates of Northern hams that they were hauling to Baton Rouge. It was the end of the cotton season and they had just completed a large trip of cotton up to the mouth of the Ohio River, and this, along with three thousand bales of cotton that they had collected on the way back downriver, was some of what they were bringing into port. There was more, of course, including hundreds of small parcels, all of which the clerk had properly recorded in his ledger.

The clerk!

Hamilton had almost forgotten! Belding had said that his mud clerk had put in his notice, and this would be his last trip. Hamilton made a mental note that he'd have to find a replacement mud clerk before they started down the river again.

The red glare from the open fireboxes danced among the cargo. The woodpile beneath the boiler deck was nearly spent, and the black firemen were working furiously at transferring what remained of it into the eight furnaces that fed steam to the two engines.

As Captain Hamilton made his way back to the furnaces, Chief Mate Lansing's voice sang out above the clangor of the firemen lobbing cordwood and the scratching of firebox rakes. "Put your backs to it, you sons of perdition! We're coming to port and Seegar is going to need all the pressure he can get to roll those paddles. Hump! Fill those fireboxes! Why, I've seen schoolgirls toss wood faster than this sorry lot. Hump! Hump! H-U-M-P!"

"Morning, Mr. Lansing."

The chief mate broke off his never-ceasing prattle and came about, his brow glistening with sweat from the heat of the furnaces in spite of the chill in the morning air. "Captain," he said briefly.

Hamilton glanced at the row of huffing men, stripped to the waist, sweating in the red glare of the roaring fires. Their sleek brown skin seemed to flow in the bloody light as massive muscles bulged and flexed. The men worked on tirelessly, like well-oiled machines, yet Hamilton knew the strain they were under. Lansing was a fair man, but a demanding taskmaster.

Of the twelve men working the furnaces, one stood out in stark contrast. Clifton Stewart was not nearly as tall as the other men and built along less bulky lines, but in the time that Hamilton had known him, he had seen an amazing change come over the man. Drawn out from a pampered past, Stewart's once-soft hands were now rock-hard, his slim chest and shoulders had swelled in the year and a half since he had come to work on the *Tempest Queen*. Now, like his comrades, beneath the flowing skin that streamed with sweat, strong muscles rolled and flexed. His naked chest showed the rugged landscape that heaving ten cords of firewood a day produces. His stomach was banded with muscles, like the steal hoops encircling an oaken keg.

Beyond these obvious physical changes, Hamilton had

been amazed by the other changes that had come over the once prissy, aloof man who had boarded the *Tempest Queen* as a pampered passenger, who had fallen in love with a chambermaid in a matter of a week, and had lost her in a moment because of a few foolish words. Stewart had grown as a man, and as a comrade he was unswerving. His dedication to the *Tempest Queen* was faultless.

He had remained aboard to take up one of the lowliest jobs on a steamboat in order to keep up his Quixotic search for his vanished Dulcinea, and other than this single reason for remaining aboard the *Tempest Queen,* one blatant fact separated him from the rest of the Negro firemen he worked with.

He was white.

At first, Hamilton had little regard for Clifton Stewart, but over the months, he had grown to respect this tenacious man.

"Mr. Lansing," Hamilton said, returning his attention to the chief mate, "once in port I want to off-load this agricultural cargo as quickly as we can. Everything but the cotton. Belding will be down shortly with the manifests. I have contracted to take on another large trip of cotton; thirty-five hundred bales, this time down to New Orleans, and I'd like to be loaded and on our way as soon as possible. I'm running a tight schedule, and we will be bringing some *special* passengers back on the return trip. We are scheduled into Memphis in twelve days with a one-day layover, and then up to Illinois."

"Thirty-five hundred added to what we already are carrying will just about take us to our limit, Captain."

"I am aware of this. If we need to, we will take a tow alongside. I would not be surprised to find additional cotton looking for a lift down to New Orleans. And there will be two thousand sacks of cottonseed as well."

Lansing whistled softly. "That will keep the boys hopping these next couple days."

Hamilton grinned. "It's the season, Mr. Lansing. It is what we are in business for. The rest of the year is the gravy. But this is the meat." He left his chief mate and dropped in on Seegar, but the chief engineer was occupied with his snorting, hissing engines and the insistent jangling of the signal bells from the pilothouse where Grimes was busy tucking the big riverboat into her berth.

Hamilton made his way through the boat and the growing gray mist of dawn. Up in the great, main cabin, less than a half dozen tables had been pushed into a line and set out for breakfast. Their passenger list was short, and everyone would be disembarking at Baton Rouge, anyway, but there were always those few who lingered. The tables were mainly meant for the officers and crew. Hamilton stopped by the galley for a cup of coffee and carried it up to the hurricane deck where now the misty dawn had spread across the river, and the busy Baton Rouge riverfront had emerged from the shroud of night. It was a lively place with twenty steamers lining her wharves and already an army of workers moving about, pushing crates, jockeying drays that were piled dangerously high with cotton. The wharf road was a solid wall of them, and more were waiting in lines along the lanes from the city down to the riverfront.

King cotton: the lifeblood of the South. Hamilton never ceased to marvel at the sight: the mountains gleaming white that suddenly grew here in the fall. All destined for Northern mills or the textile giants in Europe and England. And he was part of it.

The *Tempest Queen*'s steam whistle signaled the wharf of her final approach. Below, deckhands leaped to the guards, some with hawsers in hand, others with fenders to drop overboard as the big packet docked. They all knew their jobs, and they went about them with clockwork precision.

On shore, workers in the employ of the wharf master stood ready to receive the hawsers and to guide the *Tempest Queen* into her berth.

The boat stopped her paddles, and then they began wheeling in reverse, suspending her momentarily in the water until the river's current grabbed hold and eased her the rest of the way in. An instant before she contacted the wharf, fenders were tossed overboard and half a dozen men turned the hawsers about the pilings. She touched gently and pulled to a stop, straining the thick ropes.

The whole affair hardly rippled the coffee in Hamilton's cup where he stood up in front of the bronze bell at the head of the hurricane deck. Now that they were officially at port, he once again resumed command of his boat. The pilots would go ashore while the boat was being off-loaded. Their job was finished, their authority temporarily suspended. They had money, and they had prestige, and when in a port, riverboat pilots usually used both to their advantage.

Below, Lansing's rousters were busy manhandling the landing stage into place. Hamilton could hear the chief mate raging and railing at his workers. The roustabouts and firemen responded well to the chief's manner of running things. They respected him, and Lansing understood them. All in all, it was an equitable arrangement, Hamilton mused.

Hamilton went to his stateroom for the paperwork that had to be presented to the wharf master, and he was about to leave the *Tempest Queen* for the wharf boat where he would take care of it. Before he disembarked, he found Clifton Stewart on deck working with the other rousters and firemen to get the cargo off-loaded.

"Mr. Stewart, might I have a moment?"

Clifton set down the corner of a crate he was about to heft

onto his shoulder and dragged his dirty arm across his forehead, slinging the sweat aside. "Of course, Captain Hamilton. What is it?"

Hamilton stepped out of the way of the unloading, and Clifton took the opportunity to ladle up a drink of water from a keg nearby.

Hamilton said, "When Mr. Lansing gives you some moments to yourself, I would like you to come and see me."

Clifton grinned, the soot of his sweating face accentuating the lines that wrinkled at his eyes and the corners of his mouth. "When does Lansing ever give us time to ourselves except when we are ready to drop and have hardly the energy left to pull ourselves into our bunks?"

Hamilton grinned, for he understood the truth in that. "I'll see to Mr. Lansing. Meanwhile, you had better get back to work or he will be on *my* back."

Stewart went back to the gang of deckhands working to clear the deck for the cotton waiting on the wharf to come aboard. Hamilton sought out Lansing and found him at the bow, overseeing a group of sweating Negroes maneuvering part of a gin toward the landing stage.

"Captain?" Lansing said when Hamilton drew up at his side.

"Looks like you are progressing splendidly, Mr. Lansing."

"You keep these boys in line and they'll do a decent task of work, Cap—Here now, easy on that end boys, you're not hauling bricks, you know! Don't stumble about it like a bevy of clumsy women! It's a gin, mind you, and if you break it, it'll come out of your pay!—Yep, keep them in line, Captain, and they'll work for you. Take your eyes off of them one minute, though, and they go to sucking their fingers."

"I can't think of anyone more qualified to keep them in line, Mr. Lansing."

Lansing dove in and got the wheels on the gin straightened. When he came back to his place on the bow, Captain Hamilton said, "When you can spare him, I want you to send Mr. Stewart up to my stateroom. I'll be off the boat for a couple hours, so sometime this afternoon will be fine."

"Stewart? Right, I'll send him up to you lat—*Hold up!* Don't you women see what your doing there? She's about to topple over now!" The Negroes scrambled around to the other side and pushed the gin straight. Lansing plunged in and grabbed up a pole to lever the gin straight again.

Hamilton left him with the deckhands and made his way down to the wharf, then along it a quarter mile to where the wharf boat was moored, and took the bridge out to it to see to the business end of running a steamboat.

CHAPTER TWO

"Lemme hep you hef dat keg onto yo' shoulder bone, Mr. Cliff," the big fireman said, halting his own work to give Stewart a hand settling the awkward oaken cask onto his shoulder.

"Thank you, Zachary," Stewart said, shifting under the weight to balance it. His body ached, but no more so than any of the other two dozen men hauling the cargo down to waiting drays on the wharf. They just seemed to handle the pain better than he did. The deckhands, firemen, and stevedores were powerful men, some having grown up under the overseer's whip, hauling cotton bales and sugar sacks, and they plugged away at the task that Chief Mate Edward Lansing had given them without complaint.

But Clifton Stewart was still new to this way of life, and although a demanding year and a half was now behind him and he could almost work alongside the best of them, he still faltered beneath the heavier loads. He had learned all too well what it felt like to go to bed bone-sore and exhausted, and to sleep like the dead until shaken awake for his work shift.

Stewart staggered into the line; a steady procession of sweating sable backs tramping down the landing stage like a trail of black ants, and like ants, they all seemed to be carrying burdens too great for them. Just the same, they worked without complaint, chanting a happy song in time to the bounce of the gangplank. They called it *coonjine,* and it did seem to make the work go easier.

Oh, I thought I heard the Kate Adams *when she blowed,*
She blowed jes' lak she ain't goin' to blow no mo'.
The reason that I lak the Kate Adams *so,*
She carries a chambermaid an' a watch below.
Come on boys with yo' neck out long,
Show me what shoulder you want it on.

Stewart hauled the cask down to a waiting dray, heaved it off his shoulder, and muscled it in place alongside the others. Then it was back up to the deck of the *Tempest Queen* for another one.

Zachary stuck near him and gave him a hand with the next keg. Stewart had worked alongside Zachary ever since Captain Hamilton had given him a job aboard the riverboat. To Stewart's complete amazement, there had developed a bond between the colored fireman and himself that he did not fully understand. The only thing they had in common, other than their present jobs, was that once, a long time ago, Zachary had been a slave on a plantation, and once, not so long ago, Stewart—or at least his father—had owned slaves on a plantation. But Stewart had left all that behind.

He tried not to think of the tall, Ionic columned house with its whitewashed brick facade and neatly trimmed grounds, or of the army of black slaves that tended the place inside and out and worked the sugar and cotton crops. He particularly tried not to think of his mother and father. He had not seen them, had not even written them, since that spring day when he had confessed his love for Mystie Waters, a beautiful mulatto chambermaid. His father had driven him from the house and told him not to return until he came back to his senses. So far, his senses had remained as elusive as the beautiful woman that he had sought in every port along the Mississippi River where the *Tempest Queen* had landed. In spite of his failure to find her, he was certain Mystie was still on the river somewhere, working on a steamer, he suspected, much as she had been on the *Tempest Queen* when he had met her.

Stewart tipped the cask off his shoulder and with a grunt, shoved it up snug against the one that the man ahead of him had left off. He slung the sweat from his eyes and started back toward the landing stage when a tug at his arm pulled him aside.

"Zachary? What is it?"

Zachary pulled Clifton Stewart around behind a cotton dray, out of sight from Lansing, who was still aboard the *Tempest Queen*, barking his sharp commands. Stewart could hear him, although not so clearly now above the workers' coonjine.

"What is it?" he asked again.

Zachary's eyes rounded and he glanced furtively from side to side. Clifton could see that Zachary was scheming again, a bothersome quality that kept him forever the object of Lansing's wrath. His view came back to Stewart. "A nigger jes' whisper to me dat dere is a cockfight over yonder. I got me two nickel in my pocket—"

"You can't just sneak away like this," Stewart said emphatically, hoping to keep his friend out of the trouble he knew would crash down upon Zachary if Lansing should discover him missing.

"I can double my nickel if'n I only git a chance to put 'em on one of dem scrappy roosters."

"Lansing will have your hide!"

"Fiddle! Him talk loud, but him don't hurt him niggers none. Anyway, I freeman. Me old marster, him say so in de will paper him write down afore him die."

"Perhaps Lansing won't take a lash to your back, Zachary, but he'll work twenty pounds off your ornery black hide—and mine, too, if he finds me gone!"

"No matter. I gonna try dem birds, anyway. You comin' along, Mr. Cliff?"

Stewart shook his head.

"Den I am goin' alone." Zachary started off through the maze of cotton-baled piles mountain high and waiting to be put aboard the *Tempest Queen*. He was a headstrong man, and no man could ever turn him aside from his goal once his mind was made up. Zachary stood six feet seven inches tall, with shoulders wide as a singletree and arm and back muscles like the knots the boatmen tie in the huge hawsers that hold mighty ships to their pilings. His tan canvas pants were frayed at the cuffs, held up at his narrow waist by a piece of rope. He wore a pair of tattered boots with no laces or stockings, and that was all.

Stewart watched his friend lumber away in search of the cockfight. Zachary turned his huge shoulders sideways to pass between two closely parked drays, and then he was gone.

Stewart grimaced, shaking his head. He knew that what he was about to do was going to get them both in trouble with Lansing, but maybe, just maybe he could talk some sense into his friend.

"Zachary! Hold up there."

Zachary drew up and looked back. Stewart came through the maze of drays and said, "I'll give you two nickels right here and now if you come back with me and forget this foolishness."

"Shucks, Mr. Cliff, I don' want yo' to give me no nickel." He sounded offended. "I win me own nickel."

Stewart frowned. "I didn't think it would work, but it was worth a try. I best come along to keep you out of trouble."

"Zachary can take care of his own self."

"Yes, well, I think I'll tag along just the same."

Zachary grinned and said, "We have us a fine ol' time, Mr. Cliff!" Zachary went off, sniffing around for the cockfight. He found it down at the end of the wharf behind a warehouse. A dozen Negroes were circled around a flurry of dust and feathers, cheering, rooting, and booing as the birds tore at each other with claws and beaks.

The fight, it appeared to Stewart as he looked around, had been organized by two white men in rumpled gray frock coats, wrinkled trousers, and dirty cravats. There were four wooden cages piled nearby; two contained birds that looked every bit as disheveled as their owners. Amid the squawking and slashing and blood and feathers, one of the white men was mingling among the Negroes, puffing on a cigar, collecting the pennies and nickels that the black men were freely handing over.

"Next fight, Old Red takes on Black Andy. Three to one on Black Andy," the man was chanting, collecting the money and making marks on a piece of paper as he did so.

Zachary shot an arm in the air. "Two nickel on Black Andy!"

The man came over and took Zachary's money. "Ten cents on Black Andy," he said around the cigar in his mouth, scribbling. "What's your name, boy?"

"Zachary, suh."

The man wrote the name. He glanced up at Stewart and his view narrowed a bit, suspiciously. "Care to place a bet, mister?"

Stewart shook his head. "No, I don't think so." He was about to tell the fellow that a fool and his money were quickly parted, but thought better of it. Such an adage would not have been appreciated here. Just the same, Stewart disapproved of gambling, except for the civilized wagers men of breeding place on horses of breeding. He wished he could persuade his friend to forget this, but Zachary's eyes were round and glistening, his grin a mile wide. He was a determined man.

The barker moved on, calling out the names of the birds and the odds in the upcoming fight.

"Why not yo' put a nickel on dem birds, Mr. Cliff?"

"I do not wager on cockfights, Zachary," Stewart said impatiently. He was worried that Lansing had already discovered them missing. Although Stewart did not personally know these two men who were staging the fight, he did recognize a quality in them that he knew well in another man of his acquaintance, Dexter McKay. It was the easy spiel that instantly put Stewart on guard. Obviously, these fights were being staged for the benefit of the colored dock workers. It was just as obvious that their intentions were to fleece their victims of their pocket cash.

In an explosion of feathers and dust, one of the cocks leaped on the back of its opponent and pecked a bloody hole in the back of its head. The unfortunate bird squawked and scrambled out from beneath the deadly attack, ran in a blind circle that made the men leap back, and with a shudder, dropped over, kicked its legs three times and died.

There was a roar of laughter. The white man gathered up the victor, shoved him unceremoniously back in a crate, kicked the loser aside, and went around passing out the winnings. Stewart noted that of the dozen or so men present, only two collected any money.

Some of the Negroes complained, but the man with the list of winners said, "I got it all wrote down here. Any man can check it," and he held out the paper. There wasn't a black man among them who could read, and apparently that was what the white man was counting on. "Now, cheer up, boys, there is still another fight coming. You'll do splendidly if you put your money on old Black Andy. He's a real firecracker of a scrapper. Never been defeated in twenty-three fights. Now, ante up, boys!"

The mumbling receded as hands dug deeper into pockets and came up with an extra penny or two to wager. While the one man collected their money, the other poked at the roosters through the bars with a stick, antagonizing them and getting them into a combative mood.

Finally they were ready to begin the next match. Both men took a bird in hand, held them in place facing one another, and then let go, jumping back out of the way.

The two birds clashed like a pair of locomotives on the same track. Amid the squawking and exploding feathers, they tumbled across the ground, half obscured by the cloud of dust that their flapping wings boiled up beneath them. Old Red was on top, then Black Andy. Back and forth they went, claws digging viciously, beaks hammering away at eyes and skull. Of the two, Old Red seemed quicker on his feet.

The Negro spectators were as a single voice rooting Black Andy on, but the favored bird appeared to have trouble right from the start, and as the fight progressed, the three-to-one hero was making a mighty poor showing. He seemed sluggish, unable to dodge and swerve and leap as deftly as Old Red. Stewart could see concern filling Zachary's narrowed eyes as the battle progressed, and Black

Andy faltered. It was soon apparent to Stewart there could be only one outcome to this match.

The champion of twenty-three fights was driven into the dust. Old Red pounced upon him, pinning him beneath his strong talons. A half dozen quick thrusts, and it was over. Old Red flapped his wings, strutted a circle around the fallen rooster, crowing and jabbing his bloody beak into the dirt.

"Well, now, don't that beat all," one of the shabby orchestraters of the battle said, gathering up Old Red. "Looks like the underdog whupped that strutter real good." He laughed, shoved the bird into its crate, and then eyed the list of names he'd recorded, grinning. "Looks like we was all made humble this time, boys. Not a one of you put your money on Old Red. Ha! Reckon that will learn us a thing or two, heh? Never can tell what's likely to happen in the cocking main." He shoved the crumpled paper into a pocket and said, "Give these two winners a spell to ketch their breath, and we'll let 'em have a go at each other. Any man here want to put his money down?"

Stewart figured there wasn't a nickel left between them all because they just wagged their heads, dejected, and began to drift off.

"We better get back to work, Zachary."

"I done lose all my money, Mr. Cliff."

"Consider it well spent on furthering your education."

Zachary looked at him, vaguely confused.

"Come on, let's get out of here." Stewart started back to the *Tempest Queen,* but Zachary remained standing there, staring at the rumpled, bloodied carcass of Black Andy. It was already beginning to draw a fair number of flies.

"Zachary?"

The big fireman hunkered down and after frowning a moment at the dead bird, began to poke at it with his finger.

Stewart came back. "What are you doing there?"

The swindlers were gathering up their crates, preparing to move on to mine new territory, no doubt, Stewart mused. He dismissed them and hunkered down next to Zachary. "Leave that bloody thing alone."

"Mr. Cliff," Zachary said, keeping his voice low, "I do not know how dey did it, but dey done cheated us niggers."

"No doubt you are correct. There is an old saying, Zachary, 'Live and learn.' "

"I do not want to be cheated."

"No one does, but you can't prove a thing, Zachary, and if you accuse them, all you'll do is make trouble for yourself. Come on, let's get back to the boat before Lansing adds to your list of woes. Now, stop jabbing at that dead thing."

Zachary picked up Black Andy, turned him over, and his scowl deepened. He wrapped one of his huge hands about the bird's abdomen and to Stewart's dismay, began squeezing it.

"Don't do that, Zachary! It is disgusting!"

The fireman continued squeezing the dead bird, pulling at it like it was a cow's teat. His persistence attracted the attention of the white men who put down the crates and wandered over, peering curiously past the fresh cigars in their mouths.

"Here, now, what's that nigger doing? What's that you're doing to that dead bird, boy? Stop that now, and leave it be."

Zachary continued, getting more excited as the moments passed.

"I said stop that, boy!" one of the white men said, suddenly angry.

At that moment, Zachary's efforts were rewarded, and a round, gray bullet popped out of the bird, landing with a thump on the ground. He picked it up, looked at it, then turned his eyes to the two white faces glaring down at him. Zachary pulled at the bird again, and this time six more lead bullets plopped to the ground. He dropped Black Andy, gathered up the bullets, and stood, towering over the two white men a good six inches.

"I figured dat ol' bird was a might slow. Now I knows why. Yo' done slugged him. Yo' cheated me an' I wants my money back."

"Sure, we cheated you, you big, thick-headed nigger," one of them said, coming forward boldly. "We cheated you real good, you and all your nigger partners, and now what are you gonna do about it?"

Zachary's fist balled into a knot the size of a melon. The man saw that and grinned, taking the cigar from his lips. "Go ahead, hit me. You know what they do to a nigger who hits a white man? They'll buck you and whip you 'til your hide peels . . . if you're lucky. If you ain't lucky, they'll stretch your worthless neck on a wet rope. Go on, take your best shot." He thrust out his chin, tempting Zachary.

Zachary hauled back. Stewart caught his arm and said, "He's right. A colored man striking a white man can be mighty unhealthy here in Baton Rouge. It isn't worth it."

Zachary hesitated, and Stewart felt the big man quaking, dearly wanting nothing more than to drive his massive fist into that taunting white face.

"But him cheated we nigger folks. Him deserves to have him white nose bloodied."

"That he does, Zachary, but you can't be the one to do it, not without making more trouble for yourself than it is worth."

The white man laughed, worked up a wad of saliva in his cheek, and spat it out onto Zachary's worn boot where his big toe was poking through. "That's right, boy. There ain't a damned thing you can do to me—"

Stewart's fist shot out in a long, sweeping blow that lifted the sneering man off his heels and cartwheeled him backward onto the ground where he landed like a sack of potatoes, stunned. Clifton moved in swinging, remembering the advice that his friend, Dexter McKay, had given him about dealings that concerned knuckles and brawn. Without breaking stride, his other fist drove up short, finding soft muscle just below the second man's rib cage.

The swindler buckled.

Swinging up again, Stewart caught him on the point of the jaw, which arched him backward, and the next instant he was sprawled out on the ground next to his partner. A year and a half ago it would have been even money that Stewart would have been the one sucking up the dust, but eighteen months of hard living on the river had worked its ways on the once-pampered planter.

"Perhaps Zachary cannot do anything about it, mister, but I can."

Stewart stepped over them, dug the coins from their pockets, and dropped them into Zachary's hand.

"You two gather up your gear and get out of here. Zachary here will see to it that your ill-gained winnings are returned to their rightful owners. Now, get moving."

Groaning and spitting blood, they picked themselves up, muttering vague threats, and scurried away leaving their roosters and cages behind.

When they had gone, Zachary said, "I surely did ache to do dat, Mr. Cliff." He flexed his fist as if vicariously delighting in the sting of the punches that Stewart had thrown in his behalf. "But dey would stretch me neck for certain if'n I done it."

Stewart grinned. He was a little weak in the knees now that it was over, but it was a good feeling, just the same. "Perhaps *now* we can get back to work, and pray that Lansing has not discovered us missing."

"I tink we better do dat, Mr. Cliff."

They started back through the maze of waiting drays and the mountains of cotton bales, Zachary passing out coins to the black men who had seen what had happened and had now come out to slap their backs and tip their tattered hats. Back at the *Tempest Queen,* Stewart and Zachary slipped into the moving line of sweating workers and made their way up the landing stage.

"Mr. Stewart! Zachary!" Chief Mate Edward Lansing's voice lashed out at them with the suddenness of a striking snake when they tramped aboard. Stewart drew up, gave Zachary a wan glance, and looked over at the scowling first mate.

Lansing planted his fists on his hips, glowering. "Well, well, the two of you. We have decided to finally come back to work, have we?"

"I can explain—" Stewart started, but Lansing cut him off.

"I don't want to hear your explanations, Stewart. You have been a sluggard since the day the captain took you on. You always did figure yourself too good to put in a fair day's work for a fair day's pay. I half expected you to sneak off, but Zachary here, well that's another story."

Lansing directed his attention to the black man. "You are picking up some bad habits from your friend, I'm afraid, and I reckon it is time I break you of them . . . both of you. It's double duty for the two of you until we are under steam again.

"Yes, sir," Zachary said, lowering his eyes, not returning Lansing's fiery gaze.

"Now, hop to it! Get this cargo off-loaded, and let's get that cotton on board!"

Stewart turned to leave with Zachary, but Lansing stopped him. "Not so fast, Mr. Stewart."

He wheeled back as Zachary hurried away, out of range of Lansing's guns.

"I intend to work you harder than I do any of these

coloreds, Mr. Stewart. I have been patient with you, I even deceived myself into thinking there was an improvement in you, but now I see I was wrong. I've given you hell, and still you remain aboard. I know you are pining away over that gal that used to work for us, but I have had it with you. You are an arrogant aristocrat, or so you fancy yourself because your daddy owns land and slaves, but aboard the *Tempest Queen* you are no better than the niggers you work beside, and I intend to either break you or drive you off. One or the other, it don't matter to me."

Stewart drew himself up straight, and the hairs lifted off the back of his neck. Where Zachary had feared to look Lansing in the eye, Stewart had no such problems. "You may try to break me, sir, or drive me off, but I intend to stay on until I find Mystie. I will not be forced off this boat one minute before I am ready to leave."

Lansing grinned, as if relishing this challenge.

"Is that all, Mr. Lansing? If so, I shall return to work."

"Is that all?" Lansing gave a short laugh. "My boy, it is only the beginning. But before you get back to work, the captain left word that he wants to see you up in his cabin."

"Do you know what about?"

"Don't ask me what it is about. He don't confide in me. Just be off with you and see to his bidding. Then I want you back here, and don't expect to get any sleep these next couple days."

Lansing wheeled about on his heel. Stewart watched the chief mate bound down the landing stage to oversee the progress his men were making.

Frowning and wondering what Hamilton wanted with him, he turned toward the wide stairway and headed for the captain's stateroom.

CHAPTER THREE

Clifton Stewart made his way up to the boiler deck and took a ladder to the hurricane deck. His fist still stung from his encounter with the two swindlers down on the wharf as he neared the texas, where Captain Hamilton's stateroom was, and he suddenly realized he was thinking about his friend, Dexter McKay. It occurred to him that he hadn't seen McKay since the day before, nor had he seen him disembark after they had put into dock. Stewart wondered briefly if McKay was still aboard. It was very unlikely, he mused, knowing McKay. Whenever the *Tempest Queen* put into a port, the gambler was always first man off in search of a game, his ebony walking stick in his gloved hand, a deck of cards in his vest pocket, and his special dice. . . .

Stewart paused and grinned to himself. How ironic that recalling those two swindlers had so easily brought Dexter McKay to mind. He continued on his way, putting thoughts of his gambler friend aside and turning instead to wondering what it was Captain Hamilton wanted to see him about.

He mounted the texas deck and went forward to Hamilton's stateroom at its head, near the two black chimneys that soared skyward. If they had been under steam, those two stacks would be billowing massive gray clouds, but just now they were emitting only a fine, smoky veil, nearly invisible. The chief engineer, Barney Seegar, always kept some pressure in the tanks while in port, to turn the compressors and pumps and to keep heat flowing to the radiators this time of the year. It was late in the season, nearly November, and although the days were pleasant enough, the night brought on a chill; the *Tempest Queen* was one of the few packets on the river that kept her staterooms heated.

On Hamilton's porch, Stewart lifted his knuckles to the door, then stopped, his eye drawn to a flash of red and green and purple. The bird flickered overhead and landed on the bronze bell out on the very end of the texas. Stewart moved to the porch railing, his brain automatically ticking down a list, finally coming up with a name. Painted bunting. *Passerina ciris.* It was a male of the species, and its plumage was striking. Stewart forgot Hamilton's summons and stood there entranced, watching the little bird flit to the bell cord, then begin to preen itself. Suddenly he was wishing that Mystie could be here with him. It was in Vicksburg, he remembered, a beautiful spring day more than a year and a half ago, that he had discovered that she was, like himself, an amateur ornithologist. Thinking back on it now, Stewart knew it was at that moment that he had fallen hopelessly in love with her.

He drew in a breath, and a great sadness swept over him.

He would give everything he owned—which at the moment was not a whole lot—to have Mystie Waters at his side again, to see her wonderful smile, to hear her sweet voice.

Passerina ciris! No doubt she would have come up with the scientific name before he had. He remembered that afternoon clearly, and how he had marveled at her tremendous knowledge of birds, and their Latin names that fairly flew from her tongue as they had strolled along.

The door opened behind him. The painted bunting flitted away at the sound of it. The vision of that happy afternoon faded back into his memory.

"Mr. Stewart?"

Slowly he turned back. Captain Hamilton was standing in the doorway, watching him curiously.

"Are you all right, Mr. Stewart?"

He blinked and came out of his trance. "Yes, Captain. I am quite all right, thank you. Mr. Lansing tells me you wish to see me?"

"Come on inside." Hamilton stepped aside for him. "Have a seat," he said indicating a chair near his desk, and closing the door. The room was compact, efficient, comfortable. A stenciled burlap carpet was tacked to the floor. A coat tree stood near the window where Hamilton's blue jacket and gold-braided cap presently resided. The captain's bed was pushed up against one wall, his desk against the other. A wardrobe stood near the bed, and on the wall opposite the door, next to the desk, was a second door, presently shut, that opened onto the texas passageway where the *Tempest Queen*'s officers and crew lived.

Upon the disordered desk was an ancient brass picture frame, green from age. It held a fading daguerreotype of a beautiful woman, Hamilton's wife Cynthia, long dead. Folded among the clutter of the desk was a newspaper that Hamilton had apparently been reading. Its ominous headline was visible: "South Carolina Vows Secession if Lincoln Elected!"

Stewart sat straight and uncomfortably in the chair as Hamilton settled himself at his desk and shuffled papers aside as if looking for something. He found an envelope from which he extracted a letter and silently read it at arm's length.

Stewart grew apprehensive. What did this letter have to do with him?

Hamilton finally folded it and returned it to the envelope without explanation. "I must admit, you have surprised me, Mr. Stewart."

"I have?"

"When I first took you on as a member of this crew, I never expected you to stay as long as you have. I knew your reasons, of course. Noble as they were, I thought them a passing thing, and that in a month or two you would tire of your quest, return home, patch up your differences with your family, and carry on with your life."

Stewart grimaced. He could think of nothing to say to that.

"I told you then that I had no positions open aboard the *Tempest Queen* but that I could find work for you somewhere, and sent you on down to see Mr. Lansing."

"Yes, you took me on as a fireman."

Hamilton frowned, his bright blue eyes beneath thick, gray eyebrows studying the young man. "To be perfectly honest with you, Mr. Stewart, I did not much like you when you first came aboard. You were an arrogant cuss. Too pampered for your own good. I think I gave you the job as a fireman just to satisfy some perverse reasons of my own. Perhaps it was my way of teaching you the lessons I figured you needed to learn."

Stewart frowned and said, "The job didn't matter to me,

Captain. All that was important at the time was that it gave me the chance to remain upon the river, and to seek out Mystie. I appreciated whatever you could give me."

"Yes, Mystie Waters." He closed his eyes a moment as if remembering. "She was an odd sort, very pretty, very serious, if I recall."

"She was perfect."

"Hmm." Hamilton narrowed his view at Stewart, then grinned suddenly. "I can see now that you truly did love her."

"I have given up everything for Mystie."

"Indeed, you have. Yet in all this time you have not found her, have not even uncovered a trace of evidence that says she is still on the river."

"I did leave a letter with her parents in Cairo last year."

"But it has come to nothing. She has not tried to contact you—"

"I . . . I said some things back then, which I truly regret. I was wrong . . . about a lot of things, Captain. I see that now. But surely you didn't call me up here to dredge up the past."

"No, of course not. All this is leading up to something." He paused, then, "I wish to know what your intentions are now."

"My intentions? They have not changed."

"Then you aim to remain aboard the *Tempest Queen* until you find Mystie Waters again?"

"Yes, I do."

Hamilton pulled thoughtfully at his white beard, then tapped the envelope upon his open palm and said, "It is true that in the beginning I did not like you, Mr. Stewart, but as the months have come and gone, you have changed, and perhaps so have I. In all honesty, I have become quite fond of you. You have proven yourself on more than one occasion to be a loyal member of this crew. In fact, I think it is safe to say that this boat would not be here today if it was not for your loyalty and bravery—"

"You mean that affair on the Missouri River last year?"

"Precisely."

"I only did what any other crew member would have."

"Regardless, you have come a long way, Mr. Stewart, and now there is a position coming open, and I am offering it to you first, before I advertise it."

Stewart straightened up in his chair. "A job?"

"Mr. Belding's mud clerk is leaving, and if you want it, his position is yours."

"Me? Mud clerk?"

"I know it is not much, but it is better than the position you currently hold."

"I will take it!"

Hamilton smiled. "I thought you might."

"Thank you, sir!" Stewart was exuberant. To be out of the dark belly of the boat where the furnaces turned day and night into a continual hell, and to be out from under Lansing's demanding thumb, was like seeing sunshine finally through black storm clouds.

"I will tell Mr. Lansing that he will have to fill your position. In the meantime," Hamilton eyed Stewart critically, "you will need new clothes, and please pay a visit to the barber as well. I like my officers well groomed."

"Yes, sir. I will at once!"

Hamilton removed a pouch of coins from the drawer of his desk and spilled them into his palm. Counting through them, he pinched six gold pieces between his thumb and forefinger and handed them to Stewart. "Here is an advance on your pay. Use it to renew your wardrobe. Take the rest of the afternoon off. In the morning, report to Mr. Belding."

"Yes sir, thank you, sir." Stewart stood.

Hamilton returned the money pouch to the desk drawer and said, "Baton Rouge is where your home is, is it not?"

"It is."

"After you have purchased your new attire, why don't you pay a visit to your parents. I am certain they are concerned about you. You have not contacted them since you came aboard, am I not correct?"

Stewart's sudden exuberance left him. He stood there sober-faced, looking down at Captain Hamilton. "It is true, I have not been in contact with my parents. And I don't think I am ready to . . . at least not yet. My father made it perfectly clear that I am not to return until I 'came to my senses.' No, I think the time is not yet right, Captain."

"As you wish. It is your affair, Mr. Stewart." The old captain pursed his lips and then stood as if to show Stewart to the door, but instead his hand fell upon the newspaper and he handed it to the younger man. "Have you seen this?"

Stewart glanced at the paper. "Just a moment ago as it lay upon your desk. But it is very much like all the headlines I have been seeing these last few months. Sentiment is burning hot for secession, especially now with the elections only a few weeks away. Fire-eater newspapers like this one are helping fan the flames."

Hamilton nodded his head wearily, and there was concern in his blue eyes. "I have lived over six decades in the South, Mr. Stewart, and I have heard the cries of secession before. They come and they go, but I do believe that this time the South intends to do something about it."

"And about time," Stewart said.

The old captain grinned. "If I was thirty years younger, I'd probably be raising a battle cry, myself, Mr. Stewart."

"How does age make a difference, sir?"

Hamilton considered this. "I don't know how, it just does. I have been thinking of late that it is about time I put away my weather boots and finally build that little house on that hilltop overlooking the river, like I have been talking about all these years. And I'm thinking that if the South does secede—"

"Which she has every right to do," Stewart interjected.

Hamilton nodded his head. "True, she does. Only, there are folks up North who believe the Union to be indissoluble, and I think they will take up arms to prevent any state from pulling out."

"Then let them. We will fight for our rights."

Hamilton put the newspaper back on his desk. "And fight we will, I have no doubt. Only, I'm thinking that going to war is a poor way to start one's retirement, don't you think so?"

"I see your point, Captain."

"Well, perhaps all this tension will settle down again . . . as it has in the past. I have been studying up on this Senator Douglas these last few weeks. It seems to me that if Douglas is elected, he may yet bring some sanity to the problem."

"Douglas will try to pacify the South. He has about said as much. He is certainly the lesser of two evils, but I believe his election will only delay the inevitable. It will never correct the problems, nor will it alter the North's arrogant ways, or her heavy-handedness."

"Hmm. Perhaps, but at my age, a delay is all that is required." Hamilton smiled then. "Ten or fifteen years should be long enough, I should think. Well, you better go on into town and outfit yourself with appropriate clothing, Mr. Stewart. I will have a proper jacket fitted for you, and a cap as well."

Stewart pocketed the gold coins, thanked the captain again for the promotion, and left.

*   *   *

Clifton Stewart made his way into Baton Rouge, leaving the levees and the wharves and the wagon trains of cotton drays with their black-faced drivers behind him as the road climbed away from the river. The October sun was warm upon his back as he strode along, elated at his new position. The thought of leaving the searing furnaces and the never-ending job of heaving firewood into their fiery mouths—not to mention Chief Mate Lansing—had lifted his spirits considerably.

Stewart had never gotten along well with that man. He was not like the Negro firemen who did not resist Lansing's overbearing attitude. The firemen had little choice, even though some of them were freemen. But others were still slaves, and their meager wages were paid to their owners, with only the smallest amount allotted to them to get by on.

All in all, Stewart could not be happier than to be free of the task, but a bit of melancholy tugged at him as he made his way from the wharf district into the heart of the city. He would miss the company of his Negro fellow workers: their coonjine that made work less burdensome, their easy ways and sad faces, and their strange superstitions that Stewart never failed to find amusing. He'd miss their tales about past overseers and masters, too, and how they got around them. But he would not miss the despair in their voices when they recalled the women and children sold off and taken away from them, or the bitter memories they would tell in front of him that they would never think of telling in front of another white man.

Especially, Stewart knew, he was going to miss working alongside Zachary. How two men of such entirely different backgrounds could become so close was a mystery that still befuddled him.

For the moment, however, he put that thought aside. He

had worked his way into the town and found himself strolling along a busy street high above the levee. Here were shops aplenty for him to buy the items that he would require for his new position as mud clerk. The names of the shops were as familiar to him as his own name. He had grown up in this city, and no doubt he would encounter many old acquaintances as he procured his new outfit. He didn't particularly relish that thought, for he was certain the truth about why he had been driven from his home would be common knowledge throughout Baton Rouge by now. His mother and father would have never spoken of it outside the house, of course, but the house had many ears itching to gossip about what the master had done to his only soon-to-be-landed son.

The gold coins lay comfortably heavy in his pocket as he walked. It was a feeling he had almost forgotten in his year and a half aboard the *Tempest Queen*. Since he was in such a fine mood, and likewise since he happened to be passing by The Seigen House, one of the finer drinking emporiums in Baton Rouge, Stewart turned aside and stepped through the wide double doors.

He entered a long hallway with carpet on the floors and silk paper on the walls. Flanking the doors like a pair of black statues were two Negro doormen whose job it was to check hats and coats. They merely glanced at him as he entered and turned their eyes to the ceiling of if he was not there. Stewart grinned. He did look disreputable with neither hat nor coat to check. He felt fortunate just to have shoes on his feet and a shirt on his back. Never mind, his pocket was heavy with gold and in a matter of an hour or two he would emerge from this town a new man. But first, a drink to celebrate.

The hallway ended in a pair of batwing doors and he pushed through them as if he owned the place, glanced briefly about the saloon, which was deep and wide and mostly in shadows as the lamps were turned low to add an air of elegance. He didn't immediately see anyone he knew and made his way past the tables over to the long, walnut bar where gleaming twisted brass rails reflected in a scrupulously polished mirror upon which was etched a picture of a three-masted schooner bounding across ocean waves, her sheets billowed, sailing powerfully past tiers of neatly stacked crystal glasses.

Stewart was made somewhat self-conscious by his attire as he glanced around for the proprietor, a ex-sailor by the name of Cagney, whom he had known most of his life. Cagney Seigen had come to Baton Rouge almost twenty years earlier after his ship had foundered in a squall out in the Gulf and put him afoot. In that time he had turned a once run-down bar into a prosperous saloon and gaming house.

The bartender came over—not Seigen—looked Stewart up and down disapprovingly, and said, "You in the right place, mister?"

"I think so." Stewart was in too fine a mood to be put off by this man's surly greeting.

The bartender gave a snort beneath his breath and said, "You'll find the River Raft down by the wharf to be a might more to your liking, I think. The drinks are cheap. It's where all the boatmen go."

"Indeed. A place where the riffraff hangs out. A den of thieves, I might add. No, I am in the right place, thank you."

The bartender eyed Stewart again, and a hint of doubt was suddenly upon his face. "You don't talk like a boatman, mister."

Stewart shrugged his shoulders and grinned.

"All right, what will it be?"

"Glenlivet."

"Glenlivet? That's expensive stuff. Don't get much call

for that, mister, but you're the second fellow today to ask for it." He turned away, then abruptly back, a suspicious glint in his narrowed eyes. "Lemme see the color of your money."

Stewart slapped one of the gold coins upon the bar. "I trust you can change this?" he said. A note of audacity had crept into his voice, which he did not try to hide.

Upon seeing the glint of yellow, the suspicion fled the bartender's face and his manners immediately improved. "I can change that, all right. I'll be right over with your drink, sir."

Sir! The sound of that was music to Stewart's ears after all these months.

His drink was before him almost at once, and he took a small sip of the Scotch whiskey, relishing its smoothness and the pleasant bite as he worked it about in his mouth before sending it coursing down his throat.

"Ah! That is good."

The bartender said, "You've got expensive taste in sipping fare, friend."

"It was my father's doing, I must admit. He simply ruined me for anything else. Say, would Cagney be around?"

"Cagney?"

"Yes, Cagney Seigen. The owner."

The bartender frowned. "I reckon you must have been away for a while, sir."

"A year and a half aboard the steamer *Tempest Queen*."

"So I gathered from your clothes that you was a boat-man."

Stewart looked down at himself. "I am about to do something about these clothes as soon as I finish my drink."

"If you been away working a steamer, then I guess you haven't heard."

"Heard what?"

"Cagney, he up and sold this place. Almost a year now. Mr. Brandon Deavers is the new owner."

"I hadn't heard. Where did Cagney go?"

"I don't know. Don't reckon anyone knows. Someone said he bought himself a boat and sailed out to the Caribbean. He hasn't been back."

"The Caribbean? Well, that doesn't surprise me. Cagney's heart has always been on the sea." Stewart saluted the bounding schooner in the mirror with his glass. "To your health, Cagney," he said and tossed back a mouthful of whiskey. The bartender went off to see to another customer while Stewart worked on his drink, peering at the ship in the mirror, wondering about Cagney, wondering what else had changed in Baton Rouge in his absence.

Caught up in his thoughts, Clifton Stewart only half noted the reflection of the three men in the mirror, coming up behind him, and it was not until after they had expertly braced him at the bar did Stewart become fully aware of them and the fearsome look of revenge etched upon their faces.

CHAPTER FOUR

Stewart glanced to his left. He did not recognize the fellow standing there, but noted wryly that he was a big man, and that the shoulders of his dusty black coat seemed to strain at the seams.

Then a voice that he only vaguely remembered came from his right. "Well, well, if it ain't the nigger lover. Never did expect to run into you in a fine place like this here one."

Stewart turned and recognized the speaker. It was one of the two swindlers he had exchanged blows with earlier. Stewart set his drink on the bar with forced casualness, aware that the big man behind him had sidled up closer— close enough now to smell.

"You two wish to speak to me?" he asked, keeping his

voice even, glancing at a third man who had come up now—the second of the swindlers; the one who had collected the money from the black dock workers. Stewart had learned a few hard lessons in eighteen months upon the river, and thanks to Dexter McKay's tutelage, he had come to recognize when a man only meant to bluster, and when he meant to back up his words with fists and knives. These two, it was plain, were out for blood—his blood—and they had brought along an oversized buddy to make certain it went their way this time.

One of them carried a battered walking stick. He moved in close now and said, "There is a small matter of fifteen dollars you took from us—"

"You stole that money."

"It was fair gain."

"You slugged those roosters. I hardly call that fair gain, sir." Stewart's anger was on the rise, and he wished he could see what the big fellow behind his back was up to, but they had effectively surrounded him. Out of the corner of his eye he noted the bartender scowling from the far end of the counter, yet he made no move to stop these three. Stewart braced himself. He suspected that these two cheats were only the distraction, and when it came time to fight, it was going to be the big guy to watch out for. He chanced a glance in the mirror; the big man was looming dangerously near.

"We mean to have the money back, and then to give you a lesson in manners," the first man said.

Stewart put on a grin; to show his true feelings now would have been a mistake. "Your ill-gotten gains have been returned to the men you stole them from." In the mirror he thought he saw the man behind him grinding knuckles into his palm. He couldn't be certain, and he didn't want to take his eyes off the two gamblers who faced him long enough to see if he was correct.

Stewart mustered his control and put a sharp ring of confidence in his voice. "As for a lesson in manners, you have already tried that, and have failed miserably. Run off now, before I get angry with you." It was brazen bravado of course, but he said it anyway on the slight chance that it might change these three thugs' minds.

It didn't.

The man with the battered stick swung out without warning and cracked Stewart upon the kneecap. He should have been expecting that, and he cursed himself for his inattention as he staggered back against the bar and stifled a moan. The blow brought a glint of moisture to his eyes. The burly man behind him caught up his arms and pinned them back. He struggled against the powerful hands that held him and heard a short laugh from one of the swindlers. When his eyes finally cleared, the man with the stick had swung it back over his shoulder, taking aim at his head.

"Now for the lesson I promised you—"

Across the darkened room came a crack that sounded like a large firecracker exploding. There was a flash of orange fire and the walking stick leaped from the swindler's fist. At the same instant, the etched mirror behind the bar splintered, and a spider web of cracks shot through it.

The startled gambler yelped, grabbed his wrist. A trickle of red slowly emerged from his clenched fingers and for a moment he stood there, stunned, as if uncertain what had happened.

In a dark corner of the saloon, illuminated only by a flickering oil lamp overhead, a tall man stood out of his chair. He was all in shadows except for an edge of his fawn colored frock coat and a sliver of the tall hat upon his head. Across his vest a heavy gold chain crossed from pocket to pocket, catching the lamplight, casting it back in yellow glints. Other than this, and the small revolver in his hand, Clifton Stewart could make out nothing else of the man.

The man came forward, and as he stepped into the light, his features suddenly stood out clearly: his handsome face, the dark brown wedge of his neatly trimmed imperial beard, his gray eyes that seemed to be smiling now, his russet silk handkerchief in his breast pocket.

"Mr. McKay!" A wave of relief engulfed Clifton Stewart, and there was no hiding his surprise.

Dexter McKay looked them over and smiled. "Mr. Stewart, I did not expect to see you here. You are having some disagreement with these three men, hm?"

"Some," he admitted. "I caught them cheating a few hours ago and took them to task for it."

McKay clucked disapprovingly and lowered his voice. "You exposed them? I must say, that *is* bad form, Mr. Stewart." Then he glanced at the fellow with the bleeding wrist. "I can certainly understand your anger, sir, but really, cheating is something not to be tolerated by honorable men."

Stewart noted that McKay had spoken that last phrase overly loud. No doubt, for the benefit of the men still sitting around the card table that he had just left.

McKay turned his Remington pocket revolver on the big man.

"Let go of his arms, please."

The big man glanced at the little .31 revolver, snarled as if to say its piddling bullet was hardly a concern, but he released Stewart just the same.

"There, now, that is better. If you three have differences, I am certain they can be settled in a gentlemanly fashion, without resorting to the use of sticks. Now, if you care to continue, have at it."

Stewart had learned that among boatmen, when a fight was inevitable, the victory usually went to the man who strikes the first blow. He figured the same advice applied to gamblers and bullies as well. He didn't expect any trouble from the man with the wounded hand, and his partner was still momentarily confused himself, so that left only one.

With a glance in the cracked mirror, Stewart measured the big man's position and drove his elbow backward. His aim was perfect. He struck him in square the gut—there was plenty of him to hit. Immediately, Stewart knew that what strained the seams of this man's clothing was not muscle, but fat.

His elbow rammed deep into the man's stomach, driven by powerful muscles that had been hardened at the mouths of the *Tempest Queen*'s furnaces. A grunt exploded from the startled man's throat. Wheeling, Stewart drove a fist up, but the man managed to knock it aside. From behind, a fist slammed into his kidney. Stewart crashed into the bar and rebounded, coming around like a cornered cat, his bunched knuckles driving into the swindler's nose. A gush of warm blood covered his hand.

Stewart caught a glimpse of the bartender scooting around to the door. His white apron flashed across the room like a flag, and then the bartender plunged through the batwings and was gone.

The big man managed to grab hold of Stewart's arm, and although his bulk was mostly flab, his hand closed like a vise about his wrist. He engulfed him with his second arm and began to squeeze. Crushing pressure nearly halted Stewart's breathing.

The fellow with the smashed nose recovered from the shock, and his face turned murderous as he grabbed up a chair and lifted it toward the ceiling.

This wasn't anything at all like the proper fisticuffs that Stewart had been taught in college while on the boxing team. But then, he had learned the hard ways of the river early on; nothing that passed for fighting along the Mississippi ever resembled the Marquis of Queensbury Rules. McKay had tried to teach him that, but it had taken butting heads with a few leather-tough rivermen for the lessons to finally sink in. Stewart had been an avid pupil after that, and he had learned quickly. Working the woodpile aboard the *Tempest Queen* for eighteen months helped, too, building strength into his arms and back, and nicely wearing away all the civilized edges that his position in life the previous twenty-four years had so carefully chiseled in place.

The chair hovered a moment. Stewart tossed his head back and cracked the big man in the mouth. The squeezing pressure let up at once, and without an instant's pause, Stewart slipped out of the bear hug and ducked as the chair crashed down, shattering across the big man's head and driving him to his knees.

McKay was watching it all with a sanguine smile. It irritated Stewart to see his friend casually leaning against a post that supported the ceiling, enjoying the show as much as he was. He had no doubt that if McKay had had a few moments of warning, he would have convinced at least some of the patrons there to place hefty sums on the outcome of this fight.

The swindler stood there with shattered remains of the chair still clutched in his fists, stunned to discover it was his friend crumpled beneath the wreckage, not Stewart, and Clifton didn't give him a chance to figure out what had gone wrong. He dove in with both fists flying, and when he finally drew back, the third man was on the floor with his eyes closed and an overturned cuspidor for a pillow.

Clifton stood up out of his crouch, shaking his fist, his short, quick breaths burning his throat. "This is the second time today that I have hurt my hand on that fellow's jaw."

McKay threw back his head and laughed.

Stewart shot him a narrow glance. "You were a lot of help, Mr. McKay. You could have at least lent a hand."

"I did. I kept that fellow from spilling your brains with that stick of his, remember?" McKay returned his revolver to its holster hidden beneath his coat.

Stewart nodded slowly and gave a grin that was not far removed from a frown. "I suppose that is something. I was fortunate you happened to be nearby." Stewart moved back to the bar where, miraculously, his whiskey had survived the fight and tossed it down his throat.

Dexter McKay stepped over the sprawled shapes on the floor and glanced at the third man who was still standing, holding his bleeding wrist, looking dazed, his face white as talc. "I daresay, sir, you ought to get yourself to a doctor."

No sooner had he spoken than the man began to sway on his feet. McKay leaped to his side in time to catch him as his eyes rolled up and he fell back in a swoon. He laid him out on the floor. Some of the saloon's patrons came over for a curious look, then returned to their tables and their drinking and their cards, and the low murmuring background resumed. McKay ripped the man's shirt and fashioned a tourniquet about the wrist.

The other two men were beginning to move upon the floor now, coming groggily back to consciousness, groaning as they levered themselves up on their elbows and shook their heads.

The batwing doors burst open and in came the bartender and right behind him a second man in a black coat with a dark vest and collarless shirt beneath. He wore a small round hat upon his head. He was stocky, with a short neck, a round head, and a walrus mustache that hid his mouth completely. On his vest, half hidden by the lapel of his jacket, shone a dull nickel badge. Under his right arm he carried a short double-barreled shotgun.

He and the bartender surveyed the wreckage a moment, and as the sheriff's view came to rest upon Stewart and McKay, the apparent authors of this carnage, the bartender spied his mirror, gasped, and plunged around the end of the bar, stopping in front of it, gaping, and uttering unintelligible sounds.

"You two done this?" the lawman asked.

"Us, sir?" McKay asked innocently. He flung his palm to his breast, glanced at Stewart, and looked stunned.

"Yes, we did it," Stewart said setting his empty glass back on the bar and coming forward. He could see one of McKay's famous fabrications coming on, and he didn't even want to guess how his friend intended to talk his way out of this one.

McKay rolled his eyes and gave Stewart an impatient scowl.

Someone in the saloon shouted, "It was them three what started it. The lad was only defending himself, and that other feller, why he only evened up the odds a mite."

The sheriff looked back. "Is that the straight of it?"

"It is, Mr. Johnson."

At the sound of his name, the sheriff squinted at Stewart, then fitted a pair of spectacles upon his nose and squinted again. All at once recognition burst upon his staining eyes and a smile lifted the ends of his mustache. "Why, if it ain't young Mr. Stewart! I almost didn't recognize you." He paused and stared up and down, as if not quite believing the identity of the man he had discovered beneath the ragged clothes. "Well, well, well, what do you know. I heard you was gone off somewhere. What are you doing back in Baton Rouge? Come home finally? Your mam and pap know you're back?" He let the barrel of the shotgun tilt to the floor and stuck out a meaty hand. "It is good to see you again. I saw your pap only last week, he was in with the niggers you know, had him a mighty pile of cotton to put aboard a steamer bound for the Gulf. Well, let me look at you. Hm, put on some muscle, didn't you? You look good, but my, my, them clothes . . ."

"I was about to buy a new wardrobe when I stopped in here for a drink."

"Oh, yes . . ." The sheriff suddenly remembered his reason for being there and looked down at the men still on the floor, then spied the pool of blood by the unconscious one.

"What happened to that one?"

"Er . . . he was about to knock Mr. Stewart senseless with his walking stick. I . . . er . . . shot him . . . in the wrist only." McKay smiled guilelessly.

"Shot him?"

"Just in the wrist. It is a very small wound."

"It ain't bleeding like a small wound. Someone run off and find the doctor," Johnson said to no one in particular. He glanced back at McKay, but when he spoke, it was to Clifton.

"You friends with this fellow?"

"Yes. This is Mr. Dexter McKay. He lives aboard the *Tempest Queen,* the boat upon which I am employed."

"Well, if he is a friend of yours, Mr. Stewart, then I reckon he must be all right." He stuck out a hand. "Thad Johnson, deputy sheriff."

McKay shook the offered hand. "Most honored to meet you, sir."

Johnson looked askance at McKay's beaming face, then returned his attention to Clifton. "You on your way home, Mr. Stewart?"

Clifton shook his head. "No, I shan't be going home, at least not this time through. Perhaps in the future. And I would be grateful if you don't mention to my parents that I have been here."

"Well, I heard there was some sort of trouble between you

and your pap. I reckon it must be true then. Hope you get it all worked out."

"I do, too, Mr. Johnson."

"And as far as this here mess goes, well, I reckon there are men in this room who will say these characters begun the fight. Ain't that right, boys?" he said raising his voice.

The deputy sheriff got a general consensus from the crowd, and that was good enough for him. Thad Johnson pumped Stewart's hand one more time and was about to leave when the bartender threw up his arms and said, "Who's gonna pay for my mirror, Thad? Look what that fancy-pants done to it." He was pointing an accusing finger at McKay.

McKay instantly took two gold eagles from his pocket and laid them upon the bar. "This should cover it, I think."

The bartender ceased his flustering, his eyes widening, and he snatched them up. He turned them over as if to assure himself that they were genuine, and immediately dropped them in his pocket—and the charge against McKay as well.

"There, that settled that. I'll be off, now. It was truly a pleasure to run into you again, Mr. Stewart." The sheriff tipped his hat and started for the batwing doors. Halfway out of them, Thad Johnson stopped and came about with a sudden jerk. He thrust a forefinger into the air as if he had suddenly remembered something and said, "I almost forgot!" He strode immediately back. "I almost forgot, Mr. Stewart. I've had it so long now that I didn't even think of it."

"Think of what?"

"The letter."

"Letter? What letter?"

"It was given to me oh . . . now, let me think. Must have been eight months ago."

"A letter for me?"

"Left by a young lady, it was. Very pretty, she was, too.

She asked me if I wouldn't keep it until I should happen to run into you again. She said she couldn't give it to your family to hold. I thought that strange, but I took the letter anyway and stuck it in my desk." He paused and his expression turned uncertain. "I think I stuck it into my desk. I reckon it must still be there."

Stewart became excited. "Her name! What was her name?"

"I don't remember."

Stewart leaped for the door, stopped, and turned back. "Are you coming, Sheriff?"

Johnson started after him.

Stewart said to McKay. "Are you coming?"

Dexter McKay glanced at the darkened table he had left a few minutes before and instantly declined. "My dear Mr. Stewart, I am engaged in a game of cards with the famous George Devol! I don't believe even a summons from the Almighty Himself could persuade me to leave just now. No, my business is here, and yours is with the sheriff. I do hope this is what you have been waiting for." McKay smiled and returned to his table, but by that time Stewart was already making his way to the sheriff's office as briskly as his legs would carry him.

"Why are we stopping, Jackson?"

The driver looked back at her. "It is near onto noon, missus. De girls in de kitchen packed a dinner t' eat along de way. I was goin' to fix it for you now, missus."

"Is it noon already?" Genevieve St. James had removed her shawl an hour ago as the morning warmed. She had folded it upon the seat next to her, atop her reticule, and now she dug beneath it until she found her small gold watch. Its mother-of-pearl dial shimmered like a rainbow in the sunlight. "You are right. It is past noon."

Jackson set the brake and put the reins down.

Gen looked over her shoulder, peering down the ribbon of road behind them. "I am not yet hungry, Jackson," she said. That wasn't entirely true. She was hungry, but for the last couple hours she had had an unexplainable feeling of vulnerability on this country road, something she had not experienced before, and she was anxious to be on to New Orleans.

The old man halted, his long leg halfway out the carriage upon the step-up. "Yo' don't want Jackson to get yo'r dinner?"

"No. I want to be on our way."

Jackson frowned, and Gen had the distinct feeling that the old man was stopping more for his comfort that for any concern of her own. Stiffly, he pulled himself back up onto the seat and without a word of complaint or protest, he picked up the reins and toed off the brake.

"How far are we from New Orleans, Jackson?"

He got the carriage rolling again. "Oh, I say 'bout two hour, missus, mebbe tree."

Gen was quite familiar with the road to New Orleans. This trip, however, she had not been paying attention to the scenery. The plantation houses along the way, set far back off the road, could hardly be seen, and the fields had mostly been stripped of their cotton and abandoned for the winter. It wasn't the monotony of the drive that had made her inattentive, but the thought of tomorrow and the following days—however many there might be before she would accomplish her mission and return to the safety of Carleton Manor.

A shiver raced up her spine. She tried not to think of what she was about to do.

The carriage rattled on.

They passed a caravan of drays laden down with cotton, making its way to the river landings. The cotton was bound for great ships that cross the oceans. So much of the South's products were feeding European textile factories these days that the general feeling was, if the South went to war, the British would step in on her side to ensure the steady flow of cotton across the waves.

Gen averted her eyes as her carriage rattled by the curious Negro drivers. At the head of the caravan was a white man in tall, shiny brown boots, riding a fine chestnut mare. He gave them only a fleeting glimpse as their carriage sped by. Jackson swerved around them and expertly maneuvered the carriage back into the middle of the road.

Gen peered over her shoulder into the cloud of dust the wheels kicked up. She watched the overseer shrink as the caravan receded in their wake. Her view went past him to scan the line of pines that followed the ridge they had descended a few minutes earlier.

There, upon the brown cut of the road, Gen thought she caught a glimpse of a distant rider, but when she looked again, he was gone. On any other occasion she would not have given it the least notice, but this was the third time that morning that she had *thought* she had seen a rider.

"Jackson."

"Yes, missus?" He kept his eyes on the road, canting an ear in her direction.

"Have you noticed anyone?"

"Anyone, missus?"

"Yes, anyone that might appear to be . . . following us."

He glanced at her, then spent a moment squinting back down the road before returning his attention to the road ahead. "I ain't see'd no man followin' us all de mornin' long, missus."

Gen tightened her grasp on the armrest, feeling suddenly foolish. "I must be letting my imagination run away with me, Jackson. I don't like traveling without Robert."

Jackson didn't comment.

CHAPTER FIVE

He had to force himself to sit in the chair, to keep from wearing a path in the floor, and had the chair been constructed of any lesser wood than oak, without a doubt he would have permanently embossed it with the imprints of his fingertips.

"Surely, Sheriff, you must be able to recall where you placed the letter!"

Thad Johnson swept off his hat and scratched his head where thinning hair revealed the pale skin of his skull. "I thought for sure I had stuck it in that drawer, Mr. Stewart." He pursed his lips and narrowed his eyes, thinking. "I did go through this place last spring and got rid of—"

Stewart could take no more of this. He bounded to his

feet, "This is impossible! You cannot have lost it!" He began rifling the desk drawers hanging open.

Johnson shrugged his shoulders. "I don't think I would have thrown it away."

Stewart rounded on him and stopped just short of shaking the deputy sheriff by the shoulders. "Think, man, will you!"

Thad Johnson had finally had enough of this. "Hold up there, Stewart," he shot back. The formality of a *mister* was pointedly absent in his sharp reply, and it rang like a cracked bell in the tight confines of the cramped office. "You go off on a lark to work a riverboat and then come back here a year and a half later and expect me to mind your correspondence? My duties end at keeping the peace in this here parish, not doing the postmaster's duties as well. Now, you either settle down and let me go about looking for that letter in my own way, or get out of here and I'll send it along to the *Tempest Queen* once it turns up."

Stewart backed off and dropped into the chair again. "I am sorry, Thad. The *Tempest Queen* pulls out in the morning and I simply must have that letter before then. I have waited so long for something like this to happen, and now that it has, I can hardly contain myself."

"Work at it, boy," was Johnson's unsympathetic reply. He dragged a box from a closet and flipped through the papers stored there. It didn't appear to Stewart that Thad ever threw anything out.

Not finding it in the box, the sheriff turned an eye around the office and his view came back to a file cabinet in the corner. He had already searched the cabinet once, but now a fresh thought seemed to come to his mind, and he stood there pondering it for a while.

Suddenly he pulled open the second drawer, lifted out a double fistful of papers, and flipped through them until he found a dog-eared brown portfolio. Stewart craned his neck and read "Miscellaneous ?????" penciled on the corner of it. Johnson unfastened a wire clasp and pulled a handful of papers from the large folder. From between several sheets of papers he removed a simple white envelope.

"Here we go. I told you I'd find it my own way." A note of smug vindication crept into his voice.

Clifton snatched it from him, but stopped short of tearing it open. He could do no more than stare at it at first.

"Well, ain't you gonna open it? You were just itching like a hound to get it two minutes ago."

Stewart swallowed down a lump and looked again at the handwriting. A handsome, tight script that had been written in pen and blotted dry.

Mssr. Clifton Stewart.

It almost seemed too formal. The lump rose in his throat again. What could that mean? Turning it over, he stared at the wax seal, then broke the seal with great care to avoid ripping the envelope, and extracted the single sheet of paper. His hand shook as he unfolded it and began to read:

September 18, 1859

Dear Mr. Stewart:

I am at a loss as to how to begin this missive, for in truth, I did not expect to ever hear from you again, nor had I imagined the torment of your heart as you so eloquently expressed it with pen and paper. When my father gave me the letter that you had left with him I was stricken with confusion. Your parting words that awful night still echoed in my brain—I can hear them even now as I write to you. As I read your plaintive remorse, your plea that I should allow you to come to me, if only you knew where, my confusion deepened. At first I flung your letter away and raced down to the river's edge. I always seem to fly back to the Mississippi when my heart is heavy. She gives me strength, she clears my thoughts, and she has carried away my tears on more than one occasion. I know I shall never be able to stray far from her banks for very long.

Afterward, I retrieved your letter from the basket, and taking pen in hand, composed this reply. I do hope you are well. Life aboard a steamer has it perils as I am sure you well know by now. Father said you looked as if you had been ill when you showed up at the house. He said you were well mannered and courteous, and my mother said you tried very hard to be gracious. They tell me you have secured a position aboard the Tempest Queen *only so that you may search the river for me.*

In truth, I have not forgotten you either, Clifton, even though I have desperately tried to. Still, I fear that our worlds are too far apart, our principles too different, our lives following ever diverging paths. I wonder if absence has not made your heart grow fonder, and I worry that familiarity might—well, you know how the rest of that goes.

These fears aside, however, if you truly wish to see me again, and I do not know if this would be wisdom or folly, I will in no way spurn you. Just the same, I cannot tell you where I shall be, or how to find me. My life goes on, and I have—work—that I must be about. I can tell you only that I currently am employed aboard the steamer Guiding Star. *Captain Antone is her master and he is a true and righteous man, and is well spoken of along the river. He reminds me very much of Captain Hamilton, although much younger and quite dashing. Any wharf master can help you find the* Guiding Star *I am sure.*

I do not know how long it will be before this letter finds you; much can change in a short time. I will leave it in Baton Rouge with someone who will know how to get in touch with you. I think it best not leave it with your parents. Your letter makes it quite clear how they feel at the present.

Until—or if—we meet again,
Mystie Waters

P.S. I saw a brilliant Carduelis tristis *yesterday. The first of the season. Does that mean a hard winter up north?*

Stewart had read it so quickly he had to go back and read it again, and then he wasn't certain what Mystie was really trying to tell him. He carefully returned Mystie's letter to its envelope. Johnson was studying him and Stewart knew the man was being consumed with curiosity, but it was a private matter. Mystie's reply had left him cold. It was not at all what he had hoped for. Yet she had not completely dashed his hopes, only tempered them with her shrewd and absolutely impeccable logic. He wondered briefly if absence had not made his heart grown fonder, and that perhaps he should cease this quest now and try to forget her. The letter had been written over a year ago. Could the small flame that at that time flickered in Mystie's heart be expected to survive all these silent months?

He didn't see how.

"Thank you, Thad," he said and left the sheriff's office.

He had intended to complete the task he had come into town to do, but before he realized it, his feet were treading the long pier out to the wharf boat.

Stewart found the wharf master in his office, shuffling papers upon a wide desk that appeared at first glance to be a maze of cubbyholes, each hole filled to capacity: pens, pencils, folders, ink bottles, dividers, charts rolled into long tubes, a brass boatswain whistle, a cluster of dusty peacock feathers—the collection of a lifetime on the river. The wharf master was well up in years, bald—his blue cap was shoved into a cubbyhole as well—and he filled the air inside the office with the rich aroma of tobacco from a pipe clenched in his teeth.

Near the windows that overlooked the river stood a brass spyglass on a wooden tripod, and at its ocular was the eye of another fellow, equally aged, appearing to have nothing more to do with his time than to watch the passing boats. Both men looked up when Stewart rapped upon the jamb of the open door.

"Aye?" asked the man at the desk, removing the pipe and narrowing a bushy brow. He had a milky right eye, and a full, white beard bisected by a livid scar down his left cheek.

"Are you the wharf master?"

"Aye. I am Harry Beardburn. What can I do for ye, young man?" Beardburn closed the bad eye and looked Stewart up and down with his good one, and must have read correctly the signs that he was employed upon one of the boats moored at the wharf. "Your master sent ye? What boat are ye with?"

"The *Tempest Queen,* sir."

"Ah. Captain Hamilton's boat, eh?"

"Yes, but he did not send me, Mr. Beardburn."

"No? Then what is your business here, young man?"

The fellow at the spyglass went back to viewing the river.

Stewart said, "I have come for some information on a boat, sir."

"Hm. Which boat did ye have in mind?"

"The *Guiding Star,* sir. I was wondering if you could tell me her home port, and when she will be coming into Baton Rouge."

"The *Guiding Star?* Well, let me see." Beardburn reached for a clipboard and began riffling the pages there. "There is no *Guiding Star* scheduled into Baton Rouge according to my itinerary. Of course, that don't mean she won't show up."

"Her home port, then?"

Beardburn hung the clipboard back on its hook and he went to a shelf of bound volumes. He limped as he walked, and Stewart noted that the sole of his right boot had been built up a good three inches thicker than its mate on the man's left foot. Beardburn took down a thin ledger with a gilded *G* upon the spine and returned to the desk. Shoving aside his paperwork, he opened it flat and began flipping the pages. Beardburn's lips moved with each page and Stewart could hear the man softly pronouncing the names that appeared in the upper right-hand corner. There seemed to be no order to the names, as if they had been penned upon the page with blatant disregard to anything that resembled an alphabetical listing.

"Guiding Star," Beardburn said aloud finally, stopping. His yellowed fingertip traced down the page, and he said, "Sunk off of Island Number Ten in July of 1851."

"That must be a different boat," Stewart said.

"Hm, so it must." Beardburn frowned and continued his search.

A dozen pages or so later he stopped again. *"Guiding Star."* Then, "No, she was dismantled in December of fifty-seven. Her hull was made into a wharf boat, it seems." Beardburn continued flipping pages.

The old man by the spyglass looked over. "What be the name of that boat, Harry?"

"Guiding Star," Beardburn said, methodically turning pages, not bothering to look up.

"Hey?" The man cupped a hand behind his ear.

"Guiding Star!" he said louder.

"Guiding Star?"

"Aye!" he shouted back, and then stopped again upon a

page. "Here, perhaps this is the boat ye are seeking, young man. The *Guiding Star*. Built in the New Albany shipyards, in fifty-eight. Registered to the Central Illinois and Keokuk Packet Company. Her home port is Rock Island, Illinois. Her master is Captain Barnabas Antone—"

"That's the boat!" Stewart said. "Rock Island, Illinois, is her home port? Why, that . . . that is over a thousand miles from Baton Rouge!"

Beardburn glanced at a chart of the river on the wall, "More like one thousand five hundred and fifty-eight miles . . . well, since that chart was drawn, at least. Who knows what Lady Mississippi has done to change that by this time, eh?" He laughed and stuck the pipe back between his teeth.

Rock Island was about as far up the river from Baton Rouge as Stewart could imagine. He had not traveled any great distance above Saint Louis, but he had heard of the famous rapids far north, and he seemed to recall that Rock Island was located somewhere between what is occasionally spoken of as the Lower Rapids and the Upper Rapids. In some vague way he imagined Rock Island to be deep in the heart of the Great Northern Wilderness, and he had visions of the Mississippi River petering out not far above it.

No! He was allowing his emotions to take over.

He stopped and forced himself to think rationally about it. He knew that the Mississippi ran clear up into northern Minnesota, and hadn't Schoolcraft discovered its source in a lake he had named Itasca?

Stewart chided himself for allowing the formidable distance to unsettle him. He said, "Thank you, Mr. Beardburn. I suppose now I shall have to find a vessel going north and make my way to Rock Island."

"Hey?"

Stewart glanced over at the old man by the spyglass, who

had a hand cupped around an ear and his head turned sideways toward him. He said louder, "I shall have to find a way north so that I might find the *Guiding Star!* I have urgent business with her!"

"North?" The old man chuckled. "You'll be goin' the long way around, if you do."

"Sir? I don't understand."

The old man hooked a thumb at the wide river beyond the dingy window panes. "My meaning is, you'll be headed the wrong way if you go north, son. I seen the *Guiding Star* steam past here only yesterday. Seen her through this very glass." He patted the spyglass affectionately. "I'll wager you two bits to a cat's tail that she is tied up at the wharf at New Orleans this very minute."

"New Orleans!" The name burst from him. Stewart rejoiced at his splendid luck, for on the morrow the *Tempest Queen* would be steaming to that very port, and by nightfall he would be in New Orleans. Instead of thinking weeks ahead, it would only be a single day! He thanked Beardburn, pumped the hand of the unnamed man there with him, and skipped off the wharf boat, hardly aware of his feet pounding the pier.

The rest of the day as he dove from shop to shop, purchasing his wardrobe, thinking not of the new position he would be occupying aboard the *Tempest Queen,* but only of Mystie Waters, her lovely face, her perfect olive skin, and the long tresses that shone like a raven's wing in the sunlight.

At one point he fretted over how he was going to tell Captain Hamilton—once he had found Mystie—that he was leaving the *Tempest Queen.* He suffered through a brief surge of guilt over leaving the boat after the good captain had just promoted him to mud clerk, but the wave passed quickly. He could not dwell on these things. Instead, he went about his business, heady with the thought of Mystie being so near, and imagined a dozen different scenarios, each ending with himself and Mystie embracing and going off to be together forever.

He wanted to tell McKay right away, and Zachary, too, for both men had known him since he had come aboard, and both showed more than a passing interest in how this melodrama of his would eventually play out. He would have to tell Captain Hamilton as well, but he decided to wait until after he had found Mystie. He briefly considered the possibility that she was no longer aboard the *Guiding Star,* and immediately tossed that disquieting notion aside. This was no time to derail his elation.

In an hour, his arms were filled with paper bundles: shirts, trousers, stockings, undergarments, a new pair of shoes. A new frock coat would have been appropriate as well, but his coins only went so far. In the end, he had purchased a complete and proper wardrobe, except for a coat, and still had a few pennies left jingling in his pocket.

Feeling gay, he stepped into a confectionery and purchased a bag of pralines, and as he paid for them, he spied a stack of newspapers on the counter and bought one of them as well, folding it into thirds and shoving it under his arm among the brown paper packages, to be read later. He had lost track of the news while as a fireman aboard the *Tempest Queen,* but now that his stature had been elevated to that of a mud clerk, he decided a more cosmopolitan awareness would be required of him, and besides, the talk of secession was buzzing like a mill saw throughout the land and he didn't want to appear a complete dolt on the current happenings in Washington. With the elections right around the corner, he was curious what the fire-eaters were saying about Lincoln this week. When he found his Mystie, she, particularly, would be well informed on these matters.

Looking like an overworked porter, Clifton Stewart waddled as he toted his day's shopping back down to the wharves where the *Tempest Queen* was slowly losing her wedding cake appearance and beginning to put on weight as the bales of cotton came aboard and the mountains of Southern wealth rose upon her guards, already obscuring all of the main deck, climbing now halfway above the boiler deck.

On the dry, flat Texas ridge, Alex Strider reined in his mustang pony and leaned forward in the saddle, stretching. His spine crackled, and he lifted himself from the brutally hard saddle for a few moments of relief. He was a lean man, gaunt by some standards, tall, unshaven, and hard as the ground that he slept upon. He had spent the last three months working his way through West Texas and around to the hot central grasslands near the Red River. This was to be his last stop, according to the dog-eared and sweat-stained list in his shirt pocket.

It was October, and still the land burned. Strider swept off his wide, dusty hat and sleeved the sweat from his forehead, leaving a muddy smear. He stepped stiffly down off his horse to adjust the cinches. It was a light saddle, really no more than was needed to work cattle in this part of Texas. Bare wood mostly, covered sparsely with leather upon the seat, over the fork, and across the rear jockey. Its fenders were small but adequate, its stirrups sturdy, unadorned, steam-bent hickory. About the only prominent feature on the saddle was the heavy wooden horn, wrapped in leather and capped with a bronze shield.

Strider carried little food. His canteen was almost empty. A bedroll was tied behind the cantle, across a pair of saddlebags. The right bag held a change of socks, a pound of black powder, a bullet mold, and three hundred copper percussion caps. The left bag held gold—all that was left of the ninety thousand dollars he had taken away from Baton Rouge with him.

He sipped some water and swung back atop the mustang. The land dropped away ahead of him, and in the distance lay the colorless buildings of the cow camp, like bleached bones beneath the hot Texas sun. Strider eyed the barns and outbuildings and studied the corrals strung out behind the barn. They reminded him of the gray ribs of the dead cattle he had encountered on this trip. The camp was too far off for him to see men moving, but he knew they were there, too. Where else in this barren country would men be? Strider grinned at the thought, but it was soulless humor, more like a grin a man might give upon finding a rattlesnake curled beneath a rock. His eyes, shaded from the sun by the wide hat, did not smile.

Instinctively, he drew his revolver and checked the caps. Satisfied, he lowered the hammer on an unloaded chamber and shoved it back into his holster, but he left the hammer thong hanging free.

Strider got his pony moving again.

He passed under the portal into the yard and reined in. How very much like the dozen or so cow camps he had visited in the last three months, he decided, surveying the place, not missing a detail. The buildings were a mix of unplastered adobe and splintered wood, dried to tinder beneath the relentless sun.

A dog barked.

A woman's face peered out behind drab yellow curtains from one of the unpainted tinderboxes.

Strider urged his horse forward, past the corrals, toward a dogtrot at the far end. He was aware of the movement in the shadows of an open barn door. He did not turn his head, but watched out the corner of his eye as if he had not noticed the men gathering there.

One of the men stepped out into the sunlight. He was not armed, so Strider ignored him until the man called out. Then the weary traveler pulled up and turned his mustang back to face the man.

He approached Strider dragging a long rope that he was winding about his hand and elbow. He wore a broad hat, threadbare gabardine vest, a collarless shirt open at his neck, which was encircled by a dirty bandanna.

"You talking to me, mister?"

The man spat a stream of brown tobacco juice at the dust. "Well, now, you don't see nobody else about, do you?"

Strider glanced at the barn where the other men remained in the shadows, then turned his horse away and continued on toward the dogtrot.

"I said hold up."

Strider stopped again, this time not turning back. The man came around in front of the horse. "Who the hell are you, mister? You can't come riding in here like you own the place."

"Who the hell is asking," Strider's low, even voice rasped menacingly; his lips barely moved.

"I'm Chase Everly. I look after Mr. Dunbar's place."

"I'm here to see Percy Dunbar."

Everly glanced at the house that Strider had been riding toward. "Mr. Dunbar know you are coming?"

"He will in about half a minute—that is, if you're done talking."

Everly must have seen the challenge in Strider's flint-gray eyes; if not, he surely did not miss Strider's hand moving back to rest upon the butt of his Colt Navy revolver.

"He's . . . he's up to the house, mister."

Strider tapped his horse's flanks with his long Mexican

spurs and Everly leaped aside as the horse pushed past him.

The little house was typical of the area: two separate cabins, connected by a roof over an open patio, built to face the direction of the prevailing winds to help keep it cool during the hellish summers. They called them dogtrots, and just then a brown, long-haired dog that looked as if it had never felt the tug of a brush came trotting out from behind the house. It barked, warning Strider back, and stood its ground at the very edge of the porch. The animal was about the size of a small sheep, with a tail that had been cropped short. Probably nipped off by an old cow horse, Strider mused. The dog sat there staring at Strider, its lips curled back, showing a brace of yellow teeth.

Strider halted at the hitch rail, waiting until the dog's yapping had summoned his owner out onto the porch. It didn't take but a moment.

He was probably sixty, heavy in the belly, short-legged. The ends of his trousers were stuffed into the tops of his tall boots. Suspenders held up the trousers, and a pair of meaty shoulders beneath a plaid cotton shirt held up the suspenders. In his hurry, he had left his hat inside, but not the shotgun that lay in the crook of his arm, cocked, but pointing down at the flat, red paving stones of the porch that continued on back between the two halves of the house. He sized up Strider in a glance and said, "What can I do for you, mister?"

"Percy Dunbar?"

"That's me."

"I'm Alex Strider."

Dunbar gave him a blank look, as if waiting for more, then suddenly he seemed to remember. "Strider? Oh, yeah, you're the . . . the agent? From Mr. St. James?"

"Uh-huh."

"I got his letter awhile back that said you'd be stopping

by. Frankly, I didn't pay it much mind. Your Mr. St. James, he sounded like a crackpot, if you want to know the truth, but now I recall. You are here on account of that business he mentioned?"

Uh-huh."

"Well, step on down and come inside. I still think your Mr. St. James is cracked, but I'll listen to what you have to say."

Strider lifted his himself from the saddle.

The dog growled.

Strider stopped.

"Go chase a damn pack rat, Harriet!" Dunbar snapped and gave the dog a nudge in the ribs with the blunt toe of his boot. The dog immediately sat down and began to sweep the porch with her shortened tail.

Strider dismounted, untied his saddlebags, and climbed to the porch while the dog smelled his boots and wagged the stubby tail some more.

He stepped into the little house behind Dunbar, but not before pausing to study the men out in the yard, who were gathering together and talking guardedly among themselves.

CHAPTER SIX

The floor of the dogtrot was hard adobe mud that at one time had been troweled smooth, but now was cracked and gouged. A single table stood in the middle of the floor, and it seemed to tilt slightly with the floor. A fireplace had been built into the back wall, and next to it sat a battered bureau with an embroidered doily on top where a cluster of framed pictures of family and places far away were carefully arranged. On the wall above the bureau was a double row of pegs, currently holding two rifles, a holster and revolver, and an old army saber.

There were two windows in the small cabin: beneath the one that faced the yard was a small table with a beige porcelain vase containing some dried Texas weeds. Near the other, across the room and looking out onto the sparse, brown grass prairie, stood a heavy iron stove . . . and a woman.

When Dunbar and Strider came in, the woman glanced up from the griddle where she was preparing a meal. Strider couldn't guess her age. She might have been thirty or fifty. She looked like the land: sun-beaten and withered. But she smiled pleasantly when Dunbar introduced him to her. She brushed at her dusty gray dress as if embarrassed by its poor condition, and offered coffee from a battered blue pot at the back of the stove.

"Sit down, Strider," Dunbar said, indicating a chair. Dunbar set his shotgun on a pair of pegs beneath the rifles, went to the little table with the vase, and pulled open a drawer.

Mrs. Dunbar brought over two cups of coffee.

"Margaret, where is that letter from St. James?" he asked after a moment of rummaging through the meager contents of the drawer.

"I think you put in your possibles box, on your chest of drawers," she said. Percy remembered then and went outside, across to the other half of the house, and was back in less than a minute, holding an envelope that to Strider appeared to have passed through many hands and much distress on its journey from Carleton Manor to this dusty cow camp in the vast state of Texas.

Dunbar sat at the table, reread the letter as if to satisfy himself that it actually said what he thought it said, and then looked across at Strider.

"Suppose you tell me exactly what this Mr. St. James has in mind—and how the devil did he find me, anyway, and why?"

"You are only one of a dozen cowmen that Mr. St. James has been in touch with." Strider said. "In fact, you are the last on my list."

"You mean to tell me he has made this outrageous offer to eleven other men?"

"He has, and they have all thought it sound enough business to have taken him up on it."

"They have?" Dunbar narrowed his eyes suspiciously. "Suppose you explain it to me."

"It is simple. Mr. St. James wants to purchase all the beef you have on the hoof. I'm his agent, and I will negotiate a fair price with you."

"That much was clear from his letter. What ain't clear is his delivery date."

Strider allowed a faint smile to lift the corners of his mouth. "That is because he has no delivery date in mind— yet. In brief, Mr. Dunbar, he is only buying an option on your cattle."

"A what?"

"He is paying you for your beef now, with the right to take delivery of it at some date in the future."

"I never heard o' such a thing. How is that good for me?"

"It is very good for you, Mr. Dunbar. I negotiate a price for your cattle here and now, and pay you up front for them. You do nothing but keep the beeves on your range, fed and healthy, until Mr. St. James calls for them. All the calves they produce, you keep. You avoid the expense of herding up with the other small cattlemen, hiring a crew, driving them to market, and haggling with the purchasers at the railhead in Missouri. You avoid drowned steers, stampedes, broken legs, Indians, cattle stealers, unhappy squatters. In fact, you only have to do what you do best, Mr. Dunbar, stay on your land and raise more cattle."

"That don't make such good sense to me. If'n I keep all these cows on my land until this St. James fellow wants 'em, I won't have no grass left to raise up another herd. And then, when he does come to collect his beeves, how am I gonna get 'em to him clear over there in Louisiana, on the other side of the Mississip'? How long does he expect me to hold 'em for him?"

"A year, no longer."

"Then what?"

"Then, if he wants to take the cattle that he has bought, I will return with men to collect them. You bear no expense of driving them to Mr. St. James."

Dunbar considered Strider suspiciously. "What do you mean *if* he wants 'em?"

"He might not want them," Strider answered bluntly.

"But he paid for 'em. If he changes his mind, I sure as lightning ain't gonna return his money, especially after nursemaiding 'em for a season."

"If Mr. St. James does change his mind, and I do not return within one year, the cattle revert back to you, Mr. Dunbar. You can do as you please with the cows. You can drive them to market and sell them if you wish, or take them out and shoot them. It is all explained in the contract."

"I keep St. James's money?"

"You do."

Dunbar stared at Strider as the gaunt man sipped his coffee, absolutely at ease with himself, as if in no hurry for Dunbar to make up his mind.

"That don't make any sense," Dunbar said finally.

"It does to Mr. St. James."

"What does the man got up his sleeve?"

Strider shrugged. "His business is his business. I don't ask questions." But like Dunbar, Strider was curious as to what Robert St. James had "up his sleeve." He'd done some work for Carleton St. James before the old man had died, and when his son had contacted him with this job, Alex Strider had taken it on without inquiring too deeply into Robert's motives. But he intended to find out, just the same. The St. Jameses had accumulated several huge fortunes through shrewd business dealings, and Strider had no doubt that this affair would prove vastly profitable for Robert St.

James as well, in spite of how it appeared to him, or to men like Percy Dunbar who only looked a day—or a season—ahead.

"Let me get the straight of this," Dunbar said. His wife had come up behind him and stood silently, listening. Strider knew she was searching for a flaw in the plan as well, as every other cattleman before Percy Dunbar had suspected, for the offer sounded too good to be true. "You pay me for my cows. I get the money now. I keep them on my land for one year, let them calve, and then maybe you come back and take them away—except the calves. Maybe you don't come back, and then I keep 'em, keep the money, too, and sell 'em all over again?"

"That's the short of it. It is all explained in clear English in the contracts I have brought along." Strider removed two sheets of paper from his saddlebags and slid them across the table to Dunbar. "Read it over. Take your time. If you agree, we will settle on a price, and the number of cows you are willing to sell." Strider stood, slung the saddlebags over his shoulder, and stopped at the door. "I think I will just step outside now for a breath of air. You and the missus talk it over."

He left them looking at each other, and stood awhile near his horse, gazing out at the dusty, ramshackle spread. It was in desperate need of repairs; the corrals were down at one corner and an old freight wagon had been placed there to keep the horses inside. Off to his left, the windmill wobbled and clattered and sang out for oil as the brisk Texas wind spun the vanes.

Strider allowed a small grin to crack his face. Dunbar would take the deal, just as the eleven other cowmen before him had. These small-time businessmen had more expenses than they had money to cover them.

Strider peered across the road at the darkened barn. In the shadows he saw that four men had gathered and were watching him, talking among themselves. He was not surprised by their curiosity, but something in their manner made him wary. A sudden movement caught the corner of his eye and he shot a glance to his left in time to see a fifth fellow—the man he had met in the yard—sprint behind a small mud hut not far from the main house. The man remained there, not showing himself, and Strider knew the man was watching him.

Strider took his horse across the yard to a trough for water, ignoring the men who lingered just out of the sunlight, watching him. Before he had finished, Dunbar came out onto the porch and called, "Mr. Strider." He beckoned him to return to the house. Strider knew that the Dunbars had decided to accept St. James's offer. And why not? It was fair, and by far the best deal Percy Dunbar could hope for.

At the table the two of them negotiated a cash settlement on five hundred head of cows that Dunbar was willing to sell. Margaret Dunbar stood at Strider's back where he could not see her, and although she said not a word, she and Dunbar kept up a steady back-and-forth conversation with their eyes as Dunbar and Strider hashed out what each considered a fair price. In the end, Strider penned in the number of animals and the full selling price in the blank spaces of the contract, and Dunbar read and reread it as if certain Strider had slipped in something that would show his and St. James's true colors. But all was exactly as it had been presented to him, in simple language, spelled out plainly.

Dunbar signed the contracts—both copies—as did Strider, and Margaret Dunbar witnessed them. The cowman was paid in gold from Strider's saddlebags, and when the business was completed, Margaret insisted he stay for dinner.

Not a man who was overly fond of his own cooking, Strider accepted the invitation.

*   *   *

Chase Everly made his way back to the barn where the four wranglers waited.

"Well?" one of them asked when Everly came in and hunkered down in the cool shade of the adobe wall.

"It appears as if that fellow is gonna stay for vittles. Maggie is setting out plates for the three of 'em."

"What in the devil is he doing here, anyway?" a fellow with a ruddy face and a hole in his felt hat asked. "We don't hardly never get strangers riding in this far out, and none I can remember looking like that feller. See the way his hand fell casual-like to the butt of his revolver when you stopped him? He's trouble for sure, Chase, and I ain't never known Percy to take the likes of him in and feed him supper."

Everly gave a short laugh. "You better believe he's dangerous. He's got to be." Chase paused to build their curiosity. "And if you'd seen what I just seen through the window, you'd know why Percy and Maggie have asked him to stay."

"Well, you jest gonna let us squat here wondering, Chase?" an eager boy named Carroway said. "What *did* you see when you went over?"

"You know them saddlebags he keeps always on his shoulder?"

"We saw 'em," the man with the hole in his hat said.

"They're full of gold."

"Shit!" Carroway said. "You telling it straight, Chase?"

"I seen it. They haggled awhile about something, then all three of them put their names to a piece of paper, like they was making a pact, and then that feller digs out two sacks of gold coins. He counts out a nice, big pile of 'em, and Maggie takes it and puts it in that old kettle she keeps above the stove. He puts the rest of the gold back into them bags, and they still seemed pretty heavy when he set them back onto the floor."

"The teakettle. So that's where they keep their money," a fourth fellow said, picking his teeth with a stick of straw.

"Don't get no ideas, Brand," Everly said. "The Dunbars have always done right by us."

"I wouldn't take their money." Brand sounded offended that Everly would even consider him capable of such a despicable deed.

"Yeah, the Dunbars have been fair with us," the eager boy said, "but this stranger, we don't owe him nothing, and I sure could use a small sack of gold for my own."

There was general agreement on that, except for the fellow with the hole in his hat. He had kept his thoughts to himself until finally he said, "I'd think twice about what you're considering, boys, if I get your drift straight. He don't appear to be a man to trifle with."

The fifth man there hadn't spoken yet, and now he said, "I wouldn't want to take that stranger on all by my lonesome, but there is five of us here, and only one of him."

The man with the hole in his hat glanced at him, pushed the battered hat to the back of his head, and sleeved the sweat off his brow. "You can count me out, Cassidy."

"All right, then that makes it four to one," Brand said. "I don't see no problem in that."

"Yeah," the eager boy seconded. "You in with us, Chase?"

Chase Everly had been brooding ever since the stranger had ridden his horse past him as if he'd not been worth talking to. It had humiliated him in front of the men, and it was why he had risked incurring Percy Dunbar's wrath by sneaking over to the house and spying on the stranger through the window. He didn't have to think long on the matter before he said he was in with them.

The ruddy-faced man who had declined their offer stood now. "I reckon I'll go out east and check that new dirt tank we just put in, and make sure Mr. Dunbar's cattle has got water." He strode out and mounted a horse tied to the corral railing. Chase knew it was his way of letting them make their plans in private and showing that he wanted nothing to do with it.

That was all right by him. Gold split four ways was always better than gold split five.

It was late afternoon when the stranger left Percy and Margaret Dunbar on their porch and rode out of the compound, heading north. Chase Everly waited until he was a mile ahead and hardly visible on the rolling land before moving out with his men. The four riders kept their distance at first and, as the shadows stretched out across the land, they closed in on him.

"He's making for Kermit Creek," the eager young man said. Ahead, the stranger had descended a cut in the land and had dropped out of sight.

"That should make this easy," Chase said.

Brand rocked forward in his saddle. "Me and Cassidy will head west. Following that creek will only slow him up. We can cut ahead of him and wait while you two come up behind. Squeeze him between our guns."

Chase nodded. "Let's do it." The four men split.

Down by the creek, shadows had gathered, but Chase had no trouble following the hoofprints along the sandy bank. He had to slow his pace more than once when he saw the stranger's stout mustang turning a bend just ahead of him. Chase figured that by now Brand and Cassidy had dropped into the cut ahead of them, and he half expected to hear them any minute.

It was almost dark in the deep defile of Kermit Creek when Chase spied the mustang again. It was tied to a half-dead cottonwood tree near the creek, its head dipping down to the water. In the shadows was the hunched shape of the stranger, not far from the horse, bent over for a drink of water as well. Just then Chase spied Cassidy and Brand emerging from the deeper blackness of the narrow canyon beyond. He caught their attention with a raised arm, motioned them off their horses, and drawing their revolvers, the four men advanced.

The stranger's horse shied away but then quieted. Chase eyed the saddlebags still tied to it, then directed his attention to the stranger who apparently had not yet seen them, nor had he moved from his place by the water.

Run me down, will you? Chase thought, halting silently. The others waited as Chase raised his revolver, aimed, and draw back its hammer. The clicking of the weapon being cocked sounded loud in the narrow place, but Chase did not give the stranger a heartbeat to reach for his gun and fired immediately. Orange flame spat from the muzzle in the gloom and the roar of it echoed from the high walls around them. Instantly he thumbed back the hammer and fired again, and then a third time until the stranger tumbled face first into the stream.

The four rushed forward. In the darkness they stopped above the body half in the creek. The black hat that had been upon his head was bobbing on the water, slowly making its way downstream.

"That's done," Chase said with a nervous quaver in his voice. He bent down to roll the stranger over and rifle his pockets.

"What the hell is this?" Chase said suddenly, standing and holding a blanket. When they stared back at the body, they saw it was the twisted branch of a tree. It had been propped in place with the blanket draped over it. "Where the devil did he go?" Chase glanced about as if he still expected to find the body there.

"I'm over here," came a voice from the darkness behind them. The tone was low, unhurried, and carried with it an edge that cut like a razor.

The four men spun around, bringing their revolvers up. At first they saw nothing, and all at once the canyon seemed to burst before their eyes. Orange flame flashed and danced upon its straight, sandstone walls. The four shots came so quickly that they sounded as one long explosion, and then the defile fell deathly silent as the sound of gunfire faded away. In his last few seconds of life, Chase Everly watched the tall, gaunt figure separate from the darkness and come forward.

Then Everly died.

Strider halted a few feet away, his revolver ready, but no one moved, and after a few moments it was plain that no one was going to. He studied their faces one by one—faces he did not know until he came to Chase Everly. Here was the man who had stopped him in the yard, who had sneaked up behind the Dunbar's home—the same face that had watched him through the Dunbar's window.

Were Percy and Margaret in on this as well?

Strider didn't think so and holstered his Colt.

He collected the revolvers from their dead fingers and flung them into the stream, then retrieved his hat from the water where it had hung up on a rock. Taking up his bedroll from beneath Everly, Strider rolled it up and tied it back over the saddlebags and swung up onto his horse.

In half an hour he had left the canyon with its dead men behind him and was riding beneath a bright moon.

Strider made camp a few hours later. The next morning he reached the Red River where he boarded a flatboat. The flatboat took him to Shreveport where he purchased passage on a small steamer that carried him the rest of the way to the Mississippi River, and then down to New Orleans.

His work in Texas done, Carleton Manor was Strider's destination now.

CHAPTER SEVEN

The wharves at New Orleans stretched on forever in either direction from where Canal Street descended onto the river—or so it appeared to Gen. She had no idea how far the city docks and wharves actually did extend, but from where she sat waiting in the carriage, where Jackson had parked it near the port authorities building, she could see no end to them either up the river or down. She could, in truth, see very little of the river, and nothing beyond a few hundred feet of wharves. Anything further away was obscured by the forest of tall-masted sailing ships and the black chimneys of a hundred steamers, pumping clouds of sooty smoke into the air.

The docks seemed an incomprehensible jumble of cargo, and Gen had no idea how anyone was able to keep track of it all. Even this late in the season, piles of cotton still overwhelmed the place, and bales by the hundreds were being loaded onto ships flying foreign colors. Everywhere she looked, stevedores were hurrying with burdens on their shoulders or in handcarts.

In the scant eleven months that she had lived at Carleton Manor, she had made the thirty-eight-mile trip to New Orleans exactly four times, but she had visited the city many times before her whirlwind courtship, engagement, and marriage to Robert, and she did know something about the city. New Orleans was the South's premier port, the hub of international trade, with a population of 168,000 people. It also housed some of the finest gaming parlors—and the bawdiest—along the river.

A smile flashed fleetingly across Gen's face and was gone as she recalled those days. Ah, life had certainly settled down for her. She didn't really miss all the excitement, but still the exhilaration of the chase lingered in her soul, always struggling a bit to be let free again.

She put her mind on other things. She was going to have more excitement than she would know what to do with if everything went as Robert had planned.

And why should it not?

She straightened herself on the leather seat of the carriage, feeling the heat of the afternoon coming through its dark canvas top, and studied the boats down on the river, reading the names upon their paddle boxes. The boat she sought was not there—or, at least not visible from her vantage point.

"Newspaper, missus?" a young voice said, distracting her. When she looked around, a little black boy was standing there, a bundle of papers under his arms.

"Yes, I think I will, thank you," she said, giving the boy a nickel. He went off to hawk his newspapers at the next carriage parked up the road while she turned to the back page where the arrivals and departures of the scheduled steamers were listed. She scanned the list, which took up two full columns, frowned, then tried the listing of steamer companies that maintained private wharves out of New Orleans—thirty-three companies, she discovered, reading their announcements. She still did not find the name of the boat she was seeking.

"Where can she be?" she said aloud, folding the paper onto her lap in exasperation. She wanted a drink, but that would be impossible now . . . well, at least inappropriate, with Jackson expected back any moment. She looked for Jackson on the busy street and didn't spy him. Her eye caught the flutter of a handbill that had been tacked to a telegraph pole. She left the carriage to read it:

SENATOR STEPHEN A. DOUGLAS

Democratic Presidential Nominee

to speak on

Common Sense and Compromise on Slavery in the States and Territories

8:00 P.M.

The Riverman's Club

New Orleans

Gen read the notice with deep interest. The date at the bottom of the bill was today's date. She turned to a passing gentleman in a tall, gray silk hat and said, "Excuse me, sir, but can you tell me where The Riverman's Club is located?"

He swept the hat from his head and smiled at her. "The Riverman's Club? Why, it is on Chartres Street, near Toulouse. Are you to meet someone there?"

"No, but Senator Douglas is speaking there this evening, and I wish to hear him." She indicated the handbill.

"Oh." His smile faltered.

"Is there something the matter?" Gen asked.

He firmed up his smile and said, "No, ma'am, only that The Riverman's is a gentlemen-only club. No ladies allowed."

"I see."

He bent at the waist, bid her good day, and turned to leave.

Gen said, "You don't happen to know where Senator Douglas is staying while in New Orleans, do you?" Her blue eyes widened hopefully, and she gave him a coy smile.

"I do," he said. "Senator Douglas and his entourage are staying at the Saint Charles, and I understand that the day after tomorrow they will be boarding a steamer to take them campaigning up the river."

"Thank you. You have been most helpful." Gen returned to the carriage. Spying the Douglas handbill had been an unplanned stroke of luck, and she considered the various ways she might take advantage of it.

Jackson returned to the carriage. "De *Tempest Queen* she still not at her berth, Missus St. James." He handed her a telegraph embossed with the imprimatur of the New Orleans port authority. "De wharf master, him wired upriver. De *Tempest Queen* is still at her berth at Baton Rouge, but she is expected in tomorrow afternoon."

Gen glanced at the telegraph, which confirmed what Jackson had just told her.

"What do yo' want to do now, Missus St. James?"

"Well, there is not much I can do but wait on the morrow. I shall have to take a room."

"I can stay at de livery with de horses—"

"No, Jackson. Robert will be expecting you back at Carleton Manor this evening. You can drive me to a hotel and I shall take a room for tonight, then you can be on your way. I will be all right, really." She noted the uncertainty in Jackson's dark eyes, the unhappy dip to his lips, the downward hitch to his gray brows.

"I don't tink I ought to leave you here by yo'rself, missus."

"Nonsense. I will be just fine, Jackson. Now, let's find a proper hotel . . . er, I think the Saint Charles will do."

"Yes, ma'am," he said unhappily and climbed stiffly back up onto the seat. Taking up the reins, Jackson turned the team around and drove away from the river.

In her room, Gen changed out of her traveling dress into a loose frock and unpacked a more fashionable dress for dinner that night. She would have liked to have taken a real bath but settled instead for a sponge bath from a pitcher of hot water that she had sent up from the kitchen. Afterward, she propped the pillows up on the headboard of the bedstead and rested from the long drive, thinking and watching the afternoon shadows lengthening across the buildings beyond her second-floor window.

The trepidations that she had felt that morning after she and Robert had made love were gone, and in their place was a sharpened awareness and the exhilaration that comes from embarking on a well-planned caper. They were feelings she had almost forgotten while living safely and comfortably all these months at Carleton Manor, so far from the river.

She wanted to hear what Douglas was going to say tonight, but if she was going to enter The Riverman's Club, it would require a plan—or at least an escort.

She rang for a boy. When he arrived, she inquired as to which rooms the Douglas party occupied. He told her they had three rooms on the top floor. She thanked him with a coin from the bottom of her reticule and when he had left, Gen returned to the bed to think.

In a little while she took up the newspaper and carefully read every word. There was not much of interest in it. She read about a fire in one of the freight warehouses along the river, and of a shooting in a saloon on Bourbon Street. A riverboat had burst a boiler at the New Orleans wharves. There were no survivors, and all the bodies had been taken to the warehouse of the salvage company recovering the wreckage and were awaiting identification.

All the usual news.

It told her nothing of importance concerning the movement of Douglas and his party, although there were a torrent of articles on Southern rights, and deriding the Lincoln candidacy, and the threats coming far and wide of the dire consequences of a Republican in the White House. Nothing she did not already know. The South hated Lincoln. They didn't particularly like Douglas, either, preferring instead the incumbent vice president, John Breckinridge. But no one really expected Breckinridge to win. Only two men were serious contenders: Douglas and Lincoln.

Douglas was the moderate, and he'd work hard to appease the South. Lincoln was a firebrand, however, and his election was surely going to plunge the South into a bloody war, one Gen was certain the South could win through sheer strength of character, but oh, the cost would be high! She found herself frowning as she folded the paper and placed it upon the nightstand.

As evening drew on, Gen dressed for dinner in gray silk taffeta and pulled on black leather shoes, working the hook impatiently to get all sixteen buttons through their tight holes. She combed out her hair and pinned it up on top of her head, powdered her face, and when she had finished, she stood in front of the mirror.

At least I can still manage to dress myself, she thought, turning to study her image and approving of what she saw.

Eleven months at Carleton Manor had not completely ruined her, after all, although it had not taken her long to grow comfortable with the servants helping her into and out of her dresses. All the buttons were a bother, but they could still be managed with perseverance.

In his proposal of marriage, Robert St. James had offered Gen the life she could have only dreamt of before. She had jumped at the opportunity and had not regretted it. After so many years of playacting, she finally had the real thing. She no longer had to fake her pedigree by summoning "the colonel," her father, and by dropping the title during casual conversation in the practiced way she had used before marrying Robert. Her father, in truth, had been a poor sharecropper, and the only colonel she had ever known was the old landowner who had fought in the War of 1812.

Robert was rich, and he could give her everything she ever wanted, even the thrill of a scheme like this that would make them both infinitely richer. She had the respectability of his name, yet she could still flirt with the excitement of the old way of life. It was perfect.

Gen found a piece of hotel stationery in the desk drawer, removed her leather secretary from her traveling bag, laid out pen and blotter, and shook a little black powdered ink into a vial and added a few drops of water to it, mixing it to the proper consistency.

She thought a moment with the end of her pen pressing upon her lower lip, then dipped it into the ink and wrote:

> Hon. Stephen A. Douglas:
> Dear sir,
> I have been informed by the hotel staff that you and your entourage are staying at this very hotel. This is indeed pleasant news to me. For many years now I have admired you, your sensible views on the problems facing

the South, and your solid solutions. You will make a very fine President, indeed, Mr. Douglas, and my prayers are for you, and for a successful election.

Elections, however, require not only prayers, but money to finance them, and votes to win them. Since I am a woman, and cannot help you by casting my vote, I wish to help in the only other way that I can. I wish to make a monetary contribution. I will be boarding a steamer soon to take me up the river to visit my sister in Alton, Illinois, so if we can meet tonight, I would be happy to do what small part I can to ensure you the White House come November. I am staying in room 209.

Yours faithfully,
Miss Genevieve

She stopped. In her haste she had almost penned her true name. That would not do. She thought. Perhaps her maiden name? No, that might be even more disastrous. She pondered a moment longer, and then on a impulse decided on a play on her maiden name and penned *Summers.*

Miss Genevieve Summers. She liked the sound of that and was pleased with her choice. She folded the note, placed it in an envelope, lit a red candle from her secretary, and sealed the flap. On the front, she wrote Douglas's name and rang for the boy again. The same young man showed up at the door, took the letter along with a half dollar tip, and was gone.

Now all she could do was wait.

She seated herself at the desk again, fingered the silk petals on her bonnet, and drummed her nails upon the desktop as the minutes passed. More than before, she wished she had thought to bring along a bottle of something from Robert's liquor cabinet, but then, perhaps it was for the best she had not. Whatever would Douglas think of her if he smelled Scotch on her breath?

*   *   *

Captain Hamilton stood at the head of the hurricane deck, near the *Tempest Queen*'s big bronze bell, looking out across a broad expanse of baled cotton that had been loaded on his boat. In the failing daylight, he saw that most of the cargo had been brought aboard and stacked as high as prudence would permit. The load completely engulfed the main deck, had swallowed up the boiler deck, and now threatened to bury the hurricane as well.

She will be dipping her guards this trip!

He grinned. A most satisfactory season this had been. He had paid all his bills and had banked more than twenty thousand. A tidy nest egg. He could live quite comfortably the rest of his life on it and on his other investments and with the cash the *Tempest Queen* would bring when he sold her.

Now would be a good time to retire, he thought. "Quit while you are on top, Bill," he said aloud to himself as if to bolster his resolve.

He had been courting the idea of retirement for several years, and each time it appeared that the notion was about to win him over, he had backed off. The pull of the river was always too strong, the *Tempest Queen* too much a lady to cast aside like one would a worn pair of shoes. She was only wood, iron, and glass, it was true, but there was life to her as well.

Hamilton discovered his fingers clenching into a fist. He relaxed them, grinning. It was happening again. It always happened when he thought of selling his boat.

He started across the hurricane deck and took a ladder down to the boiler deck. The promenade that encircled the cabins there was now a dark tunnel through the bales of cotton; brown burlap walls that smelled of moist hemp and of money. Strolling forward in the dark—the lamps were never lighted when they had a "large trip" of cotton aboard—he met Clifton Stewart coming toward him.

The young man's arms were overloaded with brown paper packages, and he said happily, "Afternoon, Captain Hamilton. This has been a splendid day, has it not?"

Hamilton looked him over curiously. It had been, more or less, a *usual* day for him, but Stewart appeared to be in fine spirits. Hamilton had no idea the promotion to mud clerk had been of such importance to the young man. "Well, you certainly are chipper." He eyed the packages. "Your new wardrobe?"

"Yes, sir, and I'm anxious to get a bath and put them on. I just saw Mr. Belding as I came aboard. He says you have a stateroom for me?"

"Hmm. Yes. You may have your predecessor's quarters. He is packing up this very moment. You know where they are, don't you?"

"Yes, sir. They are up in the texas."

Stewart had emphasized that last word in a way that made it sound as if the quarters of the captain and the boat's officers were only a step or two shy of paradise.

"I'm sure Mr. Tyback will not mind you moving in as he is moving out. I will have a chambermaid sent up to change your bedding."

"Thank you, Captain Hamilton." Stewart shifted the packages in his arms. The newspaper slipped out and fell to the deck, and with it the envelope containing Mystie's letter. Hamilton bent for them.

"Hmm? What is this?"

"Er, it is only a note from an old friend, Captain. The sheriff had been holding it for me," he said quickly.

Hamilton put the envelope back inside the folded paper and wedged it under Stewart's arm for him. "Take care you don't lose anything else along the way. Should I ring for a porter to help you?"

"No, I can manage. Thank you again, Captain." Stewart

headed toward the same ladder Hamilton had just descended, and with some maneuvering and curious contortions that Hamilton figured only a young man would be capable of, he made his way up it.

Once more by himself, Hamilton continued around the promenade to the wide staircase and took it down to the main deck, which had completely disappeared under more than three thousand bales of cotton. All that remained of it was a tunnel that had been constructed through the man-made mountain. The tunnel deposited Hamilton at the very bow of the boat where a narrow path skirted the bales around to the gangplank. He took it with care, for the path fell away precipitously to the river a mere footstep to his left.

Once on the wharf, Hamilton paused to turn back and gaze at the *Tempest Queen*. She no longer looked like a boat, only a massive wall of carefully stacked cotton bales, with two black smokestacks protruding above and a gleaming white pilothouse perched atop. The guards were indeed right down to the river, dipping the water.

That would make excellent armor, Hamilton thought all at once. No cannonball nor rifle bullet could penetrate it. Hamilton was startled by that notion. In over twenty-five years of hauling cotton up and down the Mississippi, he had seen thousands of boats buried under tons of cotton, and he had never before considered the potential military applications of such an arrangement. What had brought it to mind now? He didn't know, and with a bit of uneasiness, he put the conundrum out of mind.

Belding spied him then and came over, carrying a clipboard with its papers fluttering in the breeze. The clerk stuck his pencil behind an ear and immediately it was lost beneath the shaggy hair. Hamilton sighed inwardly. Try as he might, he could never seem to keep his clerk properly groomed. It was not that Belding resisted Hamilton's suggestions to visit the barber regularly, it was just that even with a proper haircut, the man seemed perpetually disheveled. Hamilton had never quite been able to figure out exactly what was amiss; it wasn't any one item glaringly out of place, just a hundred little things.

Belding smiled pleasantly as he drew nearer. Disheveled as he was, Belding was a superb clerk, Hamilton had no doubts about that.

Perhaps I am being a bit too fussy.

Hamilton did not want to scowl as he knew old men tended to do, and he tried not to let the windblown hair bother him.

"How does she look, Mr. Belding?"

"Sixty-two and thirty-seven hundred bales of cotton, and twenty-four hundred sacks of cottonseed, Captain. That's all of it. Mr. Lansing says not another bale, not another sack, or he won't board her when we shove off."

Hamilton laughed softly. "Won't he, now. Well, you can assure Mr. Lansing that I will in no way put his life in jeopardy—or my boat. He knows his business."

Belding had been out among the cargo, doing the job of a mud clerk. He looked down at his feet and scraped the edge of his shoe on the landing stage. "I ran into Stewart a few minutes ago—"

"Yes, I saw him," Hamilton said. "I am giving him Tyback's quarters. That will put him near you, should you need him."

"I thought you might."

"Stewart is a good man. He should work out well for you."

"I can believe that. After a year and a half under Lansing's training, he should be in fine condition."

They had a chuckle over that, then Belding excused

himself, saying he had to get up to the office and figure out the freight charges for this cargo.

After the clerk had disappeared into the mountain of cotton, Hamilton thrust his hand into the pocket of his blue jacket and his hand wrapped around the small pouch of gold coins there. With the river darkening behind him, he turned his feet toward town. A small pang of guilt rose in his breast as he started up the road, but he promptly squelched it as he approached the stores and saloons. He had, after all, been practicing diligently, and hadn't McKay said his card playing had come a long way from their first voyage together? Besides, he only had a small amount of gold on him, he told himself as he stepped into a well-recommended gaming parlor.

He left his cap with one of the doormen, and at the batwing doors he stopped and spied a table where what appeared to him to be a quite friendly game of cards was in progress. As he entered the busy room, he noticed the shattered mirror behind the bar and mused that the schooner pictured there looked as if she had taken a shot across her bow, and was in peril of sinking through a wide crack.

A commotion, then a roar of cheers erupted from a dark corner of the room. A dozen men were gathered about a table there. Hamilton could not see what was going on, but knew by the look of it that there was high betting and hot cards.

He at least had sense enough to avoid the kind of game that would draw such a crowd. He had participated in such a game once, and it had very nearly cost him the *Tempest Queen*. Now he was content to play simple games and keep his losses to a minimum.

CHAPTER EIGHT

Hamilton had found himself a friendly table, and he was playing a fair hand of cards an hour into the game. He had made no spectacular wins, but then, no horrendous disasters, either. They played seven-up, Hamilton's favorite game. His partner was a young pharmacist with a prematurely bald head and a nervous tic in his right eye. Paired against them were a man who owned a snag boat and a fellow who had come down from Memphis to drum whalebone corsets.

The conversation had moved amiably along in no particular direction, drifting from river commerce to politics, from the price of cotton in New Orleans to the cost of threshing machines in Ohio. They even touched briefly on the gold strikes in the mountains far west of the Mississippi

River, in Kansas Territory, and Hamilton said that he was acquainted with a fellow by the name of McKay who was recently back from the gold fields, and who was a permanent passenger aboard the *Tempest Queen.*

The pharmacist said he had once considered moving west, but his wife would not leave the South.

The snag boat owner, a quiet man by the name of Simmons, who played his cards close to his vest, said after a few moments of silence, "Any one of you here happen to know about that boat down at New Orleans?"

When he got blank looks all around, Simmons said, "I was just wondering. Heard that a boat exploded just off the wharves. Heard that the explosion knocked down folks standing two hundred yards away, leveled another steamer moored nearby, and hurled a twelve-foot sheet of iron over five blocks, clear to Canal and Front Street.

"I saw a piece in the newspaper about that," the drummer said.

"Hmm." Hamilton pursed his lips. "Was she arriving or departing?"

"I don't know," Simmons went on. "Only picked up some talk while tying up earlier. I thought someone here might know."

The pharmacist shook his head.

Hamilton's gray brows dipped. "Only a boiler letting loose would made such an explosion. She was probably departing."

The three men there looked at him, and the question was plain on their faces. Hamilton cleared his throat, vaguely embarrassed to have placed himself as an authority on the matter, but then he did have over twenty-five years on the river, more years than at least the pharmacist had been alive.

"Most boat masters," he explained, "take pride in a fast vessel, and the smoke and pomp that goes along with it. It is what the passengers and the people on shore want to see. To get that black smoke, they burn pine knots or resined coal, and to get the speed, they hold onto the steam instead of letting it off. Pine knots burn hot, the flue gets to glowing, and the water in the boiler is low. The first revolution of her wheels brings the two materials in contact and any weakness in the boilers will cause a collapse."

"I knew that," Simmons said, gathering in the cards for a fresh deal.

The drummer took a sip of his schooner of beer and said, "I thought that was only a problem with the older high-pressure boilers."

"New boiler designs have diminished the problem some, but it has not been eliminated. A prudent captain must know when he is pushing the limit of his engines, and he must maintain them in top condition." Hamilton sipped his coffee as the snag boat owner dealt out the cards. When he had them in his hand, he said, "By the way, what was the name of the boat, Mr. Simmons?"

Simmons shrugged. "I don't know, Captain Hamilton." He looked to the drummer. "You said you saw a piece in the paper?"

"I did, but I did not read the story closely. I cannot recall the name. Is it important?"

"I suppose not," Hamilton said, studying the cards that had come to him.

"Well, let's get on with our game, gentlemen," Simmons said, tasting the frappé at his elbow.

Just then, a commotion at the table with the crowd standing about it caught the attention of the entire saloon. The men standing there gave way as one of the players suddenly stood up and drew a Colt Navy from his belt beneath his vest.

"You have cheated me!" the man said, waving the revolver

at one of the seated players. He was a lanky fellow in a gray frock coat and a worn silk hat that had seen more prosperous times.

"How have I cheated you, sir?"

Hamilton heard the voice rise from among the crowd, but he could not see the speaker through the knot of men.

"You have a card up your sleeve. I watched you put it there."

The unseen speaker laughed. "If I did, I will wager you never saw me put it there. If you do not care for the temperature of the water, my dear Mr. Shindle, you should not take a bath in it. Now, stop acting poorly and be gone with you."

"Not until I have my money back."

"Sir, you shall not have one penny of it back."

The man shook in anger and drew back the hammer on his gun.

From a different part of the table a streak of ebony lashed out in the lamplight and cracked soundly upon the man's hand. The revolver clattered to the floor and the fellow let out a yelp, grabbing his fingers.

A man stood up.

He was tall and heavily built, with a shock of dark hair falling across his broad forehead. A mustache and goatee flowed smoothly together to a point at his chin. He wore a finely tailored black coat over a white ruffled shirt and a dark cravat about his neck. He said, "I repeat. You are acting poorly and you have drunk too much whiskey. Take what you have left in your pockets and be thankful for it. Perhaps next time you will be wiser in your choice of card games."

"You'll not get away with this, Devol!" the man cried, and without warning, he balled his knuckles into a hard fist and struck out.

Devol dodged quickly, but instead of moving away from

the punch, he placed his broad skull in front of it. The crack of knuckle against skull resounded in the room and instantly the man drew back his hand, fanning it in the air, then hugging it under his arm. In one swift move, Devol took the man by the shoulders and, giving a sharp lurch, butted him in the head with his own forehead, sending him straight-away to the floor.

Hamilton watched the brief encounter with interest. The name that had been spoken struck a chord with him, and he wondered where he had heard it before.

When it became apparent that the man on the floor wasn't going to get up, two men standing nearby hoisted him into their arms and hauled him out the batwing doors and onto the sidewalk out front.

Devol brushed his hands together as if wiping the dirt of the fight off of them and said, "Well, gentlemen, I find that I have grown hungry." He glanced down at the men still seated about the table. "If you all do not object, I suggest we take this opportunity to refresh ourselves." He glanced at a huge gold watch with a long, heavy gold chain that he took from his vest pocket. "It is almost half past nine o'clock. An hour should suffice."

The players at the table agreed, and the game temporarily broke up. When the men standing about wandered off, Hamilton saw that one of the players was Dexter McKay. He was not surprised, and all at once he remembered where he had heard the name Devol before. McKay had spoken of him often. Apparently George Devol was a gambler of great stature, and his reputation was widely respected along the Mississippi. McKay had said he wanted to meet the man across a gaming table. Hamilton grinned to himself. Well, it appeared he finally had.

McKay rose slowly from the table and carefully settled his tall beaver hat upon his head. He filled his pockets with the chips that he had accumulated and took up his ebony walking stick.

Devol turned briefly toward him and Hamilton heard him say, "Thank you for disarming that rascal, Mr. McKay," and then, with his own pockets likewise bulging with chips, Devol went to the bar and ordered a sandwich.

McKay remained awhile at the table, examining his walking cane. He frowned, stroked a thumb across the shiny wood as if trying to remove a scratch, and then started away.

Hamilton raised an arm and said, "Mr. McKay."

The gambler stopped, glanced about the room, spied the captain, smiled widely, and came over.

"So, that is the famous Devol," Hamilton said. "Does he live up to his reputation and your expectations?"

McKay grinned and patted his pocket. "George Devol is an excellent card player, nearly as good as I, Captain Hamilton," he said, feigning modesty.

Hamilton laughed. "I daresay you have brass, Mr. McKay, but I will wager that Devol has a harder head than you."

"A skull like a cannonball," McKay said, "and he is welcome to it. No one so far has ever bested him at head-butting."

McKay seemed not the least disturbed by the encounter, and showed only a bit of concern over his marred stick. It was more than just a walking cane, Hamilton knew; below the silver horse-head hand grip, encased within the ebony staff, was a seventeen-inch short sword. McKay never went anywhere without it, just as he never strayed very far from the tiny pocket revolver under his coat. "A worthless little thing," Hamilton had heard McKay expound more than once about the .31 Remington. "But far superior to a clenched fist!"

McKay glanced at the cards on their table and said, "Seven-up?"

"Indeed," Hamilton replied brightly, for he had accumulated a small pile of coins in his corner that he was proud of.

"Pay attention to what you have learned, Captain, and you shall go away with heavy pockets." McKay grinned, nodded his good-bye at the three men there, and said, "I am going for a bite to eat. Perhaps I will see you later, Captain."

"We shove off in the morning, McKay."

"Er, I most likely will not be aboard when you do, Captain."

"No?" Hamilton hitched up a brow.

McKay glanced at the table where their cards were still neatly stacked in the middle. "Sometimes these games run on for days, you know. But you *will* be coming back in a few days, hm?"

"Yes. We are scheduled to bring a special passenger up the river, and we shall be stopping along the way for him to speak."

"A special passenger?"

"It is Senator Douglas. The presidential candidate."

"Really? The Little Giant? Well, I shall like to meet the man."

"You shall. The *Tempest Queen* will be back in Baton Rouge in three days, Mr. McKay."

"I will be waiting for you, Captain." McKay left them, pushing through the batwing doors and disappearing down the hallway that led to the front door.

Clifton shifted his bundles and managed to get a hand free enough to knock on the door.

"It's unlocked," came the reply from inside.

Stewart transferred the newspaper to his teeth, wedged a

brown-paper bundle between his knees, and turned the handle.

Jeffrey Tyback glanced over from the bed where he was filling a carpetbag with clothes—each piece neatly folded—and as he put them into the valise, he smoothed down the material before setting the next garment upon it. "Ah, it is you, Clifton. Come in."

Stewart waddled over the threshold and stopped just inside the small stateroom. He took the newspaper from his teeth. "Captain Hamilton has given me your cabin. He didn't think you would mind if I came up and dropped some things off."

"No, of course not. Just put them anywhere. I am almost done here."

Stewart glanced around. The staterooms in the texas where the officers and some of the crew lived were not as luxurious as those that the passengers occupied on the boiler deck below, but this little room was like a mansion compared to the cramped quarters he'd been sharing with the firemen and deckhands in the cabin near the furnaces. Here he was away from the heat and the pounding of the engines, and here his bed would be his own, not a sagging cot that he shared in shifts with the other men who stoked the boilers and bucked the cargo.

He dropped his packages on the chair by the desk, which Tyback had already been cleaned out.

"I heard you have gotten my job, Clifton. It is a step up from those furnaces."

"It certainly is, and a pleasant one, as well. How is Belding to work under?"

"Belding is a right sort of fellow; easygoing, and he don't ask much of you when under steam. But when he sets you on a task, he expects your numbers to tally, and if they don't, he ain't too patient. Two or three mess-ups and you'll find yourself back stoking those boilers." Tyback folded a shirt as he spoke, taking care that the sleeves lay perfectly flat upon the body, folded back at precisely one-half the shoulder width. Then the body was folded up over them in thirds to form a neat rectangular package that was transferred to the valise.

"Now, take me, for example. At first I had troubles with the sort of precision that Belding required. My figures didn't always add up right, you see. He took me aside one day when my tallies didn't match the figures on his manifest, and he pointed at a coal barge coming downriver, passing us on the larboard point just then.

" 'See that flat of coal?' I said, 'Yes,' and he says, 'Take note there isn't but a single ragged tent at the fore where the crew live, and it's a leaky thing to be sure. And see those men fending off the jetsam with them heavy poles?' I said, 'Yes,' and he says, 'Looks like mighty tiring work, and cold and wet come rainy nights, don't it?' I said, 'Yes,' and he says, 'Next time your tallies are in error, Mr. Tyback, you'll be looking for a new job, and if you end up on a float like that one, you will remember what your carelessness has cost you—your warm cabin, your galley-prepared meals, your tick mattress—and you will have no one but yourself to blame for the loss. Do I make my meaning clear?' I said, 'Yes,' and I have not been in error since. Get my point?"

"Yes," Stewart said.

Tyback laid another shirt on the bed, buttoned it to the throat, and carefully folded it into a neat package.

"Why are you leaving, Jeff?"

Tyback continued with the folding, not looking up. "Haven't you heard?"

"Heard?" Stewart laughed. "Down at the furnaces all one hears is the clang of iron doors, the scrape of the rakes, and Lansing carrying on as if the *Tempest Queen* was about to founder if his crew didn't keep those furnaces blazing to beat the band."

Jeffrey Tyback laughed. "I've heard that about Lansing. The reason I'm leaving is because I'm getting married!"

"Really? Why, that is bully! Who is it?"

"A girl from Port Hudson, my hometown. Her name is Emma, and she is wonderful."

"What will you do if you quit the river?"

"Oh, that's already taken care of. Emma's father owns a sawmill. I'm going to take care of the books. Ralph—that's Emma's pa—he says my training as a clerk aboard a steamer is just what his business needs."

"Well, congratulations, and good luck."

"Thanks, Clifton."

Stewart turned his attention to the packages he'd dumped on the chair. He untied one of them and shook out the three white shirts he had bought. They were wrinkled, and he'd have to send them down to the laundry to be pressed.

That thought brought Mystie to mind. He remembered how she looked that first morning, a laundry basket in her arms, her wonderful black hair tied up in a bun. The sky had been gray and drizzling, but when he heard her voice unexpectedly behind him, the gray vanished beneath the brightness of her smile. He had walked her to the laundry room that morning, taking the wicker basket from her arms. How he wished he could go back to that very moment now. How differently he would have behaved at the end of that glorious week. Or would he have? Perhaps he had needed to suffer through the last year and a half. Could he honestly have been able to cast aside what he had grown up believing, had he not?

Well, that was all water under the bridge. The *Guiding Star* was in New Orleans, and so would he be in another twenty hours. With any luck at all, Mystie would still be aboard her. He would beg her forgiveness, he would prove that he loved her, he would have her back if he had to move heaven and hell to do so. Nothing would deter him now that he was so close.

Stewart wanted to tell Tyback about the letter the sheriff had given him from Mystie, for his quest was not unknown to the crew of the *Tempest Queen,* but he refrained. He'd only tell McKay and Zachary, for now. The rest of the crew would learn of it once he was certain Mystie was still aboard the *Guiding Star.*

He unpacked new trousers and pulled them on. They were stiff, but they'd break in soon enough. He changed into one of the shirts. Wrinkled or not, it was a far sight more tidy than what he had on.

Stewart examined the new shoes he had purchased and wove the laces through the eyelets.

Tyback finished his packing. He sat on the edge of the bed and glanced at the newspaper Stewart had brought along. "Anything interesting happening? How is Lincoln faring? You know, that Northerner is nothing more than a Whig in disguise. That's all those new Republicans are. I hope he don't win next month. I fear the South will finally secede if he does." He picked up the paper. "You mind if I look through it?"

"No, go ahead. I haven't had time yet," Stewart said, pulling on his left shoe and tightening the laces.

After a moment Tyback said, "Look here. Douglas is making a sweep through the South."

"It's about time, don't you think?" Stewart said, working on the right shoe now. "He's got a few fences to mend if he expects to be elected."

"He's going to speak in New Orleans, then make his way to Memphis and—" he stopped abruptly as if stunned and then said, "Well, will you look at this!"

"What?"

"Take a guess at what steamer he is booked onto."

Stewart paused and looked at Tyback, and knew at once by the surprised look on the ex–mud clerk's face what he meant. "No, you're fooling."

"I am not. It says so right here in the paper. He's booked onto the *Tempest Queen!*" Tyback turned the paper for Stewart to see. "Wonder why Belding has said nothing about it to me? He has to have known."

"Maybe to protect the senator?"

"Then why publish his itinerary right here in the newspaper for everyone to read?"

Stewart shrugged. He had no idea why politicians—and captains—did what they did, and he returned his attention to his laces. He was curious, however, to see the man the papers had dubbed Little Giant, even though he didn't fully approve of Senator Douglas's policies or the Cincinnati platform that the Democratic party had adopted. But in the entire field of presidential candidates, as numerous as they had been in the '56 election, Douglas was the least onerous—at least of those men who stood a chance of winning. Stewart would have preferred Breckinridge, the South's candidate, but he didn't think the vice president could win. No, it was going to be a battle between Lincoln and Douglas, and if only Douglas and Senator Jeff Davis had managed to heal their differences . . . Well, Clifton Stewart had more important things than the upcoming presidential election to think about right at the moment.

Tyback turned a page and went on to another article. "Here it say New Orleans wants to put in another municipal landing."

"Uh-huh." Stewart fixed the cuff of his trousers over the top of his shoes and stood to look in the mirror. "There. That is a definite improvement." He made a face at himself and rubbed the fine blond bristles scattered about his face. He never could manage a proper beard, and certainly nothing as fine as the chin whiskers his father had worn for as long as Clifton could remember.

The paper rustled. After a moment Tyback clucked disapprovingly and shook his head. "It has happened again," he said glancing up.

"What has happened again?"

"A steamer burst her boilers as she was leaving the wharves."

"Oh? Where was this?"

"New Orleans."

"When?"

"Yesterday. The story was sent up by telegraph wire, it says here. All mates aboard her were lost, scalded to death. They were still pulling the bodies from the water when this was printed. Says here she had not yet taken on passengers, only crew and cargo. She was bound for Rock Island—"

"Rock Island?" Stewart's attention was immediately arrested. He spun about to stare at Tyback, and a fist seemed to squeeze his chest. "Rock Island, you say?"

"Yes. What is the matter, Clifton?"

Stewart had to grip the corner of the desk to steady himself. "What . . . what is the name of the boat? Does it give a name?" He was suddenly shouting.

Clifton's reaction startled Tyback. "Yes," he stammered looking back at the paper. "It was a steamer called *Guiding Star.*"

The stateroom lurched beneath Stewart's feet. Everything tilted and swam before his eyes, and he staggered back into the chair.

CHAPTER NINE

The moment of dizziness passed at once. Stewart leaped out of the chair, grabbed up the newspaper, and read the article carefully with shaking hands.

"Whatever is the matter, Clifton?" Tyback asked, staring at him with open concern.

Clifton heard Tyback's voice, but his words seemed to glance off of him like a lead musket ball off a boiler plate. They could not penetrate the swirling fog of apprehension that had suddenly engulfed him. Without answering, he crumpled the paper in his fist and went out the door onto the deck. His feet took over automatically, carrying him down the stairs, and he was not aware of anything around him until Zachary's voice reached out and yanked him back into the world of cotton and steam—his world, now.

"Ho up, dere, Mr. Cliff. Where is it yo' is goin' like dat?"

"Huh?" The fog of despair dissipated, and Clifton discovered that it was night, and he was standing at the foot of the landing stage. Yellow light from a pale, flickering lamp glinted off the water a few feet below the stage. He looked back and saw Zachary standing upon the guards at the head of the stage, his ragged shirt a ghostly apparition against the dark pile of burlap-wrapped cotton bales behind him. The rest of him melded in with the dark background.

"Zachary?"

The big Negro came across the landing stage and narrowed a suspicious eye at him. "What is wrong wid yo', Mr. Cliff? Yo' look like yo' done et a mess of bad grits."

"Oh, Zachary," Clifton said. It came out as a low moan. He had difficulty keeping a steady voice and showed his friend the newspaper.

Zachary glanced at the wrinkled sheets and a grin slowly widened his lips, white teeth in the wavering light. "She-oot, Mr. Cliff. Yo' know I cain't read a lick, 'ceptin' my name some."

"Oh—yes, of course. I forgot."

"Mr. Cliff, somethin' is mighty wrong wid yo'. Tell Zachary what it is? Come along now, sit down over here. Yo' is pale as new corn."

As if he suddenly had no will of his own, Clifton followed Zachary up the wharf to a pile of crates and sat down.

"Now, yo' tell Zachary what is wrong. Mebbe I can hep yo'"

"Nobody can help me."

"Now, nothin's ever dat bad."

Clifton took the envelope from his pocket and showed it

to Zachary. "I just received this letter this afternoon. The sheriff had been holding it for me. It is from Mystie!"

"Why, dat is good news, Mr. Cliff! What did she say?"

"She . . . she says she is working aboard a steamer named *Guiding Star,* and that she . . . she would see me again, if I wanted to."

"Dat's wonderful! But why de long face? Yo' should be dancing on yo' toes!" Zachary thought a moment and caution entered his voice. "How long ago was dem words put down on dat paper?"

"It was written more than a year ago, just after I visited her mother and father in Cairo."

"I remember dat. Yo' give dem a paper, too."

"That's right."

"I see now. Yo' worry dat she not on de *Guiding Star* no mo'."

"No, Zachary. That's not it at all. I am worried that she still *is*—or *was* on the *Guiding Star.*"

Clifton's fist tightened around the newspaper and held it up. "Yesterday the *Guiding Star* exploded as she was leaving the New Orleans wharves. Burst her boilers, according to this, and all hands aboard her were killed."

Zachary was silent a moment; then in a hopeful voice he said, "A year is a long time, Mr. Cliff. Mebbe Mystie done left dat boat and is workin' another."

"Maybe," he said, but even that slight hope did not encourage him.

"Well, we will be in New Awlins come de morrow. I will go wid yo', Mr. Cliff."

"Go with me? Where would I go?"

"I was in New Awlins when de *Louisiana* busted into a million pieces and went to de bottom of de riber. Afterwards, de recorder, a man named Baldwin, he done somethin' called a *inquiry*. Him would be de man to see if'n Mystie still worked on de *Guiding Star* or not."

Stewart nodded slowly. He would have thought of that, he told himself—eventually. At the moment, his brain was in a downward spiral, like a bird shot out of the air. What made him think of birds just now, he wondered—but he knew.

"Soon as we put in, Mr. Cliff, I go wid yo'. We will find out the straight of it, don' yo' worry none. Worryin' never solved no man's problem, yo' know. Mystie probably weren't on dat unlucky boat, anyway."

In an odd way that Stewart could not define, Zachary's encouragement helped lift some of the weight from his shoulders—just like Zachary always did when he saw Stewart struggling with something too heavy to bear.

"Now dat dat am settled, what is dis I hear 'bout yo' not goin' be workin' wid us niggers down at de woodpile? Am dat de truth?"

"Yes, it is true, Zachary. Captain Hamilton has given me the job of mud clerk. Mr. Tyback is getting married and leaving the boat."

Zachary was frowning. "I reckon it is a good ting, but I am goin' to miss yo', Mr. Cliff."

Stewart managed a grin now. Zachary had helped him over the initial shock, but the dread of what he might discover in New Orleans was an anchor pulling him down. "It's not like we won't be seeing each other. We'll see each other a lot. I'll be working with the cargo just like before, only now I am going to be counting it instead of carrying it."

"It won't be like befo' at all, Mr. Cliff. Befo' yo' was like one of us niggers, dodging Mr. Lansing's dagger tongue and eagle eye like de old rooster dodges de ax. Now yo' be a of'cer—"

"An officer? Not exactly—"

"But yo' will live wid de of'cers. No mo' sharin' a cot or

a dipper of water wid us niggers. No mo' sweatin' at dem fireboxes."

"That's true. But it won't make a difference."

Zachary looked away, fingered a pebble off the wharf, and flung it out into the black water ahead of the *Tempest Queen*'s bow. The sound of its plop was muffled by the constant whisper of the river along the hulls of the steamers moored there and the creak of fenders and wood and wharf rubbing together.

"Not at all once, Mr. Cliff, but soon yo' will be busy wid yo' new job, and eatin' in de main cabin, drinking yo' coffee outta thin white cups, and playin' checkers in de afternoon. It will make a difference. Yo' see."

Stewart didn't want his new promotion to change the friendship that had grown between Zachary and himself, but in all honesty, he had to admit that Zachary was probably correct in his assessment of things. In spite of himself, he would be drawn in a new direction now, and that direction was bound to leave Zachary farther behind. He wanted to argue with Zachary and assure him that nothing was going to change, but he couldn't. His concern over Mystie was too much of a drain on his spirit, and the best he could do was shake his head and say, "I hope not."

Zachary stood. "Yo' et somethin' yet, Mr. Cliff?"

"No. I've been busy. Shopping for new clothes."

"We got some red beans an' black catfish, an' chicory to drink, too."

Stewart gave him a weak smile and said, "Thanks, Zachary, but I think I'll pass tonight."

Zachary sat back down again. "Well, den what are yo' to do?"

"I don't know. I've got a lot on my mind. I want to be alone for a while and try to sort it out."

"Ain't nothin' to sort over, Mr. Cliff. Yo' don't know dat

she am on dat boat—or am not. I told yo' befo'. Worrin' don't do no good. Bein' alone ain't what you need, Mr. Cliff. Now, come along wid Zachary. Put yo' tinkin' on somethin' else. Dat black catfish is most tasty."

"Maybe you're right. All right, I'll go with you." Stewart stood and followed Zachary back aboard the *Tempest Queen.*

Gen waited impatiently, pacing the small hotel room, glancing at herself in the mirror over the dressing table each time she passed it. She wanted to make a proper appearance when Douglas came. She pursed her lips thoughtfully.

Would he come?

Of course he would. What politician could possibly pass up a contribution to his campaign. Even though Stephen Douglas was quite wealthy in his own right, he would come down once he read her note, if for nothing more than to polish his image. It had suffered some in the South, which was why he was making this last push before the elections.

Gen stopped by the table and took her watch from her reticule. It had been over an hour. What was keeping him? As the time passed, she grew more apprehensive, and she forced herself to take a cool, detached view of the matter. This is not precisely the way she and Robert had planned it, but whether she contacted Douglas aboard the *Tempest Queen* or at the Saint Charles Hotel, she could not see where it would make a difference.

Gen forced herself to sit at the table. She touched the loose strands of her hair back in place, frowned at her reflection, and then opened her reticule again and removed a deck of playing cards. Shoving the clutter aside, she dealt the cards into two piles, her hands moving so rapidly that only she was aware of the cards that went into each pile. She ran through the entire deck, and when she examined the two piles, one contained only red cards, and the other only black, except for the seven of spades and the three of hearts, which had inadvertently found themselves in the wrong piles.

"You're loosing your touch, Genny, gal," she told her reflection, and gathered up the cards again, shuffling them together with a crisp precision that was almost musical. She tried it again, and again ended up with only two misplaced cards. Her mouth took on a determined set. Gen shuffled them together once more and tried a third time, but before she had finished dealing them out, a knock sounded upon her door.

It startled her. She said, "Just a moment," and threw back the bedspread, flung the cards under it, and covered them over. Glancing one last time in the mirror, she went to the door and opened it.

"Miss Summers?" the man on the other side said.

It wasn't Douglas. This man was much taller and younger. He had a pleasant smile and was dressed in a dark gray suit. She had expected the senator, and she supposed the surprise showed on her face, for the gentleman standing there said, "Are you quite all right?"

Gen recovered in an instant, fixed a smile upon her face, and said, "Oh, yes. I was just lying down. It has been a very long day, you understand. Yes, I am Genevieve Summers, and you are—?"

"My names is James Sheridan. I am Mr. Douglas's secretary."

"Oh. I was expecting the senator."

Sheridan smiled pleasantly. "Like you, Miss Summers, the senator has had a very long and trying day. He and Mrs. Douglas are resting up for tonight. He is trying to conserve his voice for this evening's speech, you know," Sheridan said and pointed at his throat. "The senator has been having trouble again, you see."

"Oh, of course." She tried not to sound disappointed. She should have known the senator would not come in person and she felt foolish to have thought otherwise. A small miscalculation. She would see to it that it did not happen again.

"He was, however, quite pleased to receive your note and your words of encouragement."

No doubt, my contribution as well, Gen thought, but she smiled graciously and said, "Won't you come in, Mr. Sheridan?"

Sheridan hesitated, craning his neck to see past her into the room. "Your chaperone is here as well?"

"No, I am traveling alone. I'm to board a steamer the day after tomorrow to visit my sister in Alton."

"Perhaps it would be best if I remained out here in the hallway."

"Don't be silly, Mr. Sheridan. If it will make you comfortable, I will leave the door open." He is very discreet, she thought. No doubt wishing to avoid any sign of impropriety in the Douglas campaign.

"Well, perhaps for a moment." He entered with his gray silk hat in hand.

Gen said, "I had so hoped to meet the senator."

"Mr. Douglas regrets he could not come himself, but Adéle, his wife, insisted he rest his voice. She has ordered warm lemonade sent up. Mrs. Douglas is quite firm on this." His smile spread the neatly trimmed beard.

"I understand. Only, I so did want to tell the senator how much I admire his position and his firm desire to keep the Union together. He is a man that will work with the South, I am most convinced. When I heard that Mr. Douglas was in New Orleans, well, you can't imagine how pleased I was. My father is quite wealthy, and I know that he supports the senator as well, and since I was traveling with more money than I shall need, well, I decided I would like to give the senator a contribution."

"That is very generous of you, Miss Summers."

Gen reached for her reticule and withdrew a small purse that Robert had given her the night before. She had planned to do this aboard the *Tempest Queen,* but presenting the money now might help her get near the man later.

"It isn't much, Mr. Sheridan, only a little over four hundred dollars, but it is my small way of helping the senator." She placed the purse in his palm. "Now, you will see that the senator gets this?"

"It will be absolutely safe with me, Miss Summers, I assure you."

She breathed a sigh. "I do feel good about this. I saw a handbill that Senator Douglas will be speaking at The Riverman's Club tonight?"

"That is correct." Sheridan put the purse into his pocket.

"I wanted to attend, but I was informed that it is a private club, and that no women would be permitted inside."

He gave her a conciliatory smile, but his words were blatantly bogus. This was obviously something he did not want to be bothered with. "I am afraid that is so, Miss Summers. It is the policy of the club, and certainly none of Mr. Douglas's doings."

She parried his specious smile with one of her own, sweet and vulnerable. "I was wondering if there might be some way—?"

"I regret that I cannot help in that matter. My hands are tied."

She saw that Sheridan was anxious to leave. *Take the lady's money and bolt. Well,* she thought, *the senator won't be free of me so easily. I'll stick to him like flypaper, but first I shall play out my line a little so that he doesn't know he's taken the hook.* She said, "I quite understand, Mr. Sheridan. Do give the senator my best wishes then. Good evening."

Sheridan paused at the door. "The senator is giving a speech on the Municipal Landing the day after tomorrow at two-forty-five. If you are still in town, you can hear him there, if you like, Miss Summers."

"Thank you," she said rather brusquely.

He bowed at the waist and set his hat in place and left as graciously as he had arrived. She closed the door behind him and leaned back against it, her hands grasping the knob. "We shall meet again, Mr. Sheridan," she said aloud to the empty room and went to the bed, gathered up the enameled playing cards, returned them to their carton, and put them into her reticule.

When she looked at her watch, it was five past seven. At the bottom of her reticule was a .32-caliber Sharps four-barrel derringer. It had been a gift from Robert, and its polished, silver-plated frame shone in the lamplight, its ivory grips were white as milk against her skin. Gen slid the barrels forward to check the loads in the chambers. The four rimfire cartridges were in their proper place, and she returned it to her bag.

Settling a hat upon her head and taking up a shawl to ward off the evening chill, she locked the door behind her and went down the stairs to the foyer and took a chair by the stove to wait for Senator Douglas and his party to come through.

"I didna' think it got so cold in the South, miss."

The voice at her back startled her. She turned and saw the man standing by the stove, holding his hands near to it and rubbing them together. He apparently had just come in out of the night.

"I beg your pardon, sir. Were you addressing me?"

"Aye. I was commenting on the chill." He wore a shabby dark jacket with the collar turned up to his thick, brown beard, and a dusty felt hat with a small brim and round crown. His smile was pleasant, but what drew Gen's gaze were his eyes, bluer than the sky.

"It is autumn, sir."

"Aye, lassie, that it is. I fear I have come out ill prepared to meet cold weather, though. I canna' know what I was thinking. Back where I come from, one does not go abroad in October without his mackintosh and woolens."

Just then, Senator Douglas came down the stairs. He was accompanied by Sheridan.

Gen averted her face so that Sheridan would not recognize her and said to the stranger by the stove, "Just where is it you come from, sir?"

He laughed. "Glasgow, originally, but of late, I call Chicago me home."

Stephen Douglas passed by her, and as he did, Gen stole a glance. He was indeed a short man, but of great girth. His dark hair was worn long beneath a white felt hat that seemed to glisten against his swarthy skin. He had on a neatly tailored blue broadcloth suit. His gait was labored, as if the man had just run a grueling footrace. It was a race he was running even now: against time, against Lincoln.

James Sheridan strode close by his side, and there were two other well-dressed gentlemen with him, as well. The four of them were not speaking, but appeared in a hurry to be on their way. They swept past Gen without noticing her and out the door into the night.

Gen wanted to follow them, but when she stood, the man at the stove said, "Are you traveling?"

He had placed himself in front of her, giving her no room to maneuver past him without running into a chair on one side or the stove on the other. Douglas and his party had gone. Gen stifled a frown, and her exasperation, and gave the man a burning glance.

"I beg your pardon?"

"I asked if ye were traveling." He smiled happily, apparently not noticing the irritation in her eyes.

"Yes. I am visiting my sister in Alton."

"Alton? Illinois?"

Gen nodded.

"That is close to home for me."

Gen sat back in the chair and thought over her next move. She would have to wait now until tomorrow to get close to Douglas. Well, all right. She resigned herself to defeat this evening. She would have to fall back to the original plan. No harm done.

Settle down, Gen. You still have it under control.

"It will be cold up North this time of year."

"I have a wrap with me," she said, still a little distracted.

"I, too, am going north."

Gen looked at his thin jacket. "I am surprised, sir, that you did not dress appropriately then."

"Aye." He smiled again and nodded his head. "I do have a coat along, but I left it at me berth. I went out for a wee walk after dinner, and before I realized it, the sun had gone down, and the evening grew chill. I only stepped in here to warm myself at the stove."

"Your berth? Are you a boatman?"

"Nay." He laughed. "I reckon I must have picked up that term on my trip over from Scotland. I like the sound of it, don't ye know."

"Oh." She was tiring of this conversation and wished the man would leave now.

"So, on what boat are ye headed up the river, if I might ask, lass?"

"I am riding a steamer named the *Tempest Queen*."

His face brightened. "Why, that is a lucky chance."

"I beg your pardon?"

"I, too, am booking passage on the *Tempest Queen!* We will be traveling together."

Wonderful, she thought. She wanted a drink now more than ever. There was a saloon off the hotel lobby, but it would be inappropriate for her to enter it unescorted. In a moment of weakness she considered inviting this obnoxious intruder, but decided that she really did not want a drink that badly.

"And might I inquire as to your name, lassie?"

"It is Genevieve," she said, "and I really must be going now."

"Aye. I will see you later, then, I am sure, Miss Genevieve." He tipped his shabby hat. "My name is Allan. Allan Gill."

"Good-bye, Mr. Allan Gill," she said abruptly and left, taking the stairs to the second floor. Once away from the lobby, Gen drew in a long breath and let it out slowly.

"Damn!" she said, and with anger in her steps, she tramped down the hallway and into her room.

CHAPTER TEN

Early the next morning, Captain Hamilton found Chief
Mate Lansing down by the boilers. The furnaces were now
buried in deep shadows behind a wall of cotton, but beyond
the bales a glorious sun was rising in the clear, bright sky.
Firemen were hustling fuel through the tunnel that had been
constructed beneath the mountain of cotton, and the passage
down to the furnaces was like descending into Hades. The
red glow from the open furnace doors danced off their
sweating sable skin, reminding Hamilton of the eternal fire
that the book of Revelation warned about.

Hamilton wiped his brow with a white linen handkerchief
and made his way toward Lansing, who seemed not to
notice the intense heat.

"Step lively, boys, and keep that woodpile straight. We don't want it falling over on us when we get under way." Lansing turned to the captain as he came through the gloom. "We are almost ready down here. Another four or five cords to bring aboard."

"Very good, Mr. Lansing." Hamilton patted the gray imperial beard at his chin. "I am in a hurry to shove off. When we put into New Orleans this afternoon, we are going to have a mighty push to get this cotton off-loaded. I am behind schedule, I fear, and I will have Mr. Seegar standing on every pound of steam the old girl can make. It will be up to you and your crew to see that we don't fall back."

"I will keep the boys hopping, Captain."

"I have wired ahead to the wharf master, and he will have extra men ready to help you tackle the job of off-loading this shipment. Once we have it all off the *Tempest Queen,* I want the deck scrubbed spotless, the railing paint touched up, and the bunting and pennants brought out of storage and draped about the promenade and guys. You will have to work smartly, Mr. Lansing. We will be at it all night, I am afraid, for at four o'clock the day after, we will leave the wharf and steam to the Municipal Landing to receive a special party."

Lansing looked shocked. "All of that in only one day, Captain? Impossible! We will never get it all done in that time. Why, it will take a full day alone just to transfer this cotton to the wharf."

"Perhaps, but this time it must be done in eight hours."

Lansing's shock reshaped itself into a determined frown and he nodded his head. "Very well, Captain. I will get it done for you then, so long as you have arranged for extra hands."

"I have no doubt that you will do splendidly, Mr. Lansing." Hamilton left him and reentered the tunnel, steering to the starboard wall of cotton to keep out of the way of the ant line of firemen trotting through, logs filling their bowed arms.

He heard the chief mate's voice ring out like a cracked bell: "Double-time it boys! Get that wood aboard. Don't dally now, you're moving like a gaggle of schoolgirls. Pick up them feet and hump . . . hump . . . *Hump!*"

Lansing's words faded against the tons of cotton piled about, and then Hamilton was out of the tunnel, once again breathing the cool, morning air at the bow of his boat, and patting his brow dry. He put the handkerchief away, and in his pocket discovered a handful of coins left over from the card game. He had done quite well—at least he had left with more than he had come with, and for him, that was quite well, indeed. He wondered briefly how McKay was faring in his marathon game with the notable George Devol. Knowing McKay as well as he did, Hamilton was certain the gambler was doing splendidly.

The *Tempest Queen* pulled away from her berth at Baton Rouge beneath a billowing ceiling of black smoke supported upon her twin chimneys. The black smoke was a show for the folks on the wharves who had come to expect such things from arriving or departing steamers, and Captain Hamilton had a bit of sawdust in his veins. Her steam whistle hooted her departure to the wharf, and the big bronze bell rang three times, summoning the leadsmen to their job of calling out the depth of the river bottom until it had dropped safely away beneath the riverboat's shallow hull.

Up in the pilothouse, Ab Grimes cranked the helm hard over and aimed the *Tempest Queen* at the middle of the stream where the current was swiftest and their passage would be easiest. He yanked an iron hog ring that dangled from the ceiling that sounded the bell down in the engine room to tell the chief engineer it was time to pour on the steam. The huge, red paddle wheels picked up revolutions, biting powerfully into the water, and in a few moments the boat had gathered enough speed for the rudder to take hold. The smoke from her stacks changed from black to gray as the pine knots in the furnaces burned themselves out, and Ab Grimes straightened her around and pointed her in the direction of New Orleans.

Out on top of the cotton bales prowled the cinder guards, men with buckets of water in hand, dousing the top tier of cotton wherever they found a chimney spark smoldering. Those roustabouts not so employed were lying about the cotton pile in the sun, some singing, some throwing dice, some catching up on their sleep, knowing the big push that lay ahead of them when the *Tempest Queen* pulled into the wharves at New Orleans.

The trip downriver went smoothly, and by three o'clock New Orleans appeared ahead, making its presence first known many miles away by the huge cloud of smoke that hovered over the water. There would be fifty steamers there with furnaces blazing and boilers bubbling, making ready to leave the wharves at four o'clock, which was general departure time for the packets that ran a regular schedule.

The *Tempest Queen* steamed on toward that smoky haze, and soon the city began to rise up on the banks, and the river traffic became congested with steamers and ferryboats, rafts and shantyboats, scows and the tall-masted schooners being maneuvered into their berths or withdrawn from them by powerful little towboats. She steamed past Saint Mary's Market and drove on into the congestion, headed for a berth at the wharf, her steam whistle calling out her intent, and her roustabouts and officers hopping to the guards with lines to make her fast.

Ab Grimes docked the boat with the practiced ease of a man who knew his job and did it well, and once the *Tempest Queen* was secured to her moorings, with her wheels finally stopped and the shrilling steam escaping through the gauge cocks as the pressure bled from her tanks, the pilot's job was finished and Captain Hamilton was once more supreme ruler of his realm—all four hundred feet of it.

Lansing got his crew moving at once, manhandling the landing stages into place and off-loading the cotton, while Captain Hamilton went ashore to file his arrival with the wharf master.

Clifton Stewart had always been amazed by the apparent lack of organization on the New Orleans wharves, even though he knew that was not the case. Actually, there was both rhyme and reason to the headlong dash of stevedores and roustabouts, and the merchants with their crews of black-faced men. It was just that he had never quite understood what was going on, except that a lot of cargo was being moved around, and somehow it always managed to find its way into the correct piles.

That morning, Belding had tried briefly to explain some of it to him, but even he was vague on many points, and in the end had told Stewart not to worry about it for now, and that they were not going to haul much in the way of goods up the river this trip, anyway, only people—some very important people, if he must know, and the captain did not wish to make the Douglas party's reservation on the *Tempest Queen* general knowledge yet, even though the *Daily Crescent* had printed the story for all to see.

What he did learn from Belding was the meaning of all those colorful flags he now saw scattered about the wharf with their piles of cargo mounded beneath them. The flags had always been a mystery to him when, as a boy, he sometimes accompanied his father down to New Orleans on business. Now he knew that they were for the roustabouts who naturally could not read because they were slaves. Each flag was a different color or bore a different symbol, marking a spot where a particular cargo was to be piled;

cottonseed under the green flag, hogsheads of sugar under the yellow, cloth from England beneath the blue color, cotton bound for England under the lavender, coffee from South America where the red flag flew. It all made sense now, and suddenly the bustle of the New Orleans wharves seemed less haphazard to him.

Beyond the wharf stood a city of tall, narrow buildings, with here and there the spires of churches poking holes through the smoky air. Nearby was a customs house, and scattered about it a half dozen other official-looking buildings that Stewart could not identify, but that an international port required in order to operate under American jurisprudence. When he turned and looked out onto the river, his view was filled with the jumbled forest of masts and riggings and black smokestacks—and one pair of bright red stacks that anyone familiar with the river knew belonged to Thomas P. Leathers's speedy boat, the *Natchez*. Leathers had owned a string of boats named *Natchez,* and Stewart wasn't sure if this was *Natchez* number four, or *Natchez* number five. The previous had all met their demise against the mighty Mississippi.

A wave of hopelessness washed over him. Somewhere out there at the bottom of the river lay the twisted wreckage of the *Guiding Star* and perhaps—he didn't want to think about it but he could not stop himself—perhaps the crushed and scalded body of Mystie Waters, as well.

"Ho, dere, Mr. Cliff."

Stewart turned. Zachary bounded down the landing stage wearing a grin as wide as the Mississippi herself.

"Where is it yo' is goin', Mr. Cliff?"

"I wasn't going anywhere in particular, Zachary."

"Yo' no have clerkin' work to do?"

"Not right at the moment. I will be busy with the preparations once this load of cotton has been transferred to the wharf, but that will be hours from now."

"Den yo' and me, we gonna find dat recorder feller." Zachary started off toward the city.

"Wait a minute, Zachary. Don't you have to help off-load this cargo?"

Zachary glanced quickly over his shoulder at the *Tempest Queen,* sitting low in the water and burgeoning with cotton. "Not if'n I skee-daddle 'fore Mr. Lansing sees me."

"But you will get in trouble again."

"She-oot, ain't I tell you 'fore? Dat man is all hot wind, he is."

"More like a hurricane," Stewart said, trying to match Zachary's long-legged stride and finding that he had to scramble to keep up with the tall man. "I don't think you ought to be doing this—again."

Zachary laughed. "Yo' worry too much, Mr. Cliff."

"And you don't worry enough," Stewart commented.

They left the wharves behind and followed Canal Street away from the river.

"Do you know where this recorder is, Zachary?"

The black man stopped and looked at him, surprised. "I thought yo' know'd where he be."

"I have only been to New Orleans a few times, mostly when I was a boy. I've never explored the city that well. I thought you knew. You seemed to be going in a particular direction."

"I was, Mr. Cliff." His grin widened and white teeth gleamed. "I was goin' lickety-split in dis direct'on on account dat it takes me away from Lansing's cotton pile in dat direct'on." The grin disappeared. Zachary thought a moment, his eyes narrowing beneath coal-black brows. "Well, I know where we can find out."

"Where?" Clifton fell back in step with Zachary.

"Monkey Wrench Corner. Dat's where all de boatmen go. She-oot, Mr. Cliff. Any man dere will tell yo' all yo' need to know 'bout de *Guiding Star.*"

Ahead, Stewart could see the busy intersection of Canal Street and Royal already. "Monkey Wrench Corner! You can't believe anything you hear at Monkey Wrench Corner, Zachary. You know that."

"What yo' mean, Mr. Cliff?"

"I mean there is more yarn spun on Monkey Wrench Corner than in all the European mills that buy our cotton. There is more tall tales there than you'd find in a herd of giraffes. More blarney than you would find in—"

Zachary drew up and looked at him. "See. Dat is exac'ly what I mean, Mr. Cliff. Dem people knows lots o' tings. Dey can tell yo' all 'bout dat boat. Dey might even know 'bout your Miss Mystie, too. Now come along." He strode forward and Clifton had to double-step to keep up. They had come far enough from the river for patches of blue sky to open up through the swirling gray smoke overhead, and the heavy, acrid odor of wood and coal in the air had faded somewhat, replaced now with the smells of frying catfish and spicy pepper sauces. The foot traffic picked up as well, as they drew nearer to Monkey Wrench Corner.

The buildings here took on a different look from the narrow brick and plaster row houses closer to the river. They were taller, almost massive, built of quarried stone and faced in decorative Ionic columns and stone gables with steep roofs above. Carriages and horses moved along the streets, and on first glance the corner of Canal and Royal appeared no different than a busy corner in any other big city along the river. But a closer look revealed the distinct flavor of New Orleans: the narrow streets—only fifty French feet wide, the wrought iron decorations that encircled the wide porches and the colorfully painted marquees, the deep bass Negro voices hawking gingerbread and pralines and boiled crawdads along the sidewalks. This could belong to no other place.

Groups of men stood in the shade near the buildings, talking, and ladies—both fine and coarse—strolled along the sidewalks in their winter wraps, even though to a Northerner, the November temperature might be considered balmy.

"Now what?" Stewart said, finding a spot on the sidewalk away from the traffic.

Zachary looked around and spied three Negro men up the street, standing together. "Yo' wait here, Mr. Cliff. I gonna ask some questions," Zachary said and made straight for the three men.

Stewart frowned. This was a waste of time, but he had nothing better to do, and Zachary was bound and determined to help him uncover the facts in this matter. Nearby, two men were speaking loudly enough to be heard clearly. The older man sported gray bristle-brush whiskers and wore a tattered blue billed hat with a gold star in the middle. He appeared tipsy and slurred his words when he spoke, but Stewart was at once intrigued with what he was telling the second gent there.

"Why, that ain't slow at all, son. That boat sounds to me to be a regular speed devil, if I recollect my history true."

"You don't call seven days from Bayou Sara to Natchez-Under-the-Hill slow, Captain Diggers?" the other retorted. "Then I'd like to know just what slow *is* by your book, sir."

The older man snorted, scrubbed his whiskers with the back of a hand, and fished a bottle from his inside coat pocket. After taking a long pull from it and smacking his lips, he drove the cork back in place and returned it to the pocket.

"I'll tell you what slow is all about, Mr. Albert! Back in forty-seven—now that's just a little before your time—I was master of a sorry sidewheeler that went by the name of *Escargot*. Now don't give me that skeptical eye, I know what you are thinking. It was rightly named. She was the slowest thing on the river. One day while running downriver under full steam she lost a race with a chicken coop that had been swept off in high water.

"That is pretty slow," Mr. Albert agreed.

"And going upriver, she never did win any race at all against another boat, and that includes a race she had with a leaky pirogue that showed her its tail—and it was being paddled by an old one-armed Indian! In fact, the only race the *Escargot* ever did win was against an old sugar mill built on a caving bank north of Baton Rouge."

Mr. Albert was looking fairly skeptical now. Stewart grinned and inched closer.

The captain rocked back on his heels and thought a moment. "We never did carry very many passengers. You see, they all grew old and died before the *Escargot* ever made her port."

"Now, now, Captain Diggers, I think you are leading me along."

The old captain raised his right hand solemnly. "If I had me a Bible I'd swear to it, sir. Why, she was so slow that she once lost a race to an island!"

"Now I am certain you are playing loose with your facts, Captain, or your memory has failed you."

The captain was not offended, but took another swig of whiskey and said, "Don't believe me if you wish. It is your choice, but it's true, every word of it. I have the documents to prove all that I have said, of course . . . somewhere, but I seem to have misplaced them."

Both men chuckled, and Mr. Albert started to tell a story about a boat so slow, it took the owners seven years to learn that it had sunk, but by that time Zachary had returned with a long face, drawn down in defeat. "Dey don't know nothin', dem dumb niggers. Dey say it is true de *Guiding Star* blow'd her boilers the day 'fore yesterday, but dat is all dey know."

"What about the recorder?"

"Dey don't know nothing 'bout no recorder."

"Then we have to keep asking around. I would imagine we would find the recorder at the courthouse, wherever that might be. We need to find someone who can tell us where, and the particulars about the *Guiding Star.*"

Behind them, from the shadows of a deep doorway, a voice grated, "I can save you a lot of footwork, mister." It was a vaguely feminine voice, although at first Stewart wasn't certain. He was convinced, however, that the faint accent accompanying it was French. He peered hard into the shadows and a form stepped out into the late sunlight that slanted past the porch. Still he wasn't certain.

It *was* a woman, it turned out upon closer examination. Quite portly and about five feet five inches tall, but she was dressed every inch as a man from her gum boots to her canvas britches, homespun shirt, and the wide suspenders that followed the lumpy terrain up over the broad stomach that strained her shirt, across her ample breasts, and around her wide bulky shoulders. Her hair was dark and oily, cut short and held back by a greasy bandanna rolled tightly and tied in a knot.

She had just stepped out of a ship chandler's store with a coil of new hemp rope draped over her shoulder, and as she came nearer to him, Stewart thought he detected the odor of dead fish and machine oil. She worked a knife blade through a plug of tobacco, slivered off a curl, and shoved it deep into her mouth with a dirty finger.

"Madam? You have news of the *Guiding Star?*" he asked, staring in spite of himself.

She in turn gave him a thorough looking over. Then, working the lump of tobacco between her stained teeth, said, "I have about all the news as you are likely to find anywhere in New Orleans, mister."

Stewart found he was staring at her enormous belly, and the full breast that seemed to flow naturally into it beneath the overworked shirt. He managed to shift his view back to her face. "You?"

"Me." She glanced at Zachary, then back at Stewart. "He your nigger?"

"Er, no. Zachary and I are friends."

She made a growling sound of disapproval deep in her throat as her tongue shifted the chaw to her other cheek. "I'm in kinda a hurry. What business you got with the *Guiding Star?*"

"I heard she sustained a horrible explosion of her boilers."

The woman laughed. "You might say that. I was practically looking right at her when it happened. Blow'd her into a hunder'd pieces. Sent the forward third of the boiler deck a dozen rods out to the river, blow'd part of her boiler three blocks into the city, she did. Her hull went to the bottom in five minutes, the rest of her was scattered across the water. A sizable section of cabin was left floating downriver to the Gulf."

Stewart constructed an all-too-vivid picture of the accident in his brain, and his heart sank farther. From the way she described it, no one could have survived.

"Here, now, why the long face? You didn't have someone aboard her, did you?"

Stewart's voice cracked when he spoke. "I was looking for a—a friend. She had been employed on the *Guiding Star.* The newspaper said there were no survivors."

The woman must have seen his deep distress. A filament of feminine concern came to her harsh voice, and the ruddy skin of her weathered face seem to soften some. "If your friend was aboard the *Guiding Star,* she would not have survived that explosion."

"How would I find out for certain? I have to know."

"Only one way. Go on down and take a look at what is left of that boat, and at the bodies that were recovered."

Stewart wasn't sure he wanted to do that, but he knew he must or he could never live with himself. "Where would I go?"

"Pete's Salvage is doing the job of cleaning up the mess. Go down to the end of Canal Street and follow the river upstream about a mile. They just hauled in the main cabin section, what was left of it. The clerk's office was intact, though, and that is likely where you would find the boat's ledger and portage book. Those would tell you one way or the other. Talk to the foreman there. His name is Rotney Habercorn, and don't let him give you no runaround. Tell him Maggie said you could nose through the wreckage. But you best do it soon, before the insurance company comes investigating. You won't get nothin' out of them once they impound what's left. And the city is coming tonight to haul the bodies away."

Stewart looked down at her rubber boots, her rough clothes, the tough little mouth churning diligently away at the plug of tobacco. "Are you in the employ of Pete's Salvage Company, madam?"

She laughed again, heartily, and said, "Hell, mister. I *am* Pete. Maggie Pete. I own the place."

Stewart did not know what to say except to thank her.

She shook his hand like a man, with a strong grip and callused fingers. "Go and take a look at what's left of that boat, and I hope you don't find what you are looking for."

She shifted the tobacco again, and with a gulp, it was gone, and those ambitious jaws quit their chewing.

Stewart was stunned. "You . . . you just swallowed that," he gasped.

She looked at him with mild surprise and said, "Of course I swoller'd it. Ladies don't spit."

CHAPTER ELEVEN

The afternoon shadows stretched out far ahead of them by the time Stewart and Zachary arrived at the foot of the pier. A whitewashed sign spelled out Pete's Salvage in flaking green paint. To the west, the low sunlight sliced beneath the smoky haze that swirled above the river. It glanced in blinding orange flashes off the river's surface; a pilot's nightmare, but Stewart had always thought it a pretty sight. At the moment, however, it did nothing to lift his spirits.

He peered down the long dock at the clapboard building sitting on pilings at its very end. Five hundred feet upriver a jetty had been constructed out of rock, timbers, bits and pieces of rusty machinery, and old boats—all the old pieces only vaguely discernible through the tangle of vines and the cypress trees with Spanish moss hanging from their limbs like a gauzy drape. The jetty ran at an angle to the pier, and between the pier and jetty was a little harbor of still water. A half dozen boats were moored to pilings driven into the river's muddy bottom. One in particular drew Stewart's eye: an old snag boat with a tall derrick, and there, still attached to its chain, was the shattered section of cabin that had once graced the deck of the *Guiding Star*.

Men were moving about the snag boat's deck, and as Stewart watched, a small rowboat departed it. The oars made little eddying circles in the still water as a man rowed toward the building.

Stewart put his foot to the dock, then stopped.

Zachary was growing impatient. "Yo' gonna jest dance on an' off dat pier all de day long? Dat is de six time yo' started out an' den changed yo' mind, Mr. Cliff."

Stewart grimaced. "I am afraid of what I might find at the end of this pier."

"Yo' know yo' is goin' out dere in de end. Now jes' do it an' get it over with. I am gettin' mighty hungry an' it will be dark 'fore we get back to de *Queen*."

"You're right, Zachary. I have to know. I am being a coward about this."

"Yo' not a coward, Mr. Cliff," Zachary said in a gentle voice. "Yo' jest wantin' to prot'ct yo' heart from bein' broke again. Yo' tink dat if yo' had done tings different, dat maybe Miss Mystie would have never been aboard de *Guiding Star,* and dat if yo' find out now dat she is dead, yo' will blame yo'self for it."

Stewart winced. "You are correct, of course. I would think her death was my fault. I would only be thinking of myself. How did you ever become so wise, Zachary?"

"Shucks, Mr. Cliff. I ain't wise. Don't make me out to be no Solomon. I's only a dumb nigger who don't know no more den to heave cordwood into a steamer's furnace or tote de white man's wares on dese tired old shoulder bones."

"Don't say that, Zachary. It is not true. You are wise. You are confusing wisdom with education, and I am ashamed to admit it, but it has taken me a long time to finally learn that the two are entirely different. I've got lots of education, but not much in the way of wisdom . . . yet."

"She-oot! Yo' is de smartest man I know'd, Mr. Cliff."

"And sometimes I think you are the wisest, Zachary. "Now, I've wasted both our time vacillating on this matter." Stewart put his foot resolutely to the pier and strode out toward the building at its end. It was a long walk. The pier stretched several hundred feet into the river, and when he finally arrived at the door, the building turned out to be the size of a small warehouse. He rapped upon the door. No one answered. He knocked again, then turned the handle and stepped inside.

Sunlight was struggling to get through the dingy glass of the west windows. The east windows showed only the derricks and chimneys of the work boats in the small harbor. There was a desk near the door, buried under faded scraps of paper, some old copies of *Harper's Weekly,* and piles of yellowing illustrated newspapers. A stack of ledger books towered on the left-hand corner of the desk and appeared in danger of crashing to the grimy floor. A small space had been cleared in the middle of the clutter where several sheets of foolscap had been spread out, each containing what appeared to Stewart, as he read them upside down from the back of the desk, lists of some sort.

The rear of the building ended at a wall. There was another door to a room beyond. The door was closed. Between the wall and where Stewart and Zachary stood, the floor was littered everywhere with boxes and barrels and pieces of machinery. Stewart had not the slightest clue what they were for. Over all of it, in a haphazard fashion, were draped oil-stained tarpaulins.

The room smelled of dead fish and machine oil—much as Maggie Pete had—and there was another odor that permeated the place, a sweet, biting smell. He could not identify it.

"Don't look like no one is here, Mr. Cliff," Zachary said and took a backward step toward the door they had just entered. "I get a bad feeling 'bout this place."

"Perhaps in the back room." Stewart started for the closed door, but just then the door swung open.

A man entered and drew up abruptly, startled at finding them there. He held a box in both hands and had a pencil shoved behind his right ear. He recovered from his surprise and backed up against the door, shoving it closed behind him.

"Who are you, and what do you want here?"

"My name is Clifton Stewart, and—"

"You from the insurance company?" He gave Stewart a sharp look, but before Stewart could answer that, the man said, "No, you don't look like an insurance agent. You must be from the city, then?"

"I am not. I have come to seek information on the *Guiding Star*. I am trying to locate—"

"Is that your nigger?" the man interrupted, glancing at Zachary.

"No. He is my friend."

"He can wait outside, then. In fact, I am busy now. You both can leave." The man went to the desk, set the box on the floor, sat in a scruffy caned chair and began shuffling ink bottles and quills about.

Zachary started for the door, but Stewart caught his shirt sleeve.

"Sir, I have come for information that you might be able

to supply, and I will not leave until I have gotten what I want. And Zachary will remain with me."

The man looked up from the sheet of foolscap beneath his quill. "You still here? No, listen, unless you are with the insurance company or the city, you can leave, and you can either do it under your own power or I'll toss you out under mine."

Stewart was about to return the fellow's threat with one of his own, but that would not get him what he wanted, except perhaps the satisfaction of teaching the man a lesson in civility. He considered the problem a moment, wondering how his friend Dexter McKay would handle this situation. McKay's silver tongue had talked them out of more dilemmas than Stewart cared to recall.

He said, "No doubt you must be the esteemed Mr. Rotney Habercorn."

The man's eyes compressed suspiciously. "I am Habercorn. How do you know that?"

Stewart smiled affably, as he had seen McKay do so many times before. "Well, my very good friend, the madam Margaret Pete has spoken often of you."

"Madam Margaret—? You mean Maggie?"

"According to what I hear, you do very well at managing her business."

"She says that? You are a friend of Maggie?"

"Friends! Why, Maggie and I are . . . well, I won't go into that. It was indeed good fortune that she is doing the salvage work on the *Guiding Star,* or I might never find what I am looking for. And when I spoke with her only half an hour ago, she said, 'Ask Rotney Habercorn about it. Rotney is a good fellow and he will help you.'"

Steward hoped the lies had rolled convincingly from his lips. He was knew he was most ill equipped to fabricate these fictions off the top of his head. Certainly he was not in the league of Dexter McKay. Lying was not in Stewart's nature, but more than a few times he had watched McKay use a well-placed fable to bring folks around to his side, and now the stakes were too great to not at least give the technique a try. "I quite understand that you are a busy man—"

"Well . . ." Habercorn drew out the word, reconsidering. "I reckon if Maggie sent you, and you two know each other . . . What is it you are looking for?"

Zachary was staring at Stewart with frank confusion, a if seeing someone else, not the man who had stood at his side all these months heaving cordwood into the *Tempest Queen*'s eight furnaces, and snapping-to at Lansing's commands.

Stewart gave him a wink and turned back to Habercorn. "I am trying to locate a friend, and I fear that she might have been aboard the *Guiding Star* when the accident occurred. She had been employed upon the boat, but the last word I had from her was over a year ago. She was a chambermaid, I believe. I must know if she was on the boat when the accident occurred."

"I don't know the names of crew yet, and the *Guiding Star* had not yet boarded any passengers, only her cargo. She was on her way to the landing to take on the passengers."

"Maggie said that you have recovered the cabin?"

"Only a part of it. It was blown clear. We found it floating down to the Gulf. The wind pushed it into shore about three miles south of here. Got it out on the boat now."

"Yes, we saw it as we came up your pier."

"I suppose if you wanted to, I could row you out to it and let you nose around a bit, though I don't know what you will find there."

"Was the clerk's office intact?"

"Yes, it was." Habercorn's eyes brightened a little, and he seemed to know what Stewart was thinking. "My men have been through it. In fact, I just brought some of the things that they found over. I was about to inventory them."

A surge of urgency came to Stewart's voice. "Did they find any ledgers or portage books, perhaps?"

"I don't know. Let's take a look."

Habercorn shoved aside his writing tools and lifted the box to the desk. After a moment of rummaging through it, he extracted a ledger book and said, "Well, I'd say you are in luck. Here is her payroll."

The book was wet. The pages stuck together when Habercorn opened it up, and the ink smeared, but toward the middle the pages were still dry and the ink had not run. "Here is the last entry," he said pressing the spine flat with the palm of his hand.

Stewart went around the desk and peered over Habercorn's shoulder. The page was divided into seven columns, each with headings: Name, Occupation, No. Days, Wages per Month, Amount, Amount Retained, Amount Paid.

The first entry was that of B. Antone, and under Occupation, he was listed as master. His pay had been $225.

The next two entries belonged to the pilots. They had each received $400 that month.

The list was long, over fifty names: engineers, watchmen, cooks, trimmers, carpenters, cabin boy, mate, clerks, and over half a page of names under the occupation of rousters, which included, Stewart knew, the firemen as well. Not one of them had earned more than $20 a month. What riveted his eyes, however, were those names listed under chambermaids.

There were six names in all. The last on the list was Mystie Waters.

A fist reached up through Stewart's throat and squeezed

down on his windpipe. He placed his finger upon the entry, and holding back his emotions, said, "There. She is the one."

"It would help us to know," Habercorn urged.

"I . . . I don't think I can," Stewart repeated. He had recovered from the shock, but his hands were still damp, and he patted cold sweat from his brow with his sleeve. Habercorn had given him his chair, and a small glass of brandy from a flask in the desk drawer.

It had not helped.

"Well, I understand how you might feel about this. It is plain that you a cared a great deal for that woman. Were you two related?"

Stewart shook his head, staring at the empty glass in his fingers.

"Dey was in love," Zachary said, keeping his eyes averted.

Habercorn did not acknowledge that Zachary had spoken and said to Stewart, "If no one can come forward to identify her, she will be buried in a common grave in a potter's field with the others. No headstone to mark her resting place, no one to ever know where she ended up."

That was no way for his Mystie to end up. Stewart slowly nodded and set the glass upon the desk, standing. "All right, I will do it."

"Good." Habercorn went to the door at the back wall. Stewart followed mechanically, dreading what he was about to do. When the door swung open, that odd odor he had noticed before wafted out, stronger now, and sickly sweet. He stopped and looked over his shoulder at Zachary, who had not budged a step.

"Are you going to come with me?"

With eyes wide, the whites as beacon lights against his

black skin, Zachary shook his head and said, "No, sir, Mr. Cliff. I don't go nowhere where dere is dead bodies. De lay-lows, dey lurks to ketch dem what meddle wid dead bodies. I's sorry, Mr. Cliff, but yo' is goin' to have to do it alone, an' if I can talk yo' out of it, I will."

"No, this is something I must do . . . for Mystie."

Zachary nodded his head. "I know yo' got to do it."

Stewart grimaced and followed Habercorn inside. The smell blossomed and made him nauseous. He did not look down at once, but as he entered, he sensed the long, empty quiet of the place, and although his view was straight ahead, he couldn't help noticing the rows of tarpaulins spread on the floor from wall to wall, or the unevenness beneath them—distinctive, even to one not overly familiar with death.

"Over here, Mr. Stewart." Habercorn said it in a casual manner, as if he only wanted to show him a new butter churn or ginning machine.

Stewart looked at the floor then. The boards were dark beneath his shoes, as if they had been stained many times over, and it suddenly occurred to him that the crew of the *Guiding Star* had not been the first to lie in death in this room. The sunlight slanting through the west windows gleamed red upon the canvas covers. Habercorn threw back the first sheet. The corpses there were tinged red as well.

Two men and a woman. Their skin had begun to puff up, as if they had spent a long time in the water. He looked at the woman: gray hair, a face well into middle age, her lids wide in a death stare, but the eyes behind them were sunken, and black as ink.

"No."

Habercorn put the sheet back and went to the next group. These were all men, bloated, disfigured. One was only head and shoulders, the rest of him had been severed at the chest and his entrails laid black and hard upon the stained wooden floor. Habercorn returned the sheet and moved on.

The next sheet covered four men, and except for the red tinge upon them, and the bloated skin, they appeared more or less whole. Habercorn covered them again.

"Why are they all that color?" Stewart asked softly.

"What color?"

"The scarlet."

"That? Oh, it is only the scalding, from the steam, you know," Habercorn said matter-of-factly, as if they had been discussing the preparation of crayfish.

Stewart swallowed down a lump. His stomach was churning.

"Now, I know we got some women under this tarp," he went on, casting it aside.

Stewart's view was arrested by the first body. It had been a young woman—at least he thought she had been young. It was difficult to say, because her face was missing, her features burned off. The bone of her skull, and the enamel of her teeth were all that remained. Her clothes were that of a chambermaid's, though, and Stewart knelt closer. His heart raced. He stretched out a hand, hesitated, then drawing on all his reserves, gave the deformed head a small shove. It did not want to turn because of the rigor mortis. He pushed it harder, feeling it twist tightly beneath his hand. Under the head was a hank of yellow hair, and Stewart let go of his breath, standing quickly away as if afraid the head might snap back and bite his hand.

The three other women were still recognizable, and none was Mystie.

"No," he managed to say, hardly above a whisper.

"Then we move on." Habercorn displayed not a shred of reverence in his voice. This was only business to him, and Stewart had the grim feeling that it was business as usual.

Habercorn stopped at the next sheet. "I don't know if you can do anything with this pile. It is just a collection of pieces we fished out of the river. If you got a weak stomach, you better hold onto your lunch." He flung the sheet off.

Stewart swallowed back the bile that rose to his throat. There were legs and arms, parts of arms, a hand, a head, and other scalded appendages that he could not immediately recognize. It told him nothing . . . except the head, which was not that of the woman he loved. He looked away and Habercorn covered the gruesome pile.

In half an hour he had examined every corpse there, and had not found Mystie among them.

"I am almost sorry you didn't find her," Habercorn said afterward, when they had come back into the main room. "It means she was lost in the river. At least you would have known for certain if she had been among them folks."

He brushed his palms together as if finally finished with a chore. "Well, the morgue will be sending a wagon over for them tonight, or in the morning at the latest. We've identified all the bodies we are able, and we can't keep them here any longer. Lucky the days have been cool or it would smell like a slaughterhouse in here. Once we had us a roomful of 'em floaters in the middle of July. After two days of it, you couldn't come within fifty rods of this place." He gave a short laugh.

All Stewart wanted now was to be away from there. "Thank you, Mr. Habercorn. We will be going now."

They turned to the door and, as they stepped outside, Habercorn called, "Sorry I couldn't help you out. Have a good evening."

It was almost night; the air was cool and the water moved darkly beneath the pier. Stewart and Zachary walked along it, not speaking. There was nothing left to say. Once on shore, they turned back toward the city and the *Tempest Queen.*

From the shadows growing around a row of cypress trees, a bird shot into the night sky. In the dimming light he saw the flash of pure white on its belly, the swept-back pointed wings, the notched tail.

That's a tree swallow, he thought automatically, in spite of his grief. Iridoprocne . . . Iridoprocne . . . Iridoprocne . . .

But his brain wasn't working. Try as he might, he could not come up with the species name of the bird.

Mystie would know it, he thought sadly, and he wished with all his heart she could be here with him now, walking quietly along the river that she had loved so.

But that would never be. He was grateful that it was dark, for in the dark, Zachary could not see his tears.

CHAPTER TWELVE

"Whew, I can't never remember de captain in such a stormy state, Peaches. He's a regular whirlwind. 'Carin do this, Ruby do that, Princess, make sure de big stateroom is spotless, and mind you, I'll be along to drag a finger over de door tops later.' You would think he was expectin' de King of England aboard, now wouldn't you, Peaches?"

"I hard that it was someone important, someone named Douglas, Prinie," the second chambermaid said. The boat had been in an uproar all that night, with every able-bodied crew member enlisted in the round-the-clock effort to polish up the *Tempest Queen*. Peaches was exhausted, too, but unlike Princess, she knew that complaining about it only wasted energy.

Princess shifted her hold on the wicker basket of clean and neatly folded sheets and pillowcases. The two women entered the narrow companionway that led back to the stern of the *Tempest Queen* where the laundry closet was located. "De name don't mean nothing to me. Wonder who he is, and is he important enough for me to be rubbing blisters into my feet de size of pennies? Humph. I don't think so. Oh, what I won't give right now for a basin of water to soak dese tired old dogs in."

Peaches smiled and gave a short laugh. "We are almost done here. Another four staterooms to make up, another couple tubs of laundry, and then we can sit down. It's the poor rousters that I am thinking about. They have been up all night hauling bales, swabbing the deck, painting the handrails."

Princess said, "Well, dere better be something extra in my pay envelope this month, dat's all I can say. Here we are."

"I wouldn't hold my breath, Prinie," Peaches said.

Princess shifted her grip upon the laundry basket and reached for the brass knob. She turned it and pushed the door open. But it swung in only a few inches before it encountered an obstruction of some kind on the other side and stopped.

"Now who left dat stuff on de floor?" Princess carped, giving the door another shove. It did not budge. She frowned and a line of determination came to her lips. "I's gonna get dat open even if I got to break it down! Someone is gonna be in big trouble with me." She set the basket upon the floor, put her shoulder to the door, and shoved with all her strength. The obstruction on the other side slid heavily across the floor until the gap was wide enough to slip through.

"Dere. Dat got it." Princess gave her friend a quick,

victorious nod and went inside. The next instant she cried, "Oh, Lord!"

"What is it, Prinie?" Peaches asked from out in the hallway.

After a long silence, Princess's face appeared around the door. It was several shades lighter in color than when she had entered, and her eyes were big and white. "Oh, Lord!" she cried again, louder this time, grasping the doorjamb as if she suddenly needed the extra support and staring at Peaches. Then, recovering some, she gasped, "Quick, Peaches, go get de captain!"

"What is de matter, Prinie?"

"Dere is a dead man in here!"

Captain Hamilton, First Mate Lansing, and several other crew members piled down the long, narrow companionway. Hamilton stopped at the door, which was still open only partway and gave Princess a quick look. The chambermaid was in the hallway, leaning against the wall, and she appeared to be in a mild state of shock.

"In here, Princess?" Hamilton asked, jerking a thumb at the gaping door.

"Yessuh, Captain."

He slipped inside, and after some jostling and shoving, got the door to open all the way. Within the tight quarters of the laundry closet he hunkered down over the body, sniffed the air, and wrinkled his nose.

Whiskey!

Hamilton turned the body over and immediately his heart sank.

"Stewart," he said to himself. He put a finger to Stewart's neck. His frown lengthened, and his grief shifted to anger. An empty whiskey bottle lay nearby and he grabbed it up, standing. Back out in the hallway he said, "He is dead all right. He's dead drunk!" Hamilton shoved the bottle angrily into Lansing's hand. "I have my men working 'round the clock to get this boat ready, and he is lying here, dead drunk! Get him up to his room, then go find Belding and tell him we have located his truant mud clerk. I will want to know when he wakes up."

Hamilton stormed out, taking the stairs up to the galley three at a time. The kitchen help scrambled out of his way as he came through and strode across the main cabin where his crew was scrubbing the gleaming parquet floor, polishing the crystals of the chandeliers, and standing high on stepladders, washing the stained glass skylights that encircled the long, narrow room.

Outside on the promenade, he stopped by the railing and drew in a sharp breath. Nearby, a rouster with a bucket of green paint was scrutinizing the handrail, touching it here and there with the tip of his brush. Hamilton was not a drinking man, although he did not condemn the practice among his crew, but he would not abide drunkenness aboard his boat. Stewart would have to be let go.

It saddened him. He had grown fond of the young man. If it had been any other time, Hamilton would have been lenient. But now, with the push on to get the *Tempest Queen* ready to steam by four o'clock, discovering one of his men passed-out drunk was more than he could suffer. There was no excuse!

I thought the man more responsible than that.

Hamilton reined in his rage, tugged the hem of his blue jacket straight, and adjusted the cap upon his head. He was deeply unhappy as he went on his way to once more monitor the progress they were making toward readying the boat.

Gen bought her ticket that morning from a wharf agent and was told that the *Tempest Queen* would be arriving at the Municipal Landing at three o'clock to begin boarding passengers. Her departure was scheduled for four.

Afterward, Gen went back to the hotel desk to inquire if she had any messages. It would have surprised her greatly indeed if she had, but it gave her an excuse to strike up a casual conversation about the address their Senator Douglas would be giving that afternoon from the landing before boarding the riverboat for the trip up the Mississippi to Memphis. She also asked if he had left the hotel yet. He had not.

She purchased a copy of the *Picayune* and took a chair in the lobby to wait.

At ten o'clock, Douglas, his secretary Sheridan, and his wife, a lovely woman in a peach colored silk polonaise over a matching skirt and a black, fringed cape about her shoulders came down the stairs. Gen thought that Adéle Douglas was quite beautiful, in a matronly way.

Douglas had on the same white felt hat and the same blue broadcloth suit that she had seen the night before. They paused at the desk, passed their key across to the clerk, and then, after a brief discussion, Douglas took his wife by the arm and the three of them strolled outside.

Gen tucked the paper under her arm and followed them at a safe distance. They made their way into the French Quarter. Gen waited on the sidewalk with her face to the storefront windows as they visited shops. She lingered a full hour in the doorway of an apothecary as the senator and his wife had breakfast in a restaurant down the street. The whole rest of the morning was spent shopping. After a few hours of this, they enlisted the services of a young black boy to carry their packages. For the most part, Sheridan remained with Douglas and his wife, occasionally lingering awhile in a shop, but always catching up with them after a few minutes.

Gen didn't know why she was following them, but it seemed the most natural thing, and perhaps if fate would deliver Douglas into her hands, alone, in some secluded place like an empty alleyway, well, then she might take the advantage. It would not be how she and Robert had planned it, but then, the scheme was not cast in stone, and anyway, she would rather be done with the deed as soon as possible. She had ridden enough riverboats in her life, and she would not miss in the least another trip up the Mississippi. She much preferred the serenity of Carleton Manor to the intrigue of stalking a presidential candidate.

At one point, as she waited for the senator and his wife to leave a tea shop, she wondered if Robert had yet heard from Strider. She didn't trust Strider, even though her husband seemed to have full confidence in him. She had visions of the man taking their ninety thousand dollars and never returning. But Robert had faith in the man, God knows why.

The senator and his wife spent some time in a park, in the shade of cypress trees and live oaks. Gen bought a pecan cake from a boy with a large tray of them. This was turning out to be a waste of time. She considered returning to her hotel room, checking out, and boarding the *Tempest Queen* at the wharf, but she decided against that. If nothing else, she wanted to hear what Douglas had to say when he gave his speech at the landing.

After about fifteen minutes, Sheridan stood up from the park bench and wandered out into the narrow street, glancing at the buildings, finally spying one that interested him. It sold hunting and fishing equipment, or so Gen surmised by the shotgun and dog with the pheasant in its mouth that was painted on the windows. The senator's wife also stood after a few more minutes and stretched out a hand to her husband, but he shook his head, mopping his brow with a handkerchief and settling his hat back in place.

Gen thought he looked tired and not too healthy. Considering his girth, she figured the exercise had worn him down. His wife said something, and he nodded his head in agreement. She pointed to a row of shops down the street. The senator smiled and shooed her off to explore them, which apparently was the whole point of this pantomime. She squeezed his hand most discretely, with affection that Gen could not help but notice from her vantage point at the haberdashery's display window a half a hundred feet from them.

Adéle Douglas turned away and strolled toward the shops with their young package bearer at her side. Gen's heart quickened. Was this the opportunity that she had hoped for? Is this why she had spent half a day following Stephen Douglas around New Orleans?

She shot a quick glance at the shop Sheridan had gone into. No sign of him yet. Her view leaped to Adéle's back as she stepped into the door of a shop down the street. Then she, too, was gone.

Gen licked her lips and waited, half expecting James Sheridan to step back into the street, almost wishing he would. When he did not, she began to wonder: Could she do it? Could she possibly consider such a bold scheme right here in the early noon, with people on the streets? Could she get away with it?

Yes!

She had pulled off risky schemes before, had staked thousands of dollars on the fall of a pair of dice, had risked her neck slipping her partner a pair of kings in exchange for the deuces his hand held, right in the middle of a crowded card game. It would only take an instant, and then she would disappear. Done properly, no one would even hear the muffled report.

She was sweating as she stepped away from the window

and started slowly across the street toward the park. She would wait until no one was close by. Douglas was leaning his head back as if about to nap.

Yes, it just might work.

As she walked, her hand reached inside her bag and found the little Sharps derringer. Fired from inside the reticule with it pressed tight into Douglas's fleshy body, no one beyond a few dozen feet might notice. There would be the smoke of course; there was no way to hide that.

All at once she wasn't sure she should attempt it, but her feet were already in motion, and Douglas was so near, his head tilted back, baring the swarthy skin of his throat, his eyes closed.

She was walking a little too stiffly, she thought, but that couldn't be helped, and Douglas wasn't watching her, anyway. Her brain was racing. He was now only six strides off, now five. She was doing this for the South, she told herself. *No,* the pragmatic voice inside her head countered cynically. *That is a lie, Gen, and you know it. You are doing this for yourself, and for Robert, and for his scheme, more bold—more daring—more exhilarating than anything you have ever attempted before!*

Then she was there. Her breathing quickened, her eyes darted left to right. The pistol was slippery in her moist fingers. She swallowed heavily, blinked perspiration from her eyes, and gently sat upon the bench next to the napping Stephen Douglas.

"Back already, my dear?" he asked sleepily, his eyes still shut.

Gen made a soft reply in her throat and pressed her reticule against his side.

"Aye, lassie! It is Miss Genevieve, if these peepers dunna' deceive me."

Gen gasped and was so startled by the sound of his voice

that her bag fell from her grasp, and her head flung about.

Allan Gill was grinning happily at her from behind the bench, and he tipped his hat. "It is you."

Douglas opened his eyes, a bit startled as well, and looked at her as well. "Oh, I am sorry, miss. I mistook you for my wife." He straightened up on the bench and smiled pleasantly.

"I . . . I . . ." Gen was not a woman who usually was at a loss for words, but just now speech had fled, and her heart was fairly galloping.

Gill bent to retrieve her reticule, fished around a bit under the bench, and when he finally stood, he said, "Well, isn't this a heavy piece of luggage for a slip of a lass like you to be toting about." Her grin stretched out. He handed it back to her. "I didna' mean to startle you so. I am sorry."

"It is quite all right, Mr. Gill," Gen said, regaining command of herself.

"I saw you from across the way when you sat next to this gentleman, and I—" Allan Gill looked at Douglas and his words stopped short. "Oh, my. Why you are Senator Douglas, the candidate for the presidency of the United States of America!"

Douglas seemed pleased to be recognized. "I am indeed," he said.

Allan Gill pumped his hand. "This is indeed a pleasure, sir." He glanced at Gen. "You chose a most distinguished gentleman to share a park bench with, Miss Genevieve."

Douglas said, "Do I know you, sir?"

"Oh, no, we have never met."

"Hm. You remind me of someone, then."

Gill grinned. "I have that kind of face, sir."

By this time, Gen had completely recovered and rallied her wits about her. "Why, Mr. Gill, don't be silly. I chose this seat through no accident. I recognized the senator at

once, and I only wished to make his acquaintance." She
turned to Douglas and extended her hand. "I am Genevieve
Summers. I am the woman who sent you a note last night.
I am a fond admirer of yours."

"Summers? Oh, yes, the young lady who was so generous
last night, before my speech at The Riverman's Club."

Gill laughed. "Well, well, I see that you are two jumps
ahead of me, Miss Genevieve. I like a sharp lass!"

Gen tried to ignore this obnoxious intruder. She seethed
inside at his untimely arrival, but on the outside showed
only a cool, unruffled face and a gracious smile. "I just
wanted to say how important I feel it is for you to win the
presidential race. And that I know the tensions and animosi-
ties in the South have not been easy on you or your
campaign, but there are still many Southerners like myself
who wish you well." She spoke in her most genial southern
accent, and her blue eyes captured his and held them
prisoner.

"I love this land, Senator, and I do not wish to see it
ravaged by war. I do not want to see our young men die. But
I know there are a certain breed of men, known by the
unflattering name of fire-eaters, who are calling for secession if that horrid Mr. Lincoln is elected, and I don't want
that to happen. That is why I have given you my money, and
if I were a man, you should have my vote as well."

"I would covet it, Miss Summers, and your words have
been most encouraging to me. It has been a long struggle,
and the going has been bumpy. I am not the sort of man who
seeks the presidency for his own glory. I do this out of a
sincere desire, like you, to keep this Union whole and to
reconcile both sides. The South has some grievous com-
plaints against the North, and they are not unfounded. I
intend to address them when I am president, and work to
find an equitable solution."

"I know you will, Senator. A just and honorable man such as yourself could do no less," Gen said the words with bursting pride, giving them a ring of nobility.

Gill applauded. "Well spoken, lassie. You are not only beautiful, but a patriot as well!"

Her smile faltered, but she repaired it as she looked at him. "Thank you, sir," she said, wishing the boor would be on his way.

James Sheridan returned with a small package under his arm. He appeared mildly surprised at finding the senator surrounded by Gen and Gill.

Gen flashed a smile at him and said, "Good afternoon, Mr. Sheridan."

He recognized her then. "Oh, you are the lady from the hotel."

He tried to affect a gracious smile, but Gen knew he was more annoyed than glad to see her.

"So, you finally got your opportunity to speak with the senator."

She stood gracefully from the bench, clutching her reticule in both hands. "I had no doubts that I would, sir, for as it turns out, we will be traveling upon the same boat up the river. The *Tempest Queen*."

"Aye, then we all are," Gill announced happily.

"Yes, indeed," Gen said, lowering her eyelids to hide the storm brewing there. The last thing she needed was this buffoon tagging after her. "Well, I must be getting back to my room and pack. I don't want to miss your speech at the landing this afternoon. It was so nice meeting you, Senator . . . Mr. Sheridan." She shook both their hands, and ignoring Gill completely, started back toward the hotel.

"Might I walk you back, lass?" he asked, catching up with her.

She wheeled about. "No, you might not." Immediately

she resumed her march. Fortunately, he did not follow. Finally, she thought, I am rid of the fellow.

It was almost one o'clock when she arrived in her room. Alone, with the door securely latched, she sat upon the bed, propped her back against the headboard, and let go a long breath.

That was close.

"Perhaps it was for the best," she said aloud. The powder that Robert had given her was just as deadly and certainly quieter, and she could be long gone before it took effect and anyone knew what had happened. Using the pistol was an impulsive idea, and dangerous. It *was* for the best that she had been interrupted.

She lifted her reticule from the floor and set it upon her lap, digging through it for the silver-plated Sharps.

It was not there!

She searched the bag again, fighting back a sudden panic. The pistol was indeed missing.

It must have fallen out when I dropped my bag!

She could think of no other reason for it to be gone, and it was only sheer luck that no one there had spied it.

CHAPTER THIRTEEN

Blinding white light stabbed through his cabin window and impaled his eyeballs, driving electric sparks, like splinters of glass, into his brain. His head was being compressed between the jaws of a giant vise, and his mouth contained all the sand of the Sahara, or so it seemed to him.

Clifton Stewart was not thinking clearly.

The Sahara. Thirst. He suddenly craved water almost more than breathing. When he tried to sit up, a pile driver crashed down upon his head and drove it back into the pillow. The feathers and smooth cotton muffled his low groan. When he tried to swallow, something got in the way, and after two or three attempts, he realized it was his tongue. In his mind, it had swelled to the thickness of a barber's strop.

Clifton Stewart had never before become drunk, and he never drank anything but Glenlivet if he could help it. What was it the steward had sold him the night before? Old Steamboat? Old Boiler Room? Old Bilge? He couldn't quite remember the name, but it definitely was not Glenlivet!

He tried again to rise, and with determination and patience finally maneuvered himself to the edge of his bed and put his feet upon the floor. He clasped his head in both his hands so that it would not tumble off and sat there staring at the floorboards and his bare feet drifting in and out of focus, waiting for a sudden wave of nausea to pass. It occurred to him after a few minutes of this that he was still fully dressed. Trying to think back, he could not remember putting himself to bed. He did not recall the climb up the stairs to the texas at all.

What he did remember was his overwhelming grief, and he seemed to recall that Zachary was there with him, at least for a while. It was all a blur now. He remembered, after the first few sips of Old Bilge—or whatever it was—visiting the places on the *Tempest Queen* where he and Mystie had walked that single glorious week more than a year and a half ago.

There had been a bustle of activity about him. He remembered that, and he recalled that all the lamps and candles had been lighted. He had been jostled and bumped into, but all he wanted was to be alone with his grief, and he had made his way down the companionway toward the laundry storage where that first day he had carried Mystie's basket for her.

After that, it was all a blank.

How did he get here, still dressed? He rotated an arm. It was stiff, as if he had slept on it funny.

He smacked his cracked lips and tried to work some moisture into them, but they were still as dry as the Sahara. He grabbed the back of a nearby chair and stood. Nothing dramatic occurred to launch him off his feet, and so, somewhat encouraged, he shuffled to the pitcher of water by the mirror. He didn't bother with a glass but tilted the pitcher back and drank from the rim with the water dribbling down his chin and onto his new shirt, which smelled of cheap whiskey.

He could not get enough water.

He paused after a while and wiped his mouth and chin with a dirty sleeve. The fellow that stared back at him from the mirror looked like a rogue, with bloodshot eyes, puffed and pink lids, a drawn face, and fine yellow whiskers emerging in patches. He looked ten years older, and felt it.

Stewart took another long drink, and when the white porcelain bottom was all that was left in the pitcher, he put it back and straightened up, feeling slightly better.

A knock sounded upon his door.

"Yes, who is it?" Stewart said softly.

"Hamilton," came the firm reply from the other side.

Stewart glanced down at himself, attempted to tuck in his shirttail, but had not the strength and, leaning back against his dressing table for support, said, "Come in, Captain."

The sunlight blazed in the rectangle of the doorway. Stewart squinted and put up an arm to protect his eyes. A black shape momentarily blocked some of the light as Hamilton stepped inside. The captain stood there looking at him a while before shutting the door.

Stewart lowered his arm, and said in a weak voice, "I am afraid I am not in any condition to be the proper host, Captain." He managed a smile, but saw that Hamilton was not in a humorous mood.

The captain said nothing for a while. Stewart saw that the

man was harboring a mighty anger. Stewart grabbed the chair, pulled it over and, trembling, sat in it, cradling his head again.

"You appear to be in agony, Mr. Stewart," Captain Hamilton finally said.

"I cannot ever remember feeling worse," he said, but he meant in a physical way, for indeed, ever since he read Mystie's name on the *Guiding Star*'s payroll ledger, he had been emotionally crushed, and now he cared little for whatever reprimand Hamilton had in mind for him.

"I have no sympathy for a man who drinks himself insensible."

"No, sir. And I do not expect any."

"Have you anything to say on your behalf, Mr. Stewart?"

"No." He had not yet come to terms with Mystie's death, and he could not talk about it now.

"I have had every crew member up all night, working to get this boat in shape to carry Senator Douglas and his party up the river. You knew that, didn't you?"

"Yes. I was aware of it, Captain."

"And yet you chose to drink yourself insensible?"

"I am sorry, sir." He wanted this inquisition to end. Yes, he was guilty, yes, he would take his punishment, yes, yes, yes.

"I had thought you were more responsible than that, Mr. Stewart. In light of your recent promotion, I had expected diligence from you; I thought I saw the makings of an officer in you. You possess a tenacity that I admire. I see, however, that I was mistaken on several counts. I am gravely disappointed in you."

Stewart remained silent, bearing the brunt of Hamilton's indignation. He would not cheapen his memory of Mystie by using her as an excuse to plead his case.

"I see that you have nothing to offer in your defense."

"No."

Hamilton nodded his gray head. "Then I must ask you to leave."

Stewart looked up, but he moved his head too quickly, and an invisible lead pipe smacked him across the forehead. He winced, and when his eyes once more got the focusing problem in hand, he saw that Hamilton was dead serious.

"Leave? The *Tempest Queen?*"

Hamilton nodded his gray head.

"You are firing me?" Stewart managed to say.

"I am. Consider the money I gave you yesterday as your severance." Hamilton looked at his silver watch. "It is now twenty past twelve. We will be steaming to the Municipal Landing at three o'clock to take on our passengers. I will expect you to be packed up and leave at that time."

"But—" Stewart stammered.

"I regret this decision, Mr. Stewart, but you have left me with no choice."

He had no energy to protest. Mystie's death, his pounding head, the shifting room, and the thought of returning home to his father in defeat left him helpless. "I . . . I understand." He looked at the floor, cradling his head.

A slash of brutally painful light ricocheted off the painted boards. He closed his eyes. Hamilton's footsteps receded, the door latched, the light was shut out, and he was alone.

Stewart sat there a long while considering his options, which were not numerous. In the end, he knew he had no choice but to return to his father's plantation. He had had so many grand plans before this. He had even considered someday purchasing a steamboat like the *Tempest Queen,* and with Mystie at his side, building a business that would support them and their children. Now nothing mattered, and crawling home in defeat somehow was no more repugnant than any other choice.

His head pounded, and the taste of cheap whiskey was upon his breath, but despite that, he managed to drag out a valise and begin packing his few belongings.

The woman in the crowd lifted herself upon her toes to see above the heads of the milling crowd of people who had come to hear the senator from Illinois speak. She was curious, of course, to hear what he had to say, but she had already made up her mind on the subject. Lincoln was her choice for president, and from what she had read in the papers, these two men and the current vice president, John C. Breckinridge, the South's choice, were running a neck-to-neck three-way race.

Politics, however, were not forefront on her mind, and she had only found her way into this gathering by chance. She lifted on her toes again, but not in hopes of spying the famous senator whom papers called Little Giant. She was searching the crowd for the face of the man who had gone to purchase tickets for them on the next steamer bound for Illinois.

Near the landing was a raised platform festooned with buntings and flags, and upon it was a podium. At the moment, it was empty, but by the growing agitation of the crowd, she knew it would not long remain that way.

She wore a new hat, new dress, and new shoes. Her reticule and the few items that it held were all that remained of her original belongings. At another time she would have been intensely interested in the small piece of history about to be made here on the New Orleans wharves, but now all she cared about was going upriver—going home.

The last few days had been frightful—the inquests and the questioning most uncomfortable. But they had been necessary, and she had come through all right. It was poor Barnabas who had borne the brunt of the questions and the allegations, and she was glad it was over now and that they were going home. He would have to face more questions, of course. The company would need all the details, the insurance investigators would want to know as well, but at least in Illinois they would be on friendlier ground.

She stretched again and far out across the sea of bare heads, hats, and bonnets, she saw the blue cap and the face beneath it that she knew and loved so well. She waved a handkerchief in the air, caught his eye, and kept her arm raised above the crowd until he had woven his way through it and was at her side.

"I have found us each a berth upon a steamer bound north," he said. "We were most fortunate. It is traveling all the way to Illinois, so we won't have to transfer."

His usual gay smile and happy lilt were missing. She quite understood that he had nothing to be happy about at the moment. But now they had passage home. One more hurdle was over, and only a few were left to cross. The next big fence to leap would be with the company, but Barnabas was confident that it would go well and that his job was secure. He had done nothing wrong.

"When do we depart?"

"We can board when she arrives at the landing. I was told it would be three o'clock. In fact, it is the very boat that Senator Douglas will be traveling upon."

"Really?" Her black brows lifted with interest. "That should prove an entertaining trip."

Barnabas smiled at her. Not his usual wide smile, it was small and forced, but it was the first she had seen since the accident, and it encouraged her some. He said, "We can both use a little cheering up, my darling."

She took his hand and squeezed it. "This will soon be behind us, and we will have the rest of our lives together."

"Yes, we do have that to look forward to."

"What is the name of the steamer?" she asked.

"It is a very fine vessel. One of the grandest on the river. You know the boat, I am sure. The *Tempest Queen*." He paused and looked at her, his brows knitting together in concern. "Why, darling, is something the matter?"

"The *Tempest Queen?* That is Captain Hamilton's boat."

"Yes, it is."

"Could you not have found us passage on any other boat?" she asked.

He seemed confused by her distress. "I suppose I could have found another, but why?" His tone was suddenly defensive. "What is the matter?"

There were too many bitter memories to deal with right now, considering all that she had been through these last days. And Barnabas didn't need to be burdened with them, either. "It is all right. Nothing is the matter. I once knew someone who worked aboard the *Tempest Queen,* that's all."

She had said enough. She did not need to tell him about past loves and past sorrows, and even though Barnabas shared her feeling about slavery, she could not yet tell him of her connections with the Railroad—at least not until they were safely out of the South.

"Oh, is that all? I don't see why you're fretting over that. It is only a boat you used to work on. I can't see why it should make a difference."

"It will be all right," she said. She did not want to discuss the matter further. She'd have to make do.

Suddenly the military band, which was hidden some-where beyond the crowd and below the platform, began to play.

"Look. There is the senator now, just coming to the podium. Let's hear what he has to say," Barnabas said.

But her head was swimming with memories, and although she climbed up on her toes again to see above the crowd, Mystie Water's thoughts were elsewhere.

Would Clifton still be aboard the *Tempest Queen?*

She hoped not.

Not far away, jostled by the crowd like a fish caught in a net, Gen watched the senator climb the steps. The brass band finished a martial tune, and Douglas saluted them and grasped the podium firmly in his two pudgy hands. Gen found a place close to the platform and climbed onto a bale of cotton where she had a clear view of the senator.

Douglas waved the crowd down. The silence spread along the landing until the only sounds were those coming from the puffing and hissing steamers nearby and the splash of their paddle wheels turning lazily in the muddy water. Stephen A. Douglas began to speak.

"Fine gentlemen of the South, greetings, and to her lovely ladies, I tip my hat. I am not one of those who believe that I have any more personal interest in the presidency than any other good citizen of America. I am here to make an appeal to you on behalf of the Union and the peace of the country."

"He speaks well, does he not, lassie?"

The last voice Gen expected to hear was that of Allan Gill. She glanced to her left, and down, and at the foot of the cotton bale discovered his smiling face behind the brown beard looking up at her. He tipped the scruffy hat and set his battered blue duffel bag on the bale by her feet.

Gen was at her wit's end. Was she never going to shake this flea-bitten foreign vagabond? And what was it that he saw in her, anyway? Did he know that she had money, and was he out to somehow swindle her out of it? Gen laughed to herself.

I have dealt with better than you, sir.

"Why, Mr. Gill," she said, butter and cream smooth,

showing not a hint of the annoyance that she was feeling, "you do manage to pop up at the most unexpected times."

"Aye, it does seem that way, lassie. But methinks it be only lady chance having her way with us. Really, this is no coincidence. We both admire the senator and want to hear him speak, and we both are booked on the same steamer. I'd say not running into each other would be more of a trick than the other way about, lass."

"I suppose," she drawled sweetly, returning her gaze to the senator. But she wasn't convinced.

". . . desire no man to vote for me unless he hopes and desires the Union maintained and preserved intact by the faithful execution of every act, every line and letter of the written Constitution, which our fathers bequeathed to us."

A wave of voices, both dissenters and supporters, rolled through the crowd.

"Aye, he would make a fine president."

Gen glanced at Gill. "He would keep us from war—at least for another four years."

Allan Gill shoved his hands into the pockets of his shabby jacket and grinned. "And isn't that what we want, you and me, lassie?"

"Of course." She averted her eyes and returned her attention to the little man on the podium speaking strong words.

"So, I have come south to plead for your votes! I make no promises that run contrary to my own beliefs, but consider the sectional parties, North as well as South, as the great evil and curse of this country. Is there not some holy principle, some common ground around which all Union-loving men might rally to preserve this glorious Union against Northern and Southern agitators?"

From out in the river came the deep-throated call of a steam whistle. A long, three-tiered steamboat rounded into view, gleaming white beneath the dirty yellow and gray smoke that hung over the river. On her paddle box was painted dark, roiling clouds with the sun bursting through them, its yellow rays shooting out to the curved edge of the box where the name *Tempest Queen* was painted. Her promenade and main deck were draped in red, blue, and white bunting, and pennants of the same color flapped along her guy lines and hog chains. Black smoke churned above her chimneys, and upon the hurricane deck stood a stout, gray-bearded man in the coat and cap of a ship's master. Behind him were three of his officers.

With a burst of white steam, the whistle hooted again. The magnificent packet had stopped its near-side wheel and was pivoting in midriver with its far-side wheel turning, aiming her toward the landing.

The steamboat glided into its berth, making a smooth and faultless landing, and a dozen men hurried to make her fast.

"There be our lift, lassie."

Gen ignored Allan Gill, intent on hearing the finish of the senator's speech.

". . . Would such a grievance justify revolution or secession? I tell them no—never on earth! There is no evil in this country for which the Constitution and the laws do not furnish a remedy, no grievance that can justify disunion!"

Douglas finished his speech and received a round of applause and cheers. There were a few jeering voices, but for the most part, the senator had struck a chord with the people. Gen knew that although they spoke boldly, few Southerners really wanted disunion or the bloodshed that it was likely to bring, even though the fire-eaters' voices were the ones most folks heard these days.

"No, that man, he will make this country hang together," Allan Gill said.

Gen frowned. There seemed no way to be free of the man,

and for the moment at least, she was stuck with him. "He will, if he is elected."

She permitted him to help her off the bale, taking his hand for support.

"You sound as if he might not be, lass," Gill said, grabbing up her valise before she could protest.

Senator Douglas had already left the podium, and the brass band had begun to play again as his small party, which this time included the governor of Louisiana, Thomas Moore, made their way out onto the landing and aboard the waiting riverboat.

"He has a formidable race against Mr. Lincoln," Gen said.

"Aye, but he still stands a good chance of winning."

"Yes, Mr. Gill, he does at that," she replied. "A very good chance."

And that was precisely the problem.

CHAPTER FOURTEEN

Stewart had shoved the last of his new clothes into the valise and had just squeezed it shut and latched it when a knock sounded on his door.

"Come in," he said.

The mixture of grief, a throbbing head, and the humiliation of being tossed off the boat combined to make him decidedly unenthusiastic. He knew that the *Tempest Queen* had backed away from the wharf; he felt her powerful engines drumming away three decks below, heard the rhythmic chuffing of her escape pipes. In a few minutes she would be pulling into the Municipal Landing where he would disembark. He thought Captain Hamilton had returned to make sure he was on his way out, but when the door opened, it was Zachary standing there.

"Hullo, Mr. Cliff?" Zachary stepped in tentatively. He looked around the little stateroom and whistled. "Dis here is mighty fancy cabin, Mr. Cliff."

"How are you, Zachary?"

"Oh, I's fine. It was dat same question dat I was gonna ask yo'."

"I think I had a bit too much to drink last night."

"Dat is de truth, Mr. Cliff."

Stewart grimaced. "Did you bring me up here afterward?"

"No, suh. I left yo' when dat Mr. Lansing snagged me aside an' put a bucket of soap water and scrub brush in my hand."

"Did you get in trouble for being ashore with me?"

"She-oot, no, Mr. Cliff. Dat Mr. Lansing, him is so busy runnin' around like de Christmas goose what sees de ax a-comin' at him dat him don't even know I am away 'til dark."

"Good. I am glad."

"Mr. Cliff?"

"Yes?"

"I hear dat de capt'n done give yo' de boot."

Stewart nodded his head—carefully—but the sharp pain made him wince just the same.

"I got drunk and shirked my duties. I suppose I had it coming."

"De talk am all over de boat how dem two girls, Prinie and Peaches found yo' passed out drunk in de laund'y. Dey thought sure 'nough yo' was dead. Called de capt'n and everb'y over to see. Couple de rousters carried yo' up here to sleep it off."

It sounded even worse than he feared. "I was afraid that's what happened."

"Mr. Cliff? I am gonna miss yo'."

"I am going to miss you, too, Zachary. Clifton extended his hand. Zachary looked at it as if he had never taken a white man's hand in friendship before. Then, hesitating, he clasped it in his own big paw.

"What am yo' gonna do now, Mr. Cliff?"

"I don't know. Probably go back home. There is nothing left for me on the river."

"Dat is where yo' belong, where de livin' am easy. Mebbe some day ol' Zachary will put him feet up on dry land and come see how yo' done."

Stewart managed a smile. "I'd like that. You take care of yourself, and don't let Lansing ride all over you."

"She-oot, him a pussycat what roars like a tiger. I be jim-dandy. Dis is my life. Dis is where I belong. It never really was yo'rs. Yo' belong in dat big house, not in de belly of a steamer feeding dem furnaces or even clerkin'. It time yo' go back to it."

The rhythm of the engines changed as the outside paddle wheel slowed while its twin on the other side kept turning. They felt the boat pivot forty-five degrees and then both wheels resumed turning together. Beyond his stateroom window, Clifton watched the Municipal Landing slide up alongside. A gentle nudge shook the boat as she bumped the mooring fenders, and then the long, drawn-out tug against her hawsers, as if stretching a giant gum band, pulling her finally to a stop.

He grabbed his valise. "It is time for me to go."

"I'll walk wid yo' a spell."

They went out into the afternoon sunlight that still sent needles of pain into his head. Coming around the promenade, Clifton paused to view the landing one deck below and the passengers coming aboard. The short, round figure of Senator Douglas was unmistakable, the woman at his side beautiful. She and four other gentlemen, smartly dressed, accompanied him on board. Captain Hamilton was standing at the bow to greet the dignitaries as they stepped off the landing stage. He welcomed them aboard with a handshake and a few words, and then the boat's string quartet began playing, almost as soon as the brass band ashore had stopped.

Once Douglas and his party were aboard, the *Tempest Queen* began taking on her other passengers. Stewart watched a moment and then said to Zachary, "Well, I best be on my way. I don't think the captain would want me making my way off while his passengers are boarding. I'll just go aft and take the stern gangplank. Good-bye, Zachary."

"Go'by, Mr. Cliff. God be wid yo'."

Stewart put his back to the gathering below, to the captain, to a life he had lived for the last eighteen months, and left. He took a ladder down to the main deck, mounted the aft landing stage were a couple of Negro rousters sat tossing dice upon the deck, and walked off. They watched him leave but said nothing.

As his feet stepped upon the landing, a flicker of yellow and gray and white caught his eye. The bird had been perched on one of the guy wires, and now it sailed to the jack staff at the bow of the boat.

A yellow-throated warbler, Stewart thought, and automatically his brain ran down a list and came up with the scientific name, *Dendroica dominica*.

A great sadness swept over him. For the rest of his life, every time he spied and identified a bird, he would think of Mystie. He would probably have to abandon his love of ornithology and take up a new interest—or suffer the misery that would be a constant companion.

He blinked the moisture from his eyes and carried his bag down the long pier toward town.

*   *   *

Mystie's view was suddenly drawn skyward. In the few seconds that it took for the bird to glide from the stern of the *Tempest Queen* to a perch atop the jack staff at the bow, she had identified it.

"Oh, look Barnabas, *Dendroica dominica,* a yellow-throated warbler." She pointed it out to him, smiling in spite of herself.

"Huh?" He followed her pointing finger. "What? Oh, Mystie, it is only a bird," he said with a hint of impatience. "Now come along, we are boarding."

Her smile faltered, then disappeared.

Since Hamilton was with the senator, Belding was boarding passengers. He accepted the two tickets that Captain Barnabas offered and didn't bother to look at the woman at the captain's side. If he had, Mystie was certain he would have recognized her. She followed Barnabas around to the stairway, which was draped in bright, patriotic colors. Music swelled through the main deck and followed them up to the main cabin. How well she knew this boat . . . and how much she missed her, Mystie suddenly realized as old memories flooded back.

In spite of her better judgment, she looked for Clifton among the faces of the crew, but she did not find him.

Gen presented her ticket to the clerk, was waved aboard, and waited as Gill likewise handed the man the stub of his. Allan Gill's ticket was for deck passage only, and she held back a small smile. If she could avoid the pest in no other way, at least now they would be separated by social—if not financial—station. Deck passengers were seldom permitted to move beyond the main deck. The upper staterooms and the luxuries of the main cabin would be off limits to him. They would be Gen's sanctuary.

"I'll take that now," she said, recovering her baggage from his hand. "Thank you, and good-bye, Mr. Gill."

"Good-bye, lassie. Be seeing you around." Gill tipped his hat, and as he turned to leave, he started singing:

> *O lang will his lady*
> *Look frae the castle Doune,*
> *Eer she see the Earl o Murray*
> *Come sounding through the toon.*

Gen didn't wait around to listen to the rest of it, but hurried up the stairway to the wide promenade of the boiler deck. Ahead of her were the leaded-glass windows of the four gleaming doors that opened into the main cabin. She stopped, released a long breath, and glanced over the railing. Below, Allan Gill slung his battered duffel bag over his scruffy shoulder, and now whistling the tune to the ditty he had just sung, he wandered off toward the guards and a deck chair there beside an iron spittoon. He sat down, stretched his legs out in front of himself, and laid his head back into his hands with his arms akimbo.

"Perhaps now I will be free of you, Mr. Gill," Gen said softly to herself. She glanced at the stateroom number on her stub, then stepped inside the main cabin.

Sunlight through the stained glass skylights glinted in the crystal chandeliers, showering the polished parquet wood at her feet in the colors of the rainbow. The floor stretched away in front of her for most of three hundred fifty feet. On either side to it, columned walls rose up to an arched ceiling, painted glaringly white, with green and gold trim, and a riot of scrollwork, carvings, and wood turnings. At the back of the main cabin, the gleaming parquet stopped, and a red and gold carpet continued on, marking the ladies' salon. Scattered about the salon were comfortable chairs, sofas, and settees, all brightly upholstered. At the very back of the salon was a great gilded mirror reaching from floor to ceiling. It was so intricately carved that it dazzled even Gen's eye, and she had ridden many fancy packets in her time.

She went through the main cabin where passengers had begun to arrive. Negro waiters in starched white coats were already carrying drinks on trays held high over their heads. Gen found her room about midway down and went inside. She set her bag on the floor, tossed her bonnet onto the bed, and looked around. It was a small room, with a single bed and a dressing table. There was a pitcher of water, a wash basin, and a towel. On one wall was an iron radiator.

The window was open, and it looked out over the promenade into the afternoon sun. A breeze moved the light chintz curtains. The cabin, she noted with some disappointment, had no door opening out onto the promenade. She'd have to go in and out through the main cabin. There was a door between her room and the adjoining stateroom, but when she tried the handle, it was locked. She tried to open it with the key that was upon the dressing table, but it only worked on the main door. She put the key into her reticule and went back out into the main cabin. Tables covered with cloths were arranged around the room. There was a bar with a colored bartender in a white coat standing behind it. She desperately wanted a whiskey now and headed for it.

"Yes, missus? What would yo' like?"

What she wanted was a glass of rye—a tall glass—but ladies didn't take their liquor that way. Gen hesitated, looked around, and said, "Oh, I think I'll have something sweet. A peach frappé?" She smiled at a gentleman standing nearby. The man returned her smile and moved off with his wife. When he had gone, Gen whispered to the bartender, "And spike it!"

"Missus?"

"You heard me. Put a couple shots of whiskey in it."

"Er, yes ma'am."

Gen took a long drink of the frappé, and the sting of the whiskey coursing down her throat was instantly soothing. After a few minutes, she was feeling more her old self.

Gen went outside on the promenade to look around. Toward the back of the boat she found the senator's rooms: three staterooms set apart and draped in bunting. They were larger than the rest and on the opposite side of the boat from hers. The senator's rooms had the convenience of two doors, one that opened to the promenade and the other into the main cabin.

She stepped up to the green handrails to watch the last of the passengers come aboard. She looked at her watch. It was nearly four o'clock. The other steamers nearby were already preparing to leave. The *Tempest Queen*'s own paddle wheels were turning slowly in their boxes, as if only waiting for the command to put on steam, splashing the muddy water into slow eddies that moved back toward the stern.

Above her, the escape pipes chuffed lazily. White puffs of steam burst from them every few seconds, and the smoke that curled from the tall, black chimneys only faintly grayed the otherwise overcast yellow air.

Behind them, a steamer with red chimneys blew her whistle and backed away from the landing.

All at once, as if answering the *Natchez*'s whistle, the *Tempest Queen*'s whistle shrieked. Gen flinched at the sudden shrill sound two decks above her head. It sounded the five-minute departure warning, and below, a Negro rouster walked along the deck shouting in a deep bass voice, "All ashore who am goin' ashore!"

Friends and family gave farewell hugs and kisses and departed by way of the two gangplanks. Gen carried her frappé to the front of the promenade where she had a view of the captain escorting Douglas and his party across the deck and toward the curved stairway.

"You seem unusually quite, Mystie," Barnabas said, taking her by the arm as they ascended the stairs.

"It is the stress of the last few days, that's all," she said, and immediately wished she hadn't, for that was only half true. She had been thinking about Clifton Stewart, recalling their last night together, with the sky crashing down about them, the rain driving in sheets. She remembered so clearly Clifton's confusion at first when he discovered that she had let the runaway slave, Eli, escape. And then his rejection of her once his senses had returned. His words never left her. He had spoken his intentions clearly enough. He never wanted to see her again, and he hadn't.

Afterward when Captain Hamilton had learned that she had freed the slave, he had told her she would have to leave the *Tempest Queen* or risk arrest. She thought she would never hear from Stewart again, and she had tried to put him out of her thoughts. But a few months later, while she had been away, he had visited her parents in Cairo and had left a letter for her. In spite of herself, she felt compelled to answer him.

Ever since then, over a year now, she had heard no word from him. And then Barnabas Antone had come into her life. Finally she was able to submerge her feelings for Clifton, and she had done so quite well until half an hour ago when Barnabas had informed her that he had booked passage for them on the *Tempest Queen*.

The memories came back in torrents. She was being a wicked woman! Here she was with the man to whom she was engaged to be married, and all she could think about was a love that had turned sour over a year and a half ago.

Barnabas said, "We can't go on brooding forever over the accident, Mystie."

"I keep thinking of those people, over fifty of them gone, some of them our friends. Their lives snuffed out in a moment because a distracted engineer probably let the boilers run low or wasn't watching the gauges."

"Be thankful that I had to remain ashore to make arrangement for those missing barrels of potatoes, and that you were with me at the time."

"But why, Barnabas? Why us? Why did God choose to spare us? Why did he allow all those others to die?"

Barnabas Antone gave a short laugh. "God? Well, my dear, you may attribute our good fortune to divine intervention, if you choose to. I, for one, do not. It was no more than pure chance. The word for it, I believe, is serendipity."

"Barnabas, you can't mean that."

"He smiled at her and took her hand. "You believe whatever you like, my dear, and I will believe what I like. In the end, it will make very little difference."

"You seem to be in better spirits," she noted.

Barnabas nodded. "We are leaving New Orleans and the tragedy behind us. I pled my case before the recorder and was found innocent. The company will agree with the findings of the inquest, and in short order I shall have another boat to command, and I shall have you as my wife. I can only brood for so long with those happy prospects ahead of me."

She was about to tell him that his attitude was rather callous, but at that moment one of the boat's firemen came around the promenade, making for the stairway that she and Barnabas had just left. The fireman looked her way and stopped dead in his tracks. His eyes bulged, his jaw dropped, and he stood there, staring.

Mystie recognized him at once. It had been a long time, but without hesitation his name came to her. "Zachary?"

His ability to speak seemed to have fled, as if he had been incapacitated by some force that she did not understand.

"Zachary, it is me, Mystie."

"Ooooh, noooo, it ain't yo'," Zachary finally managed to say. "Yo' is dead. Yo' is a ghost!"

"I am not, Zachary," she said taking a step in his direction.

He scrambled back a step and crossed his arms in front of him. "Don't yo' come no closer. Yo' leave poor Zachary alone. I never done yo' no wrong, an' I didn't go nowhere nears dem dead bodies. Yo' got no cause to come both'r me."

"Zachary," she said sharply. "I am not a ghost. I'm not dead!" Mystie had little patience with slave superstitions. It was a chain around their necks as mighty as any the white man had yet contrived. "Look at me. Do I look like a ghost?"

Behind her, she heard Barnabas chuckle. "Let the poor fellow be. Can't you see he's scared to death?"

"No, Barnabas," she snapped. She turned to Zachary. "Stop that trembling. Touch my hand." She extended it to him.

Zachary stared at it, his eyes still big as coat buttons.

"Go on, touch it," she insisted, and he tentatively reached out a trembling hand.

"It am warm," he said, as if could not believe his own sense.

"Of course it is warm. I'm not dead!"

"Yo' ain't dead?"

"I am not."

"Yo' ain't dead! Yo' is alive!"

"Yes! What on earth made you think I was a ghost?"

"Mr. Cliff, him did read yo' name in a book dat dey done fished up out of de *Guiding Star* cabin."

"Mr. Cliff?"

"Mr. Cliff—yo'r Mr. Cliff."

"Clifton?"

It was at that moment that the *Tempest Queen*'s steam whistle sounded the five-minute departure warning.

Zachary's head came up, and suddenly his eyes shot landward. "Ooooh, dat Mr. Cliff!" He looked back at her. "Don't you go nowhere, Miss Mystie!" and with that, he bounded down the stairs, nearly running over the captain and Senator Douglas, and dashed across the landing stage, parting the folks there as Moses had the Red Sea.

"Now, what was that all about, Mystie?"

"Oh, Barnabas. I would have told you someday."

"Told me what? Who is this fellow . . . this Mr. Cliff?"

"I already told you that I used to work on the *Tempest Queen*. Clifton is . . . is someone I used to know." She could not go into it any further than that now and turned her eyes down toward the landing where Zachary's long legs, pumping like pistons, were propelling him toward shore.

CHAPTER FIFTEEN

The road ran nearly ruler straight between brown fields where black men hoed the furrows, working the ground before it wintered over. A smell of woodsmoke was in the air, and the way was lined with live oaks and palm trees. Alex Strider turned off the main road and followed the twisting land back toward the big white house in the distance, which was only partly visible through the trees that grew thick, crowding in close to the shoulder of the road.

When he came to the arched gateway, he reined in and studied the massive building at the far end of a circular crushed-stone drive. Beyond the wide gateway the grounds were neatly groomed. The trees had been cut back from the house, opening up a lawn that was still green this late into the season. Perhaps that wasn't so unusual for Louisiana, but for a man from the territories, it was a startling sight.

Strider studied the lay of the place. Black slaves worked along the edges of the lawn, and farther back where the barns were, several black women were hauling baskets in their arms, and at the hems of their dresses little children skipped and played.

He glanced at a stand of trees farther out. A wagon was there, and three black men were busily wielding axes. Strider watched them swing, and a half second later heard the sound of their chopping echo out of the woodlot and across the long yard where he sat upon his tough little mustang. The horse had covered over a thousand miles, but he was still as game as the day Strider had ridden from these same gates more than three months ago.

Convinced that nothing was out of place in the carefully groomed world beyond the gate, Strider urged his horse forward. The gravel of the long drive crunched beneath the horse's iron-clad hooves.

Evenly spaced banana trees lined the drive, their large, ragged leaves showing glimpses of the blue sky overhead, and beneath them grew Spanish daggers with their tough, sharp leaves rising like spikes from the rich southern soil. A little distance away, to his right, was a grove of pecan trees.

Strider passed a garden that was mostly of brown and tangled vegetation, except for a border of winter roses blooming brilliant red, like a necklace of blood drops around the dead vines. Kneeling among the withered vines, a black woman in a tattered dress and bright calico apron worked with a hand trowel. She looked up as he passed, and although her eyes followed him, she did not smile, did not acknowledge him at all.

Strider kept his view ahead, on the white columns and wide gallery across the front of the house where two Negro women were sweeping with grass brooms. An elderly black man came out of the front doors just then and watched Alex Strider ride up.

Strider reined to a stop and leaned forward in his saddle. "Afternoon, Jackson. Is your master in?"

"Yessuh, Mr. Strider. Mr. St. James has been waiting for yo'. If yo' step down, please, and follow me, I will take yo' to him. One of de boys will take yo' horse around to de barn to be grained and watered."

Strider swung out of the hard saddle and arched his back. It had been a long ride from the river landing where the little steamer had put him ashore. He untied the bags from the back of his saddle, putting them over his shoulder. They weighed considerably less than they had the day he had ridden out from Carleton Manor. Jackson told one of the sweeping girls to run and bring a groom for Strider's horse, then in his bent gait, went back into the house.

Strider walked at his side down the wide hallway. A huge painting of a woman in a green dress hung in a gold frame upon one of the parlor walls: Roberta St. James, wife of Carleton St. James, and Robert's mother. Both she and Carleton were gone now, but their son Robert had done well at increasing their fortunes and expanding the acreage of Carleton Manor and his other holdings.

To Strider's left was the ladies' sitting room, to his right, the gentlemen's parlor. Jackson took him through the gentlemen's parlor, where the furniture was heavy and rifles and shotguns filled a huge oak gun case. The smell of cigar smoke clung to the draperies and upon one wall were the mounted trophies of old Carleton St. James's many hunting trips. They passed on through, with Strider having to slow his steps in order not to outpace Jackson, who appeared never to hurry for any reason.

The next room was Robert's office. The door was open,

and beyond it Strider could see the man hunched over his desk, a quill in hand, busily scribbling something upon a piece of paper.

Jackson knocked on the open door.

Robert St. James freshened his quill in the inkwell and glanced over. "Yes, Jackson, what is it?"

"Mr. Strider has arrived, suh."

"Strider? Good, good, send him in."

Alex Strider stepped past Jackson. St. James put down the quill and pushed back his chair, but Strider was standing by the desk before he could rise.

"Good to see you again, Alex." They shook hands, and St. James sat down again, motioning Strider to a chair on the other side of the desk.

Strider remained standing.

St. James said to Jackson, "You can leave us now, and close the door behind you."

"Yessuh." The heavy door shut quietly but firmly.

St. James looked back at Strider. "Well, sit down, Alex, you make me nervous standing there. Can I pour you a brandy?"

"When we have finished with business."

"Oh, very well. Do you intend to stand the whole time?"

Strider dropped the saddlebags on St. James's desk.

"Very well, business before comfort. How did it go?"

"All right."

"No trouble?"

"I ran into some at the last place—Percy Dunbar's spread."

"And?"

"I handled it."

St. James frowned. "Is that all you can say? 'I handled it'?"

"Uh-huh."

Robert pondered the tall Texan a moment, then dragged the bags across his desk and worked the buckles loose. Strider watched St. James extract a thick folder and the two pouches of gold coins that remained.

"This might take some time, Alex. You sure you don't want to sit?"

"Uh-huh."

St. James's frown deepened. "Have it your way," he said and removed the contracts from the folder. Methodically, he compared the names on each sheet to a list he had retrieved from his desk drawer. Then he took a fresh sheet of foolscap and, knocking the excess ink from his pen, wrote the sum he found on each contract in one column, and the number of animals that sum had purchased in another. After fifteen minutes of this, he totaled the two columns and spent a few more minutes working with mathematical equations that to Strider might as well have been written in Bohemian.

Finally satisfied with his results, St. James turned to the two remaining pouches, poured the coins onto his blotter, and counted them, adding that number to the mix of numbers on his paper.

Strider figured that the wealthy planter must have been pleased with the results because when he was finally all done with his ciphering, a small smile made its way onto St. James's face and the young man nodded his head.

"Very good. You have done well, Alex. I am beginning to understand why my father always had a good word on your behalf."

"Your father always paid up like he promised."

St. James laughed. "Oh, is that all you are worried about?" He shoved the remaining coins across his desk. "I pay up, too. There you go, as we agreed upon, all that you managed to bring back and—" He stood and went across the room to a safe in the corner. When he returned, he had another pouch of coins. "And a thousand dollars in gold on top of it."

Strider collected it, counted it, and for the first time since arriving, he allowed a smile onto his face. "You St. Jameses always did keep your word."

"It is the only way to assure dependable help in the future, Alex."

Strider pulled the chair around and sat down, putting his spurs on St. James's desk. "I'll have that drink now."

St. James narrowed his eye at the scuffed boots but said nothing. "Brandy?"

"It doesn't matter."

St. James poured out two glasses, handed one to Strider, and said, "To a successful completion of a job well done." He took a sip and said, "Now, tell me about this trouble you had at Dunbar's place."

"It was nothing. A couple of his hands figured they'd make a little profit on the side by waylaying me and taking your gold."

"And?" St. James prompted when Strider fell silent.

"There isn't anything else to say. They tried and they weren't lucky."

"Hmm. I see. Did Dunbar set you up?"

"No, I don't think so. This was something they did on their own."

St. James nodded his head.

Strider tasted his brandy and said, "Now I got one for you, St. James. What in blazes are you up to?"

"Whatever do you mean, Alex?"

"Don't give me that innocent look. You know what I mean. You now have claim on almost eighty thousand head of cows, and you got them for pennies on the dollar. They are just sitting out there fattening up on Texas grass waiting for you to decide what you are going to do about them."

Robert St. James smiled thinly. "It is nothing, Alex, really. Only an investment."

"Yeah, I figured that much, but in what?"

"Cattle, of course. Haven't you ever heard of the futures market?"

"I know that the price of cattle has remained stable as a Methodist preacher for the last dozen years. What makes you think it's going to go up anytime soon? And why are you willing to risk over ninety thousand dollars if it don't? No, you got something else up your sleeve, and you are fixing to make a mountain of money off of it."

St. James laughed. "Sure, I can lose it all," he said in an unruffled southern drawl. "Anytime you play with futures you are doing nothing more than gambling. If the deal was a sure thing, I wouldn't earn enough to pay your fee. I'd never make that 'mountain of money' you so picturesquely alluded to. But now, if I did hedge my bets—" He paused to let Strider think about that a moment.

"That list of cow camps I sent with you were not randomly pulled from a hat. All those men were just breaking even, some on the verge of going under, others so far behind in their bills that they would have taken any offer that was a sure thing instead of gambling on driving their cattle to market. See what I mean? Sure things don't pay off. Big risks do."

"No. That isn't it, St. James," Strider said easily. "But it's all right, it is your business and you paid me what you promised. I'm happy." Strider threw back the rest of his brandy and stood. "Only, I had me a curious thought while riding to the steamboat landing after leaving Dunbar's place."

"Oh? What sort of thought, Alex?"

Strider had started for the door. He turned back and stood there a long moment, considering his employer. "I had me a lot of time to think it over, and I got this funny notion that all those cows would sure go a long way toward feeding a hungry army." He grinned. "But then, there isn't any hungry army about that I know of, not even a war going on, so I reckon it must have been nothing more than fanciful daydreaming." He started for the door again, then stopped and looked over his shoulder. "Only, if there was a war to come, those cows would suddenly be worth a lot more than you paid for them."

St. James gave him a tight grin in return. "I reckon you must have been dreaming, Alex. It is a curious idea, nonetheless. I must give it some thought."

Strider reached for the door. "Oh, by the way, I haven't seen that new wife of yours, St. James. Is she out?"

"Gen went to New Orleans a few days ago to visit her sister."

"She has a sister in New Orleans?"

"No. Her sister lives in Illinois. She boarded a steamer in New Orleans."

"Oh, I see." Strider opened the door.

"I will be in touch if I should need your services further, Alex."

"You know where to find me," Strider said as he left.

Clifton Stewart made his way off the landing with no particular destination in mind. The busy wharfside sights and sounds—the black-faced boys hawking wharf pies, the bustle of the rousters and stevedores hauling freight upon their big shoulders or pushing it in a hand barrow, the steam whistles of departing boats, and the clangor of their deck bells—all seemed to blend into one long, meaningless blur.

He had no idea how far he had walked or even in which direction. His head ached, his mouth was boot leather, and his spirit lay crushed beneath the weight of grief and defeat. He had walked far enough, however, for the sounds of the wharf to have diminished, and when he finally looked around, he found himself on a street that he did not know. His temples pounded, his eyes teared in the sunlight. He sat on a bench nearby, hanging his aching head between his knees.

He had only been there a minute when he thought he

heard his name being called. It came from far away, faintly. He looked up, squinting against the glare, but all he saw was the steady stream of fright wagons and drays making their way to and from the river.

Clifton licked his cracked lips and wanted a drink of water. He wanted to be away from New Orleans as well, but neither one of those two desires seemed likely prospects at the moment. He looked around at the buildings nearby. If he had wanted more whiskey, he'd have had no trouble finding it. Every three or four doorways belonged to saloons.

He decided to move on, leave the river behind him, and find someplace quiet to think through his dilemma. He would have to make his way up to Baton Rouge, and with no money in his pocket, that meant a long walk ahead of him. He picked up his valise and continued on.

A few steps farther up the street, he drew up and glanced over his shoulder to listen. Had he heard his name being called? It was unlikely. The *Tempest Queen* must already be pulling away from the landing, and no one other than her crew knew that he was here in New Orleans.

He started on again, heading for a church he had spied ahead where he figured he could find some quiet to work through his next moves.

"Mr. Cliff!"

Stewart stopped. The voice was far off, but this time he was certain he had heard his name, and he knew the voice as well. He wheeled around, watching the traffic below where two streets crossed. The deep voice boomed again.

"Mr. Cliff!"

It was one block over. Stewart hurried through an alley and emerged from its shadows at a street that was busier than the one he had just left behind.

"Mr. Cliff!"

It came from the direction of the river.

"Zachary! Zachary, where are you?"

The passing pedestrians looked at him, and he knew he appeared irrational with his hair uncombed and his eyelids puffed. Whatever could Zachary want with him? What could be so important that the man would be calling his name in public?

"Zachary!"

"Mr. Cliff!"

Stewart moved in the direction of his voice. Down the street, the tall figure of a black man in tattered trousers and a muslin shirt unbuttoned to his waist suddenly dashed through the intersection.

"Zachary!"

The big fireman stopped and looked around as if disoriented. Stewart shot up his arm and waved it. Zachary spied him then and changed the direction of his headlong rush.

"What is it?" Stewart asked when his friend put on his brakes, puffing like a steam engine.

Zachary grabbed him by the shoulders and shook him. At first Stewart thought he had gone mad, but then he discerned that he was only excited.

"Mr. Cliff, yo' got to come back to de boat wid me. Mr. Cliff, she am alive!"

"Hold up there, what are you talking about?"

"We ain't got no time to waste. She am alive. Come now!" He tried dragging Stewart along.

"Wait!" Stewart dug in his heels. "What *are* you talking about, Zachary? Who is alive?"

"It is Miss Mystie! She am alive!"

"That's impossible," he said, not daring to believe it, only to have his hopes dashed again later. "I saw her name in the *Guiding Star*'s payroll ledger. No one survived that explosion."

"I don't care what yo' done see in dat book. I see her wid

dees own two eyes of mine. I touch her! I talk wid her! Mystie am alive, and she am on de *Tempest Queen* right now, and de five-minute whistle already blow'd!"

This new hope overrode the fear he had of his heart being ripped apart once more, and before he knew what he was doing, Stewart was at Zachary's shirttail, plunging down the street toward the river. The black man's longer legs carried him ahead, and although Stewart tried valiantly to keep up, he fell back just the same, and the hammer inside his head pounded a tempo in beat to his footsteps.

He fell farther back as the busy wharves came nearer. Zachary was already there.

Could Mystie still be alive?

Stewart had no time to ponder that. He had to concentrate on his running, and trying not to crash into anyone on the sidewalk. The valise was heavy in his hand and dragged him down. He came finally to the wharf and dashed across it toward the Municipal Landing.

The *Tempest Queen*'s steam whistle and bell signaled her departure, its sounds as distinctive as the voice of a lover.

The crates and bales of cotton parted for him, and then the landing lay just ahead. Zachary was already halfway down it, but even if his friend did somehow manage to make the boat, Stewart knew that he was going to be too late.

The *Tempest Queen* had begun to move out. Stewart's feet pounded the long landing as the boat's chimneys belched a mountain of smoke the color of pitch from the pine knots the firemen would be throwing into the furnaces now. Her mighty paddle wheels were turning faster, and she slipped from her mooring fenders.

He stumbled on, losing strength. His eyes blurred behind the fountains of sweat steaming from his forehead. His throat was ablaze.

The *Tempest Queen* had moved away from the landing

and the river filled the space between her and the landing, widening with each second.

He was certain his heart would burst within his chest, and his brain would explode, but he drove on just the same. He blinked the sweat away and saw Zachary reach the edge of the landing and without breaking stride, leap out across the open water. To Stewart's distorted thoughts, he appeared to hang in the air for the longest time before his foot finally came down upon the guard at the rear of the boat just behind the paddle box where water boiled out from the revolving wheel. Zachary's hand grabbed a post, and he swung about to face the landing. With his free hand, he waved Stewart on. Already the boat had moved too far out. Even in the best of condition, Stewart could never make the leap. To try now would be suicide.

But Zachary kept urging, and Stewart's legs were pumping on their own. They had long since given up listening to his brain, which was trying to get the message through to them to give up the race. He came up alongside the boat, and not caring anymore what the consequences might be, he felt his toes push off, his feet lift and leave the landing, and then all he could see was the boiling water rushing at him.

His arms flailed the air and his valise plunged into the drink. If he had been a bird he might have flown across the gap, but he was not. His fingers missed the post by a good two feet, and down he plunged toward the angry water.

His downward motion stopped with a jolt; his arm felt as if it had been yanked from his shoulder, and as the water about his knees and legs tried to pull him under, another force was lifting him in the opposite direction. Then a big hand cupped beneath his other arm and Zachary, his legs entwined in the balusters of the railing to anchor him in place, lifted him up and over the railing as easily as if he had been a sack of goose feathers, and set him down on the deck.

CHAPTER SIXTEEN

Zachary hauled Stewart back to his feet and said, "Dat was a close one, Mr. Cliff."

"Too close for my liking, Zachary," Stewart replied between gasping breaths. He looked back at the landing dropping away behind them, and at a corner of his valise still bobbing above the water. As he watched, it sank out of sight, and to the bottom of the Mississippi River went everything he owned except for the letter, which he had kept in his shirt pocket, close to his heart.

Mystie!

Once his heart and breath rate had dropped back to something that resembled normal, he remembered why he had risked life and limb to make that crazy leap from the landing to the *Tempest Queen*.

"Zachary, now tell me again, and give me the straight of it. How can Mystie be alive, and what is she doing here?"

"I don' know, Mr. Cliff, but if yo' is done huffin' and puffin', I will takes yo' to her."

Where they had landed, on a narrow horseshoe-shaped gallery that enclosed the very rear of the boat, behind the paddle boxes, there were only two ways out; a small door into the engine room, or up a ladder to the an even smaller covered deck off the kitchen, then through the galley and up another flight of steps to the main cabin. From there they could either go forward to one of the many side doors that opened onto the promenade, or out the polished oak and leaded-glass doors all the way at the front of the cabin where the formal staircase would take them down to the main deck.

Captain Hamilton, along with his esteemed guests, were gathered in the main cabin when Stewart and Zachary entered. Before Hamilton noticed them, they ducked down a small passage that took them from the main cabin and deposited them upon the promenade.

Zachary looked around and, tugging Stewart's sleeve, started forward. Clifton's brain was still in a daze, and the pounding behind his eyes had stepped up its tempo. He wasn't convinced that Mystie was alive and on the *Tempest Queen*, but certainly Zachary was. It might yet turn out to be some ugly mistake, and his heart would be crushed further, but now he had to know for sure.

All at once he had a startling thought. If she was alive and aboard the *Tempest Queen*, what would he say to her? He had rehearsed this reunion a hundred times in his imagination, but now that the long-sought meeting might be near, all those scenarios seemed strangely distant and wooden.

He would let it come naturally, he decided as he tagged along at Zachary's heels. He would bare his heart to her and hope she would forgive him and take him back.

At the front of the promenade, Zachary stopped and looked around. Here, a half dozen people stood, talking or just watching the heavy rider traffic as the *Tempest Queen* steamed through the New Orleans port, heading for the far side of the river. Ahead, Stewart saw St. Mary's Market drawing nearer, and perhaps a mile further upriver, the bright red chimneys of the *Natchez*, steaming upriver beneath a churning ceiling of black smoke.

"She ain't here no mo'," Zachary said, his eyes searching the faces of the white passengers in their colorful traveling clothes.

Stewart fought down the wave of dread, but he had half expected this. Zachary's news that Mystie was still alive had been too good to be true.

"Was she ever really here, Zachary?" he asked, unable to keep his suspicion from his voice.

Zachary wheeled on Stewart and said, "Yo' tink I lie to yo', Mr. Cliff? Yo' tink I don' know my own eyes?"

"No, Zachary, I didn't mean—"

"She am aboard, an' I's gonna prove dat to yo'!"

Stewart could see that Zachary was as upset about not finding Mystie as he was, and it occurred to him suddenly that this quest of his, over the months, had become important to the other members of the crew as well. They wanted to see him succeed almost as much as he wanted to.

"I'm sorry. I know you didn't lie, Zachary."

The big man started around the front of the promenade. Clifton followed him, knowing that Mystie was not going to show up on the other side of the boat, either, but he had to see this thing through to the end, no matter how painful it was.

They had come around the front when Zachary abruptly stopped. Stewart nearly ran into him. "What is it—?" he started to ask, and then he looked past Zachary at the woman who stood near the end of the promenade where it curved out and back toward the huge wheel box. For a moment he remained transfixed there, hardly daring to believe what his eyes were telling him. Then he stepped past Zachary and quickened his pace.

"Mystie?"

She had been talking to a tall gentleman in a dark suit when Stewart called her name. Her face came around with eyes large and black. It was the perfect face that he had held in his memory all these many months, and she was even more beautiful than he remembered; her glistening ebony hair, tied in a pink-and-green ribbon, showered to her shoulders. Stewart's heart leaped. It was her! She had not perished in the explosion!

"Mystie!" he cried again, rushing forward.

Now the man looked over as well.

"Clifton?" She came toward him a single, hesitant step, then stopped.

He instantly felt the wall that she threw up between them, but he couldn't help himself and swept her into his arms and held her tightly. She remained stiff in his embrace, and he released her and stepped back, seeing the confusion that had suddenly flooded her face. He imagined his own expression was something similar.

"Finally I have found you! We thought you had died in the explosion—and I had given up all hope. Oh, Mystie, you don't know how hard I have searched for you, have sought your face in every port, every riverside store and café, you have no idea how many streets I have walked in all the little towns between New Orleans and Hannibal!"

"But, why did you? You said—"

"I was a fool. What I said back then was the thoughtless words of someone who knew nothing beyond the world his parents had built for him. I have learned so much, Mystie. I am not the same man I was eighteen months ago."

She looked at him as if only now seeing what he looked like. "You have changed." She took his hand and rubbed a soft finger over the calluses that had grown on his palms. "You have been working hard."

"I have been a fireman all these months," he said with a note of pride in his voice.

Her view traveled down to his soaked shoes and trousers.

Stewart grimaced. "I had a bit of an accident while boarding just now."

"Him done almost fall in de drink. I catched him out of de air," Zachary said. "It am sure good to see yo' again, Miss Mystie. Mr. Cliff an' me thought yo' went to de bottom of de river wid the *Guiding Star*."

"Mr. Cliff and you?" she asked, looking at the tall black fireman.

Zachary grinned. "I gots to watch out fo' him, yo' know, Miss Mystie. Mr. Cliff is still a lit'le green an' New Awlins ain't no place fo' a boatman ain't yet in long britches."

"A little green?" Stewart said, glancing at his friend. "And just who was it who got your money back from those swindlers in Baton Rouge the other day?"

Zachary just laughed.

Mystie was smiling. "It is good to see you again, Clifton."

All this time, the man at her side had been listening with an amused grin on his face. Now he said, "This is truly a touching reunion, Mystie, but it is now time we find our staterooms."

Stewart took notice of the man for the first time. He was about Stewart's height and the same age, and he was dressed smartly in a dark suit and a black felt hat with a small brim.

He wore a self-assured grin that for some reason Stewart found irritating.

"Who is this fellow, Mystie?"

Her smile faded. She looked at the man standing beside her, then back at Stewart. "This is Mr. Barnabas Antone, the captain of the *Guiding Star* . . . and my fiancé."

"Your fiancé?" Shock, surprise, sadness, and anger descended upon him at the same time.

Barnabas took Mystie by the arm. "That is correct, sir. We are to be married in Cairo next month. Now, if you will excuse us, we must be going." He stepped past them, taking Mystie with him. Barnabas turned Mystie into the first door that led to the main cabin, but an instant before she disappeared, her face turned toward him with large, dark eyes momentarily catching the sunlight. Then she was gone.

He'd lost her once, he had agonized over her death, he had found her alive, and now he had lost her a second time. It was almost too much to bear.

Suddenly Zachary grabbed his arm and hauled him around the bend in the promenade and back out of sight against the paddle box.

"What—?" Stewart managed to say.

"De capt'n just come out. It best him not see yo' aboard."

"What does it matter now, Zachary? This is worse than when I thought she had been killed! She is in love with another man!"

Zachary glanced nervously at the bend in the promenade, then tried the door of the stateroom they were standing near. It was unoccupied, and it opened at his touch. He hurried Stewart inside, closed the door, and sat him in the bed. "De capt'n ain't gonna find us in here."

"I don't care anymore. Let Captain Hamilton throw me off. I won't fight him. There is nothing left to fight for."

"She-oot, Mr. Cliff. Listen to yo'r talk! I ain't never

know'd yo' to be a quitter! Why, dat is what I admire most 'bout yo'. Yo' stick wid someting ain' see it done to de end. Now hear yo'r words. Yo' don't care no mo'. Yo' won't fight. Dem's is de words of a loser!"

"I am a loser, and it is about time I faced up to it. I have lost my job, the captain's respect . . . and now for the second time I have lost Mystie!"

"Yo' ain't los' nothin' unless yo' up an' quits now."

"You don't know what you are talking about, Zachary. How could you?"

Zachary rounded on Stewart, anger flaring in his black eyes. "What do I know 'bout losin'? I tell yo' what I know'd. I know'd de heartache of losin' a young'un to de fever 'cause de man in de big house didn't tink he could send fo' no doct'r in de middle of de night. I know'd 'bout losin' my only precious lit'le gal to de auction block when she but twelve year old, an' I can not do a ting to stop it. I know'd 'bout seein' my wife stripped down naked and stood in a line so de white man can see what goods dey are buyin'. I know'd 'bout bein' sold myself. I had me fo' marsters 'fo' I got freedom. An' dat's just a lit'le 'bout what I know'd 'bout losin'. Yo' don't know de meanin' of losin' if'n yo' skin ain't black!"

As swiftly as it arose, Zachary's anger died, which was always the way with him, Clifton knew. "You are right. I have no place to complain. Sometimes it is difficult to see beyond your own pain, and I had no right saying that to you, Zachary."

"It am all right, Mr. Cliff. I reckon I needed to blow some steam, that's all. She-oot, I want to see yo' an' Miss Mystie back together ag'in as much as yo' do."

"But now what do I do?"

"Yo' won dat woman's heart once, yo' can win it back

ag'in. Jes' do what yo' done b'fo'. I tink she still loves yo'.
I tink right now she am as confused 'bout dis as yo' am."

"You're right, Zachary," Stewart said, coming to his feet
at once. "You are absolutely right! I will do it!" He pulled
the stateroom door open and marched outside.

Captain Hamilton was quite satisfied with the way his
crew had whipped the *Tempest Queen* into shape, and in
such short order. He must think of some way to show them
his appreciation. But what?

He ran his hand along the green railing and looked up at
the blue sky. Now that they had left the haze of New
Orleans behind, the afternoon sun was warm and comfortable upon his weathered skin.

He was going to miss this life.

Hamilton took a ladder up to the hurricane deck and
strolled toward the stern where the wide vista was inspiring.
In the distance, the yellow-brown haze of New Orleans
appeared to be sinking into the depths of the mighty
Mississippi.

Yes, he would miss this, but in life there is a season for all
things, and this season was about over for him. He ought to
be looking forward to retirement, not dreading it. He would
finally have time to travel, perhaps to return to France where
he had taken Cynthia after their wedding. Then there was
California, and the Sacramento River to see. So many places
to visit, and if he was ever going to write a book about the
river, as he had threatened to do for so many years, that
would be the time.

He turned and walked forward, stopping near the big bell
to stand in the place he had stood for so many years,
watching the river unfolding before him. Ahead, he spied
the red stacks of Captain Leathers's boat, and they seemed
to be coming closer. Thomas Leathers, Hamilton under-

stood, was a sporting man, and his boat, the *Natchez*, was reputed to be one of the fastest on the river. But Hamilton had thought that the *Tempest Queen*, with her eight massive furnaces and two powerful Baldwin engines, each pushing a forty-inch piston with a ten-foot stroke, turning two forty-foot paddle wheels, would leave any boat on the river in her wake.

But racing was a young man's sport. More than a few good boats had found watery graves in deep Mississippi mud because their masters had piled on a mite more steam than their boilers could hold. In most of his years on the river, Hamilton had resisted the urge to race. As a young man, he tried it once or twice, but not in the last twenty years had he succumbed to the urge, in spite of his crew's prodding. They would have enjoyed a good win. A boat's prowess was a point of pride among her crew; something to brag about at the riverfront bars and gambling parlors.

Hamilton laughed to himself and shook his head. A cautious man tends to live a dull life. He could not imagine someone like McKay avoiding a good race. But then, Dexter McKay would make a horrible captain. It took a certain type of man to run a riverboat: someone with a level head on his shoulders and the tenacity to stick to a course. Someone who had a vested interest in the boat above and beyond money—a soul attachment. Once, he thought he had seen those qualities in young Mr. Stewart, but the man had proved that under it all, he was as irresponsible as the next.

Hamilton looked ahead, and noted with some curiosity that the *Tempest Queen* was crawling nearer to the *Natchez*. He climbed the stairs to the top of the texas and stepped into the pilothouse. Ab Grimes was at the helm, and his partner Gip Dementor, a wiry fellow who had signed on a few months earlier, sat upon the green leather sofa near the nickel plated stove, reading a book. Grimes had steered the *Tempest Queen* near the eastern bank of the Mississippi where the run upriver had less current to buck. They were so near the shore that Hamilton could smell the smoking piles of bagasse and see crews of men working on the levees, making repairs. There were several small rowboats tied to the batture, and a gang of perhaps fifteen Negroes were digging with shovels and picks, and pushing wheelbarrows.

The levee system was a marvelous contrivance of man to resist a force as mighty as the Mississippi River—and sometimes it even worked. No doubt, since 1850, when the federal government had granted southern states all the swampland within their limits that had not yet been sold, the levee system had much improved. Unfortunately, the improvements had come too late to save Captain Hamilton's home and family from the angry river. Today, the levees were an unbroken barrier from Point La Hache up to Baton Rouge, and nearly continuous from Baton Rouge up to Vicksburg, where nature stepped in to provided its own levees.

"Afternoon, Mr. Grimes," Hamilton said to the pilot, nodding then to his partner, "and Mr. Dementor."

"What can I do for you, Captain?" Grimes said as he peered over the spokes of the helm, out the window that ran completely around the pilothouse.

"I am just making my rounds. Our passengers are presently occupied, enjoying a drink in the main cabin, and the entertainment of our musicians. The air is clean and sweet up here now that we are away from New Orleans."

Dementor laughed and looked up from the book. "What's the matter, Captain, don't you like all that smoke? Reminds you too much of fire and brimstone?"

"At my age one does not care to contemplate such things," Hamilton said, smiling.

"Oh, you still got a lot of years left in you, Captain," Grimes said, pulling one of the hog rings overhead that rang a bell down below in the engine room.

Hamilton sat upon the high bench and watched the river around him. "I feel fit, Mr. Grimes, but it would be arrogance to presume on tomorrow—especially at my age." He picked up the spyglass from the windowsill and put it to his eye.

"Hmm."

"Something the matter, Captain?" Grimes asked.

When Hamilton looked over, Grimes seemed to be holding back a smirk.

"Nothing is the matter. I know my boat is in the finest hands, only . . ."

"Only what, Captain?"

"We seem to be creeping up on Mr. Leathers's fine boat."

"We do?"

Hamilton looked over sharply. This time he was certain he saw a restrained smirk. "And a moment ago you signaled the engine room for more steam."

"Did I?"

"Hmm." Hamilton raised the glass to his eye again and trained it on the *Natchez*'s stern boom where her lifeboat hung off its cables.

"I know her pilot," Grimes said. "He's a lazy dolt, and he is probably napping at the helm, not watching the river."

In Hamilton's experience, riverboat pilots might be a lazy lot once ashore, but not while at the wheel of a steamer, and there was not a one of them who might be called a dolt.

"What are we turning, Mr. Grimes?"

"Oh, it feels like about forty to me, Captain."

Hamilton lowered the glass and speared him with his narrow stare. "Forty! We are turning at least fifty, Mr. Grimes."

"Weelll, Captain, perhaps a couple over forty . . . but I am sure we are below fifty."

Hamilton frowned and went to the brass speaking tube that sprouted from the pilothouse's floor. He yanked a cable and a few seconds later Barney Seegar's voice echoed up the tube. "What is it now, Grimes? I got these engines running like a scared Injun as it is!"

"This is Captain Hamilton, Mr. Seegar."

A long pause, then in a more sober tone, "Oh. I . . . ah, yes, what is it, Captain?"

"What are we turning, Mr. Seegar?"

Another extended pause, then Seegar's voice echoed up from the engine room below. "Fifty-one revolutions per minute, sir."

"Thank you, Mr. Seegar." Hamilton stood away from the speaking tube and narrowed an eye at Grimes. "Forty revolutions per minute? Is that what you thought?"

Grimes gave him a wan smile. "I reckon I must have been a little off," he said, but he could not keep the humor out of his voice.

"I reckon you must have been."

They had drawn near enough to the *Natchez* now to see the faces of her passengers at the railing. Hamilton thought a moment, then said, "I know what you are up to, Mr. Grimes."

"You do?"

"You are attempting to race that boat."

"Race the *Natchez*? Me?" Grimes was shocked.

"You know I disapprove of racing?"

"I know you have mentioned it a time or two, Captain."

"Even though the crew and passengers would find great entertainment in watching two fine packets stretch their legs and make a run of it, I have never approved of putting the *Tempest Queen* in peril."

"Of course not. You are the finest captain on the river, and she is the finest boat." Grimes hesitated. "Then again, a little heavy breathing would do her good. It cleans the flues, you know."

"Cleans the flues? I have never heard that one before."

"It's true," Grimes said, straight-faced. "Any engineer on the river will tell you so. That's why I asked Mr. Seegar to put on a tad bit more steam. Just wanted to keep her flues from sooting up."

"Hmm. I see. Of course, it will appear to Captain Leathers that were are itching for a race."

Grimes shrugged. "I can't help what Old Push thinks."

"I suppose not." Hamilton pondered it a few moments, pulling at the point of his gray beard. The *Tempest Queen* was in top shape, her boilers sound, and her load was light. A brief run would do no harm, and his special guests might even find it entertaining. He had relented all these years, and now, at the end of his career, that he was even considering embarking on a race shocked him. But what could one last fling matter? It would be his gift to the crew for a job well done. Still, it went against his better judgment, and he could never openly condone it.

Hamilton said, "Proceed with cleaning those flues, Mr. Grimes."

"Yes, sir!"

Hamilton stepped out of the pilothouse onto the texas. The *Tempest Queen* was pulling up alongside the *Natchez,* and upon her texas, Captain Thomas P. Leathers looked over at him. Less than two hundred feet separated them. Without the aid of the spyglass, Hamilton saw clearly Leathers's fiery red hair and red beard. The man was dressed in a black suit and a lace-frilled, puff-bosomed shirt.

Captain Leathers stepped into his pilothouse, and when

he emerged a few seconds later he held a megaphone in his hand.

"Good afternoon, Mr. Hamilton," his voice boomed across the water, over the chuffing of their escape pipes and the churning water beneath their wheels.

Hamilton reached through the doorway and Gip Dementor put a megaphone in his hand. "Afternoon, Mr. Leathers. What can I do for you?"

Leathers put the megaphone to his face again. "You seem to be in a bit of a hurry to reach Baton Rouge, Mr. Hamilton."

"Not at all, Mr. Leathers. My pilot tells me he is only cleaning the flues."

"Oh, is that all it is."

Leathers lowered the megaphone and said something to a man who had stuck his head out of the pilothouse door. Hamilton could see the grin come to Leathers's face a moment before he hid it behind the megaphone.

"I just told my pilot. He thinks cleaning the flues is a bully idea. He wants to clean off our flues as well."

"Very good. My regards to your pilot. We shall see you in Baton Rouge, Mr. Leathers."

Hamilton turned back inside the pilothouse. "You may continue, Mr. Grimes."

Ab Grimes grinned and sounded the *Tempest Queen*'s whistle. The *Natchez* replied with her own, and in a moment the chuffing of the escape pipes picked up their tempo and the paddle wheels their revolutions.

CHAPTER SEVENTEEN

It only took a few minutes for the word to spread throughout the *Tempest Queen* that she was running neck to neck with Captain Leathers's *Natchez*. The *Natchez*'s red chimneys were a familiar sight from New Orleans up to Vicksburg, her regular run. She was one of the fastest packets on the river, so as the port side railings along the *Tempest Queen*'s promenade began to fill up with anxious passengers, and it was determined that there indeed was a race in progress, it was only natural that wagers began circulating. Those who knew anything about the river and Captain T. P. Leathers's reputation were putting their money on the *Natchez*.

The officers of the *Tempest Queen*, however, making their way to the railings, and the waiters who brought ice tea out

on trays to the throng gathering there, and the chamber-
maids up from the laundry all snapped up the *Natchez* bets.
They were a loyal crew, and they knew what the *Tempest
Queen* was made of—and it was tougher stuff than Leathers's boat.

At the railings of both steamers, the passengers leaned
out, waving hats and scarves and hands.

The *Tempest Queen* was a longer, wider boat, with bigger
buckets and heavy-breathing engines. Her escape pipes sang
smoothly while gray smoke poured from her chimneys. The
wake that formed on either side of her bow rolled smoothly
back along her hull to dip under her driving buckets at
precisely the point the engineers who had designed her had
intended it to occur. She was built for speed, a thoroughbred
of wood and iron, and her breeding was evident now. Her
load was light and she was riding high in the water. It didn't
take long for her to pull ahead.

A roar of cheers rose from her decks, and her steam
whistle blew long and lovely, answered by two short,
striving hoots of the *Natchez*'s whistle.

Up on the texas deck, Hamilton knew a surge of pride in
his boat. He briefly wondered why he had not run her like
this at least once before—but he knew the reason. The
Tempest Queen was far too valuable to risk on frivolities.
This boat was, in fact, his second *Tempest Queen*. The first,
a smaller steamer, had been lost some years back below
Island Number Ten when a cargo fire had burned her to the
waterline.

He would permit Ab Grimes to "clean her flues" a while
longer, but he'd be keeping a sharp eye on the gauges, and
would give Seegar strict orders to cut back on the pressure
at the first indication it had climbed too high. As it appeared,
however, the *Tempest Queen* might easily remain ahead of
the *Natchez*.

Hamilton glanced at his chimneys. The smoke pouring from them was a comfortable gray color. Across the water the *Natchez*'s red chimneys were spewing roiling black clouds. Leathers had ordered pine knots tossed into his furnaces to raise the temperature in an attempt to close the distance.

So long as Hamilton could keep ahead of him without resorting to such tactics, which made for excess pressure, he would permit the race to continue—but not one minute beyond what he deemed safe.

He went down to the engine room to consult with his chief engineer, Barney Seegar. The place was a clanking, steamy, hothouse. Fat, asbestos-wrapped pipes climbed up the walls and across the ceiling, three stories overhead. Like the hammers of a Roman galley's beat keeper, the two mighty engines pounded in meter with each other, driving their connecting rods back and forth, turning the iron shaft in its bearings that in turn spun the big wheel in the paddle box outside. Here, so close to the heart of the boat, the floor vibrated beneath Hamilton's feet, adding just that much more noise to the place.

Steam valves topped with bright red wheels sprouted from the machinery and the floor, and bell cords and hog rings hung from the ceiling. Near one wall a bank of gauges filled a board near the flared end of the brass speaking tube that snaked up to the pilothouse. There, studying the gauges, Hamilton found his engineer.

"Mr. Seegar."

The chief engineer did not hear him at first, which didn't surprise Hamilton, considering the noise of the place, and that years of working in the engine room of a steamer had stolen most of Seegar's hearing. He spoke his name again, louder.

Seegar came about. "Captain? What can I do for you?"

"You are doing it."

"Hey?" Seegar cupped a hand behind his ear.

Hamilton shouted, "You can keep an eye on those gauges."

Seegar nodded his head at the wide doorway and the two men stepped outside the engine room. The cacophony was somewhat muffled out on the guards, away from the heat of the furnaces. "What is going on, anyway, Captain? We just pulled away from that boat like we meant business."

"Mr. Grimes is 'cleaning the flues.'"

"He's doing what?"

Hamilton smiled. "It is his way of saying he wanted to race the *Natchez*."

"And you allowed it?"

"I know what you are thinking, Mr. Seegar. I never permit such sport. But this time I relented—just a little. I thought the crew would enjoy it, and our special passengers as well. That is why I am down here. I don't want you to push those engines too far, and I don't want you to allow excessive pressure to build up. Keep an eye on the gauges."

"Iron pages? What are you talking about?"

Hamilton raised his voice. "The gauges! I said, keep an eye on the gauges."

Seegar grinned. "No need to worry yourself on that account, Captain. If the pressure is up more than fifty pounds, I'll bleed it off, and to blazes with Mr. Grimes if he demands more." Seegar chuckled. "Cleaning the flues!"

"Good. I had no doubt you would see to the boat's safety." Hamilton went forward and found Lansing hovering over his firemen like a schoolmaster looking for insurrection among his charges. Hamilton gave the chief mate the same message. Keep the fires hot, but no theatrics, no pine knots. This is a bit of entertainment for the passengers and crew, that is all, and if Mr. Leathers wishes to blow his boat apart, that is his business."

As Hamilton strolled back up the stairway and stepped onto the promenade, he thought, *And it is a bit of entertainment for myself, as well. A year from now I will be watching the river from my porch railing, on a hilltop overlooking the Mississippi.* He ran a hand along the *Tempest Queen*'s green handrails and a lump rose in his throat at the prospect of selling her. But the time had come.

"For all things there is a season," he told himself aloud, and straightening his jacket around, and standing tall, he made his way to the crowded railing where the passengers were watching the *Natchez.*

T. P. Leathers's boat had ceased falling behind and was holding firm less than a hundred rods to the *Tempest Queen*'s stern.

Gen made her way outside with the crowd and found herself at the railing less than an arm's length from the senator. His wife was there as well, and so was the governor of Louisiana. She did not see Mr. Sheridan at once, but in a moment spied him at the railing a few dozen feet off. Every eye was slanted at the *Natchez,* which had fallen back at the start of the race, but appeared to have halted her backward slide and was slowing inching her way nearer.

"Isn't this exciting, Senator Douglas?" she said, nearly squealing. *Careful. Mustn't overdo it.* She sipped her frappé and smiled at him when he looked over.

"Ah, the young lady from the park," he said. His smooth-shaven chin was suddenly filled with dimples, and he appeared a little boy. Now that she was in better control of herself, and the whiskey in her drink had relaxed her some, she took notice of the things that she had missed at their first meeting. Douglas's head was unusually broad and very heavy, almost too large for his body. It sat upon a short neck and strong shoulders. His eyes were striking; large, dark blue, deep-set. They watched her now, unflinching. They were most distracting and she had to glance aside. When she did, she noted his ears—so small and delicate.

"Adéle, darling," he said to his wife. "Here is the young lady I mentioned to you—the one who was most generous toward our campaign."

Adéle Douglas looked past her husband and smiled at Gen, but said nothing.

"I have never seen a riverboat race, have you?" Gen lied.

Douglas gave a small laugh. "I have seen many, but I must admit, this is the first in which I have been a participant."

She heard the strain in his voice from all the speeches he had been giving lately, and although his words were not loud, they seemed endowed with a deep resonance and an energy that vibrated when he spoke. She could imagine him before the senate, and every senator there riveted by that famous voice.

A colored steward came through the crowd with a tray of ice tea and the senator removed two—for his wife and for himself. He glanced at Gen with the obvious question on his face but she showed him her frappé, and he sent the steward on his way.

The *Natchez*'s whistle blew. Gen looked over. The boat seemed closer, and those passengers aboard the *Tempest Queen* who had wagered on the *Natchez* gave a cheer now. "Oh, look, I think we are losing ground."

"I think our captain is only teasing her," Douglas replied. "I know the feel of a good boat, and I can tell the *Tempest Queen* is not even breathing hard." Douglas paused a moment, his eyes flicking back and forth as if only now noticing something. "I don't see your friend around."

"My friend?"

"Yes, the gentleman from the park."

"Oh, you mean Mr. Gill." She frowned. "He is not really my friend. Only someone I met while waiting for the boat."

"I caught a glimpse of you two boarding. I naturally assumed that you were traveling together."

She laughed. "Heavens, no," then lowering her voice, she confided, "in fact, I have tried my best to escape his attentions, but he is a persistent man, showing up at the oddest times."

Douglas gave her a small smile. "Well, I can hardly fault the gentleman for pursuing such an attractive young lady."

Gen smiled graciously.

Adéle was apparently bored with the race and said, "I am becoming chilled, Stephen. I am going back to the salon."

"I will go with you, my dear. This contest will continue for quite some hours, and I need to sit down for a while."

The senator, his wife, and Governor Moore returned to the main cabin. Gen relished a good race, especially if she had placed a few hundred dollars on it—which she had not. She hesitated to leave now, but what she must do here was more important, the prize far greater.

Sighing, she glanced once more at the *Natchez,* crawling up on the *Tempest Queen*'s stern, then tossing back the rest of her drink, she deposited the glass upon a passing tray and followed them inside.

Mystie Waters closed the door to her stateroom and looked around it. How swiftly the months away seemed to disappear before her eyes. Her view lingered upon the bed, then the little table laid out with pitcher, pan, and towel. She had made up this very room a dozen times over when she worked on the *Tempest Queen.* Now she was the passenger, and someone else was changing the sheets, laundering the towels, and polishing the window panes. She untied her bonnet, dropped it upon the bed, and opened the door and stepped out onto the narrow deck beyond.

Hers was one of the aft cabins, located behind the big paddle box, and there was no way on or off this deck except through one of the four staterooms here. It was very private and isolated from the traffic of the promenade. The soothing rush of water from beneath the paddle masked the noise and bustle of a busy boat.

She was oddly relieved that the cabin Barnabas had gotten for himself was on the opposite side of the boat. Here, at least, she could pull her thoughts together without interruption.

There was no one else on the deck at the moment and she sat in one of the chairs there and tried to enjoy the passing river and her view of the levee nearby, which was overgrown with willows and young pines. A filmy veil of gray Spanish moss hung from the older trees beyond the earthen wall of the levee. It was most pleasant, but her thoughts kept going back to Clifton Stewart's face and the tragic look of despair that had come to it as Barnabas had escorted her away.

Four days ago her future had been settled, as if carved in stone. She was to marry Barnabas and live in his home on the west bank of the Mississippi, not too far from her parents' home in Cairo. He would continue as captain of the *Guiding Star* while she remained at home to raise their children. He had met her parents, and it made no difference to him that her mother was a Negro, and a freed slave.

Then the accident in New Orleans had occurred. So many friends had died. The draining inquiry followed, and the relief when Barnabas had been found innocent of any wrongdoing. Throughout the ordeal, the strain had been more difficult for her than it had been for Barnabas, even though she was not the one answering the questions. As the days passed, he seemed to grow more callous about the whole horrible accident.

It was all so very confusing.

And then she had run into Clifton.

Mystie half expected that she would see Clifton when Barnabas told her he had purchased tickets aboard the *Tempest Queen*, but she never imagined his burst of joy at finding her. How could she have known he still had feelings for her? She had written him over a year ago, and there had been no response. Why did he still care, anyway? They were both from different worlds: she a mulatto, the daughter of a slave girl, he the son of a wealthy slave owner; she the abolitionist and conductor on the Underground Railroad, he the proper Southern gentleman who saw nothing wrong with trading in human flesh. No they could never have made a life together!

Mystie sat in the deck chair, looking at the river but not seeing it. Vaguely, she was aware of the commotion on the other side of the boat, the muffled cheers, the exchanging of whistles with another boat that she could not see from the little deck where she sat on the starboard side. Her brain was occupied with the events of the last few days, and she tried to sort through them . . . through it all, trying to find herself in all the confusion. What did she really feel, stripped of all the hurt and anger and grief that colored her thoughts?

A knock at the door brought her back to the moment. She went through her stateroom to answer it.

Barnabas was standing on the other side. "You all settled in yet?" he asked.

"I was just resting."

"Resting? There will be plenty of time for that, Myst! There is a race on. We are running the *Natchez,* and so far we are ahead of her, but Old Push is really piling on the steam. Come, let's find us a place at the railing and encourage this old girl along."

Mystie was surprised, but she was in no mood for gaiety. "Captain Hamilton is racing?"

"He is giving it a go, all right."

"But that is not like him at all. He always forbade it—at least while I worked on the *Tempest Queen*."

"Well, he hasn't tried to stop it yet. Now grab your bonnet and let's go."

"No, Barnabas. Really, I would rather remain in my stateroom and rest."

"Nonsense. Come along, darling. You will miss the excitement."

"No, Barnabas. I really would rather not at the moment."

He frowned. "Well, all right then, you can have it your way—at least *until* we are married." He laughed. "I will keep you informed, but don't blame me if you feel left out of the talk later on around the dinner table."

She closed the door behind him, and a knot slowly twisted inside her as she went back out onto the deck to be alone with her thoughts. She had only once more gotten comfortable in the chair when a second knock sounded on her door.

"He is going to insist that I go, even if he must drag me along," she said irritably as she reached for the handle. But when she pulled it open, it was not Barnabas standing there.

"Clifton," she said, discovering that she was not overly surprised to see him there. He looked solemn.

"Mystie. I have to talk to you."

She stepped back for him. "Come in."

He did, looking around the small stateroom. "Is Mr. Antone not here?"

"No, he is off watching the race."

"Oh."

"I understand everyone is crowding the larboard railing. How come you are not there?"

He managed a fleeting smile. "I reckon I am only interested in races that involve the four-legged variety of animals." He hesitated and the smile faded. "Well, that is not entirely true, but I have more pressing thoughts on my mind at the moment."

"I think I know what you mean."

"Mystie, I saw your name on the payroll ledger. How did you ever survive?"

"Sit down, Clifton," she said.

He pulled the chair around, and Mystie sat upon the edge of the small bed. "I was not on the boat at the time of the explosion. Barnabas had to settle a problem with the freight he had carried. He had come up short several barrels of potatoes. Barnabas stayed to settle the receiver's claim, and I just happened to be with him at the time.

"We had just taken on a load to carry upriver, and we had passengers waiting to board at the Municipal Landing. Barnabas did not want to delay the *Guiding Star* any longer than necessary, so we stayed ashore while the boat left for the landing. We had planned to catch up with it there."

Steward shook his head. "That is more than coincidence. It was meant to be."

"Do you really think so?"

"Of course. Don't you?"

Mystie frowned. "Yes, I do. But Barnabas thinks it was only serendipity."

"I suppose some people would think that."

She felt strangely comfortable sitting there, talking to Clifton. She had forgotten how understanding and gentle he was.

A pang of guilt pierced her.

These feelings were inappropriate for a woman engaged to be married to another man. She could not allow her heart to wander. "Well, I suppose two people will never agree on everything," she said, suddenly defensive. "You and I certainly did not."

He winced. "I was wrong, Mystie. I know that now. Is there no way I can show you?"

"It is too late now, I am afraid," she said, trying to resist the feelings rising, unwanted, within her. "Perhaps if you had found me six months ago—"

"I tried. I looked everywhere. I left a letter with your father. You know that."

"Yes, and I wrote back to you, but you never responded." She did not understand the sudden anger she felt. "I could only think that you had finally given up looking for me. What was I to do? That last night we were together you said you didn't want to see me again. I never did understand why you would change your mind. And now I discover that you have been searching me out in every port, at every landing. I wasn't hiding from you, Clifton. I told you were you could find me. For months afterward, whenever the *Guiding Star* and the *Tempest Queen* passed one another, I would stop my work and look for your face at her railing or study the men upon her deck. I never saw you."

"No, you wouldn't. I have been at the furnaces for eighteen months. And when I wasn't working, I was sleeping. Moving ten to fifteen cords of firewood a day takes everything out of a man. And as for your letter, why, I only first laid eyes upon it not three days ago, and you cannot imagine my joy when I did.

"Then I read about the accident. My first action upon disembarking was to search out word of you. Zachary helped me. Our efforts led me to the salvage yard where they had just recovered some ledgers. Your name was there. Everyone I asked said that no one aboard had survived.

"Afterward, I returned to the *Tempest Queen,* acquired some very cheap whiskey from one of the stewards, and—" He frowned and shrugged his shoulders. "And I got very drunk."

She felt his pain and embarrassment as he turned his eyes to the floor. "That is awful, Clifton. How are you feeling now?"

"This morning I wanted to die. I am much improved this evening, though. I was in New Orleans when Zachary found me and told me you were alive. I raced back and nearly fell beneath the wheel jumping back aboard. Zachary caught me at the last moment."

"You had to jump? You were still in town when we pulled out?"

He nodded his head.

"Why?"

"Because," Stewart said looking back into her eyes, "when the captain found me in a state of insobriety, he fired me."

"Oh. I am sorry," All at once she was ashamed that she had gotten angry at him. She wanted to reach out and take his hand and comfort him, but she held back. She had to prevent the old feelings from returning, restrain them any way she could.

She was engaged to another man. That she had to keep reminding herself of the fact was a serious concern to her.

"You lost your job because of me?"

"Yes, but I would have gladly given up a hundred jobs to find you alive again."

Mystie stood and looked out the window at the river moving past. This was all wrong. Her feelings were wrong. She must be strong, although her heart was breaking and being pulled in two directions. "I think perhaps you should leave now, Clifton," she said not looking back at him. "It is inappropriate for me to be seeing you now . . . now that I am engaged." She hoped she had sounded strong and determined.

In the long pause that followed, she resisted the urge to tell Clifton not to leave after all. Her confusion smothered her like a wet blanket. She didn't know what she wanted . . . or who.

Behind her, the chair scraped the floor. She sensed him coming near to her; then, hesitating, he retreated to the door. "I need to talk with you further, Mystie. Perhaps when you feel better?"

She did not need to look into his face to know his torment. She could not have looked if she had wanted to, but she managed a small nod of her head.

The door opened, then closed. When she finally looked back, Clifton had gone.

Mystie went out onto the deck, gripping the railing until her knuckles whitened, and as she always did when troubles weighed her down, she turned her confused heart to the river that she loved and gave her tears to the mighty Mississippi.

CHAPTER EIGHTEEN

Throughout the afternoon Senator Douglas received a steady stream of visitors. Editors from three different newspapers occupied him for over an hour. Governor Moore gave a short speech to the folks gathered there. Adéle answered the occasional question cast her way, and all the while, James Sheridan scribbled a record of it for posterity upon his tablet of paper.

To Gen, who had taken a table a few feet away, it seemed that no one could pass by the senator's table without offering a word or two of encouragement or shaking his hand. After two hours of this, it was apparent to her that she'd not soon have a moment alone with the man. Her frustration had grown to the point where she was ordering her whiskey unencumbered by the peach frappé.

Then James Sheridan announced to the people there that the senator and his wife were going to have dinner, and would everyone please give them an hour alone. The admirers drifted off, and Captain Hamilton, the governor, Mr. Douglas, Adéle, Mr. Sheridan, and two of his staff were shown to a long table near the ladies' salon, across from the raised platform where the string quartet was setting up music stands and unpacking their instruments.

The party passed near Gen's table and Senator Douglas gave her a smile. Gen returned the favor most graciously. They went a few steps farther and Douglas bent near his wife and spoke into her ear. By the time they reached the table, Adéle had nodded her head. Douglas took Sheridan by the sleeve and said something to him next.

Gen almost toppled over in her chair when both men looked over at her. She regained her composure only a moment before Sheridan came back across the room.

"Miss Summers," he said, giving a small bow. "The senator and his wife wish to know if you'd like to join them for dinner."

"Me?" Her shock passed in a flash. This was more than she could have hoped for. "I . . . I would be happy to dine with the senator and his wife."

Sheridan escorted Gen to the table. Douglas rose from his chair and said, "I know you are traveling alone, Miss Summers, and I hope you do not think me presumptuous, but to show my appreciation for your enthusiastic support of our campaign, and your generous financial gift, Adéle and I would be pleased if you joined us for dinner."

"I am flattered and honored, sir. I hardly know what to say."

"Nothing needs to be said, Miss Summers, except that you will accept."

"Yes, I accept."

Douglas introduced her to the men around the table as the white-coated waiter pulled back a chair and held it for her. They fitted her in on Adéle's right, where two other chairs reminded unoccupied, as if Douglas had been expecting a larger guest list than had showed up. Gen decided the money given Douglas at the hotel had already begun to pay a dividend. She was pleased with herself now for having seized that opportunity when she had.

"So, you are traveling alone," Captain Hamilton said when she was finally settled in place. He was across the table from her.

"I am, and you have a lovely boat, Captain," she said, smiling.

"I hope your trip will be enjoyable, Miss Summers. How far will you be going with us?"

"All the way to Alton, Captain. I am visiting my sister there."

"If there is anything I might do to make your journey more pleasant, let me know."

Gen thought the captain a nice old man, quite handsome in his neatly barbered beard, with smiling blue eyes that were at once reassuring, but her real interest was in the senator, on Adéle's left. At the moment, however, Senator Douglas was engaged in conversation with the governor.

At the far corner of the table, Mr. Sheridan was ordering a bottle of wine, and across and to her right the senator's two aides were discussing, of all things, a horse race that had run a day or two before. Gen discreetly listened in for a few moments. A good race drew her attention like calico and lace might draw the eye of some other woman. She wondered about the challenge being waged at present beyond the larboard railing. Her last glimpse of it had shown the *Natchez* slowly closing on the *Tempest Queen*'s stern. How Captain Hamilton could sit here, undisturbed, while his boat was engaged in the race, was quite beyond Gen.

The senator and the governor came to a pause in their conversation and Douglas turned to Hamilton. "Tell me, Captain Hamilton, how do you read the political temperature along this magnificent river?"

Hamilton gave a short laugh and said, "It is a very long river, Senator."

Everyone found that amusing and Douglas said, "You have the tact of a politician, Captain. I commend you."

Adéle leaned closer to Gen, "I am afraid this dinner will be all politics and cigar smoke, my dear. I am used to it, but you may find it a bit tiring after a while."

"On the contrary. I find politics interesting, Mrs. Douglas."

"I did too . . . in the beginning," Adéle said, but it sounded as if she had long since lost her fascination with it.

Then the food began to arrive on silver serving platters and the dinner was laid out before them. In the corner, the quartet began softly sawing at their fiddles as a Negro waiter made his way around the table filling the long-stemmed goblets with a clear white wine.

The meal was delicious, and Gen actually did enjoy the masculine conversation. It was like being invited into Robert's study when he had his friends over. There was always the talk of government and politics or business deals, and always over a snifter of brandy and clouds of cigar smoke. The wine on top of the whiskey that she had drunk before dinner made her lightheaded. She took care not to appear giddy, and when she spoke she kept her words brief and well thought out.

After dinner, the waiter poured coffee and carried over a dessert tray. Before Gen could examine the offerings there, a steam whistle shrilled. So close was it that she nearly spilled her coffee. Someone shouted that the *Natchez* had pulled abreast of them, and the main cabin immediately emptied, as if the fellow had cried "Fire!" instead. The passengers and crew alike piled up against the larboard railing outside.

"It sounds to me as if Mr. Leathers has taken the challenge seriously, Captain Hamilton," Senator Douglas said.

"He takes every challenge seriously, Senator," Hamilton said. "Where do you think he got the title Old Push from?" Hamilton stood. "I suppose I ought to step outside and see what has happened."

"I will join you," Douglas said with a sudden boyish eagerness, and as if it had been a royal command, the entire table stood in unison and made for the door. All, that is, except Gen, who hesitated. For a moment she was alone in the long, empty room. She glanced at the doors and the hallways. Even the kitchen help seemed to have taken to the railings.

Suddenly her head was clear, and the plans she and Robert had carefully worked out came into sharp focus in spite of the whiskey and wine. Gen opened her reticule, snatched out the brown-paper packet Robert had handed her before she had left Carleton Manor, and ripping a corner of it open, she dumped what amounted to a half a teaspoonful of white crystals into the senator's unattended coffee cup. Quickly stirring it with a spoon, Gen thrust the packet back into her purse.

The whole thing took less than twenty seconds, and before anyone had missed her, Gen was at the railing with the rest of the senator's dinner guests.

The river was growing dark now with the approach of night. Across the water, a mere stone's throw away, the red chimneys of the *Natchez* were belching black smoke and raining sparks and cinders upon the water. Her running lights had been lit, and they reflected off the black water. On the *Tempest Queen*'s promenade, a steward was making his unhurried way from lamp to lamp with a sputtering torch, leaving a trail of lamplight on the deck behind him.

Groans and cheers rose among the passengers at the railings of both boats.

"Captain, are you going to permit this?" the senator asked lightly.

Gen noticed that Hamilton was peering up at the *Tempest Queen*'s dark chimneys and frowning.

"I would not want to put the passengers or my boat in peril," he replied after a moment.

Douglas laughed. He was apparently enjoying the challenge, and Gen thought she detected a streak of gamesmanship in the staid senator. "I know a stout vessel when I see one, Captain, and I am sure your fine boat can stand a few more pounds in her boilers. You know what is best, of course."

"Don't let Stephen bulldog you into it, Captain Hamilton," Adéle scolded, but she was smiling at her husband, just the same.

Gen tried to calm her racing heart, and she was certain her anxiety showed upon her face. But she had passed the point of no return now, and although she wanted to flee the scene before Senator Douglas returned to the table, she knew she could not—at least not without pointing a suspicious finger her way when the senator suddenly fell dead over his dessert.

She rehearsed in her brain how she should react. First she would cry out, then she would faint. Afterward, she would tell everyone the poor senator must have had a weak heart, and that must have been what had killed him. Was there a doctor aboard? Some of the larger packets had a physician among the officers. She wondered if a man of medicine could see the signs of poisoning. Would anyone know what to look for? Robert seemed certain the poison would go undetected. But could a man of medicine be fooled?

She told herself to calm down. In all likelihood there was no doctor aboard. The senator was vastly overweight, and she had read somewhere that fat people suffered more with heart ailments than those of less portly dimensions. It would be all right in the end. She drew in a long, calming breath and tried to concentrate on the race as everyone else was doing.

Captain Hamilton said, "She has only just caught up with us, Senator. Let's give Mr. Leathers a while to see if he can keep the pace." Hamilton looked at Gen, held her in his gaze for a long while. "Are you all right, Miss Summers?"

"I am fine, Captain," she answered.

"You look chilled, the air is brisk out here. Perhaps we should return to the table."

"Perhaps," she said, but the senator's table was the last place she wished to be. Still, she had to see this thing through.

Hamilton took her by the arm and escorted her back inside where the crystal chandeliers that ran the length of the main cabin seemed to flood the long room with light. He took her to her chair at the senator's table. "There, have a sip of your coffee. These fall evenings on the river can be deceptive and can chill you before you are aware of it." He took his chair and watched her a moment longer before taking up his coffee cup. In a few minutes, the rest of the guests had filed back inside.

"A race between two mighty warriors of the river is an

inspiring sight, Captain Hamilton," Douglas said, lowering his bulk into the chair. "I have no doubt your fine vessel could easily leave the *Natchez* in her wake."

"And I have no doubt you are correct." Hamilton sipped his coffee as the waiter returned with the dessert tray. The captain said, "If you indeed find the race entertaining, I will tell my engineer to boost the revolutions a little, and then we can see just how much push Old Push has in him."

"I think that would be quite entertaining, Captain," Douglas said with a hearty laugh.

Hamilton glanced back at Gen and smiled at her. "There, you are looking much better, Miss Summers. It must have been the chill."

"Yes, Captain. I think you are correct. I am feeling much better." She was aware of his eyes lingering upon her, and she was beginning to feel uncomfortable beneath his openly fascinated stare, which he kept on her longer than she thought proper on such a short acquaintance.

She glanced away, and noted that Douglas had not yet touched his coffee. Adéle was making a selection from the tray, and the senator was eying the fare, which was deliciously rich, with hungry desire. But Gen's thoughts were not on dessert, and she doubted that she could eat anything now—not with the nervous knot of anticipation twisting within her.

Douglas made his selection, a creamy chocolate parfait, and he wasted no time filling his spoon, and then his mouth. He pronounced the dessert "gilt-edged" and dug into it with such zeal that the spoon did not stop until it clattered upon the glass bottom of the deep glass, urgently working the final traces of chocolate from the cut grooves. It was only when no more dessert was left to mine from the glass that Senator Douglas at last reached for his coffee, to wash it down.

Gen, up to now, had barely tasted her dessert. She caught her breath and forced herself not to watch the senator lift the cup to his lips, and instead made her hand scoop up a small spoonful of the parfait and transfer it to her mouth. She did not taste it. Her heard pounded in her chest.

How long would it take?

The coffee cup clinked softly back upon its saucer.

Gen took another bite . . . and she waited.

The senator's hearty voice nearly startled her as he began a story about a humorous event that had occurred in the senate chambers. He broke the tale with sips of coffee and Gen wished he would shut up and just die, as he was supposed to.

How long did it take for arsenic to take effect?

Robert had not known for sure, but he had suspected no more than five to ten minutes.

Gen braced herself and waited.

"Well, is you jest gonna sit dere on dat railing sulkin' all night, Mr. Cliff? Or you gonna tells me what she say?"

Clifton Stewart did not stir at once, then he looked up from the deck where he had been studying a crack in one of the boards for the last five minutes, and turned away from the low, stern railing. They were back on the small aft deck behind the engine room, in the only place Captain Hamilton seldom visited. Nearby was the boat's tiller, and to his left was one of the *Tempest Queen*'s lifeboats, suspended from a boom that hung out over the river above her dark wake. In the gathering night, scattered points of light began to dot the levees like lonely fireflies.

"She said, briefly, that she was engaged to be married, and that it was not appropriate that she should see me anymore. Then she told me to leave."

"Dat's good."

Stewart glanced up, startled. "Good?"

"Don' yo' see, if yo' was no threat to her, she wouldn't have send yo' packin'. She would have talked yo' along 'til yo' both was talked out. Dat gal is mix up in de baddest way now, Mr. Cliff, and yo' got to keep at her."

"I don't known, Zachary. Maybe I should face the truth. I have lost Mystie to another man."

"She-oot! Mr. Cliff. Hear yo' talk! Yo' done about turn dis river over on him head looking fo' dat gal, and now dat yo' find her, yo' gonna give up the chase jes' because she went and got herself anoth'r beau. Dat ain't the Cliff Stewart I come to know. No, suh. Dat is someone who am a quitter." Zachary turned his back on Stewart, disgusted.

After a moment, he looked back and said, "Now dis is de second time I had to talk to yo' dat way, Mr. Cliff. I don't much care to bawl out a white man like I done, but yo' need to be told the straight of it. So, get dem foolish notions out of yo'r head and go fight for de woman yo' love. If'n yo' ain't willin' to fight, yo' ain't worthy to win her love back."

"You're right, Zachary," Stewart said, feeling the vigor within himself growing stronger. "I won't quit! Mr. Barnabas Antone will have to fight for Mystie if he intends to keep her." Stewart started for the ladder that climbed up off the isolated deck.

"What am yo' gonna do?"

Stewart stopped with his foot on a step. "I'm going back to her and . . . and . . . and I am not sure what I am going to do, Zachary."

Zachary's black face was disappearing fast in the shadows growing up around the stern and overhead. To their left, where the *Natchez* had now pulled half a boat's length ahead, sparks were flying from the boats' chimneys. "Whatever it might be, Mr. Cliff, keep in mind dat gal has got a will and a soul, and if you don't handle what yo' am to do jes' right, she's likely to turn on yo' like a panther at de back of a hole."

"In other words, you are advising me to exercise diplomacy, not ardor?"

Zachary scratched his head and looked puzzled. "I reckon—if'n I cipher dem fancy words straight."

"I will keep your advice in mind, Zachary. Thanks." Stewart started up the ladder, but stopped after two steps and put a hand to his head. He clutched the hand railing as a wave of dizziness gripped him.

"Yo' am lookin' mighty peaked, Mr. Cliff. Am yo' all right?"

Stewart lowered himself back to the deck and leaned heavily against the railing. "I suddenly feel sick, Zachary."

The big fireman gave a low chuckle. "Yo' still am hung over, Mr. Cliff. Yo' ain't used to all dat drinkin' yo' done last night. Yo' woke up drunk and yo' have been goin' all day long like a runaway nigger wid de pattyrollers at him heels. What yo' need now is some sleep."

"I can't. I've got to talk to Mystie."

"In yo'r condition you are mostly likely to say de wrong ting to dat gal. No, Mr. Cliff, what yo' need now is to get some sleep. It will clear yo'r head so's when yo' do talk to yo'r Miss Mystie, yo' won't go crosswise wid yo'r words."

"I can't afford to take the time for sleep. I cannot chance losing her again."

"She-oot, Mr. Cliff, where am she gonna go between here and Baton Rouge? De boat am only goin' to make one stop, and dat am at the wood yard above Plaquemine. Besides, she has passage clear up de river to Il'inoi. Yo' got plenty o' time. But if'n it makes yo' feel better, I will keeps a eye on her cabin 'til yo' wake up."

"You would do that for me?" Stewart thought this over, and he could find no holes in Zachary's logic. It made sense for him to rest the night. Like Zachary had said, she wasn't going anywhere tonight, and in the morning, with a clear head, he could make his move—whatever that might be. He still hadn't decided the best way to attack the problem.

"All right. I will just curl up back here on the stern. If you could find me a blanket to keep back the chill—"

"No yo' won't, Mr. Cliff. Yo' am goin' to sleep on my cot."

"You're forgetting one thing. To get to your cot means that we will have to sneak past Lansing."

Zachary threw back his head and laughed. "Ain't I taught yo' nothin' dis last year and a half? Me and yo' will jes' slip past dat Mr. Lansing like two ghosts up from de graveyard and out fer a night on de town. Yo' jest follow ol' Zachary."

The fireman started up the ladder.

Stewart frowned. He knew from experience the way most of Zachary's schemes ended up. But Zachary had not left the discussion open to argument, and with more than just a little reservation, Clifton Stewart followed his friend up the ladder.

CHAPTER NINETEEN

The minutes slipped by. Gen couldn't eat. She could hardly breathe. Captain Hamilton's eye kept coming back to her . . . and his smile. It was impossible to return it; the last thing she needed now was this old man's attentions. A lump had caught and had remained stubbornly in her throat. Her brow was damp, and she knew she must look dreadfully suspicious.

And still Douglas would not die!

Five minutes passed. Ten. He had finished his story and his coffee, and was happily engaging in political sparring with the governor and Captain Hamilton—whenever he could momentarily capture the captain's wandering attention.

Did Robert say fifteen minutes? No. She was certain he had said ten. No more.

Half her dessert remained uneaten, and her coffee had chilled in the thin china cup. Finally she could stand no more of this. She stood, excused herself, and left without looking back. She aimed for the nearest door and burst out onto the promenade, into the chill fall night, and came to a sudden stop.

"Aye! Why, if it isn't Miss Summers. And how be ye tonight, lassie?" Allan Gill said.

"Oh! Mr. Gill! You startled me."

He had just turned from the railing where, apparently, he had been watching the dark levee slip by less than twenty rods away. Her sudden appearance seemed to have startled him as much as his had her. In the darkness she thought she saw him slip something into his pocket, but when his hand reappeared again it held only a pipe. Gen recovered from her surprise at finding Gill there. The chill breeze helped clear her head some, and she said, "Whatever are you doing up here?"

He drew in a deep breath as he fished around in one of his pockets for a match safe. "'Tis a grand view from up here—this Mississippi River of yours. 'Tis a lovely thing, is she not?" He struck a flame and put it to the bowl of his pipe. Its fire flickered in his eyes. When he got it burning, he shook out the match and flipped it over the railing where it was lost to the darkness and rolling water below.

"I only came up here to marvel at her, and to have a wider view. There is nothing like this to compare in Scotland. Oh, we have our rivers, but mostly they are short, rushing things, always anxious to be running down to the sea. Even the Tweed is a mere brook compared to your Mississippi."

"I suppose," Gen said, distracted. "I wouldn't know." She glanced over her shoulder at the door she had just emerged from, any moment expecting to hear a commotion and cries for assistance.

But it did not come.

There was no way the senator could have drunk all that poison and still survived it . . . was there? Gen didn't know anymore.

Allan Gill was smiling, almost as if he could see her confusion. The glow from his pipe gave a crimson cast to his features, accentuated the shadows of his deep-set eyes.

"Of course, we have our own beauties," Gill went on. "There are the Highlands; grand and lovely peaks lifting to the sky—something like your Rocky Mountains, I should think, although I have never been far enough west to see them. And we have our lochs as well. Just now, as I was looking out across this broad river, I was thinking of Loch Katrine, a bonny place not far from my home in Glasgow. I miss the mountains, ye know, lassie . . . the mountains, the lochs, the glens, and the firths. Aye, the fish I used to catch from the Clyde!" Gill smiled at her and then he laughed.

"If you are not careful, you will talk yourself into going back," Gen said. She did not wish to encourage this conversation.

"Nay, I dunna' think so, lassie. I have made a life for myself here in your country now, and 'tis here I shall stay." He drew upon his pipe, studied Gen a long moment, then expelling a cloud of smoke said, "Well, I reckon I will be on my way. I hear the view from up on the hurricane deck is even grander than from here. Good night, lass."

Allan Gill wandered down the promenade and took a ladder up to the hurricane deck. When he had gone, Gen let go a sigh of relief and looked back at the door. Something must have gone dreadfully wrong, for above the quiet music she could still hear Senator Douglas's hearty laugh. Did

Robert give her the wrong package? No, he was far too meticulous for such an error.

She was confused, and Gen did not like confusion. She always liked to know exactly what her next move would be. Like Robert, she was meticulous in such matters. She needed time now to rethink all that she was doing. She needed to be alone to trace back where she might have gone wrong, where every attempt had gone wrong. The matter had moved beyond the point where she could easily accept chance as playing a part in it.

Gen started for her cabin, then drew up abruptly. Her view leaped to the railing where a moment before Allan Gill had been standing. Had he been drinking coffee? She did not remember him doing so, and yet there on the railing was a coffee cup. She picked it up. It was empty. She glanced back at the door, heard Douglas laugh again.

Could Gill have—? No that was impossible. The pest was merely up here taking in the scenery. Still, as she turned the cup over in her hand, she couldn't help but wonder.

"Are you quite all right, Miss Summers?"

Gen turned and discovered Captain Hamilton standing there, looking concerned. She tried to smile naturally, and said, "Yes, I am fine, now. I hope I am not coming down with something."

"It is sometimes these hot days followed by the cool nights. You ought to be wearing a shawl."

"Yes. I should. I will go get one, Captain. Thank you." Gen looked at the coffee cup still in her hand. "It was just left sitting here on the railing. It could have fallen and hurt one of the passengers below."

Hamilton took it from her. "Only someone very thoughtful—someone like you, Miss Summers—would be concerned for the welfare of the other passengers." He placed it

upon the deck, next to one of the many iron spittons spaced
every twenty feet along the promenade. "A steward will collect
it." He stepped to the railing and looked out across to the dark
shore. "Have you lived in the South very long?"

"All my life, Captain," she said, impatient in his company. Old men were nice to talk to, but when they began
developing romantic notions, Gen knew the time had come
to flee.

Hamilton gave her a narrow look. "That surprises me."

"Why should it, Captain?"

He shrugged and smiled again. "Oh, it is just that I
thought I detected a lingering Northern accent."

"Who, me?" she laughed. "Why, don't be silly, Captain
Hamilton. I'm a Dixie girl through and through; born and
reared in the great state of Louisiana, raised on peaches and
honey, a daughter of the South." She laughed again and cast
about for some way to excuse herself. Hamilton's eyes
remained on her. "I really ought to retire to my cabin,
Captain."

He seemed to sense her discomfort then, and said, "You
must forgive an old fool."

"I beg your pardon, Captain?"

"Let me walk you to your stateroom."

She would have preferred he didn't, but Hamilton immediately took her arm and they started along the promenade.
Hamilton said after a moment, "I have a confession. A while
ago, as we were seated at the senator's table, it suddenly
occurred to me that, had my own daughter lived, she would
be about your age now. As a child, she had your same
colored hair, your same eyes."

He looked at her and grinned. "I am an old man now, and
old men sometimes have these foolish, reminiscing thoughts.
As I sat there, I began to imagine that you were my daughter,

and I wondered if my life would have been any different if you—she—had lived."

"I'm sorry, Captain." Gen felt suddenly foolish thinking that the captain had harbored any romantic notions toward her.

He waved a hand in the air and said, "Don't trouble yourself with it. It happened long ago. In another life—or so it sometimes seems."

"What was your daughter's name?"

"Alicia."

"A lovely name."

They came around the front of the promenade. The steps leading down to the main deck were before them, and ahead, mounted at the bow near the jack staff, were the smoky torch baskets, casting their red light upon the water ahead. Also in that direction, farther out in the water now, and showing her stern lamp, was the *Natchez*. Her deck lights blazed and her chimneys spat sparks skyward to rain back down upon the black water around her.

"How did she die, Captain?"

Hamilton paused and looked out across the dark river. For a moment, Gen thought he had drifted from this world into another—a world that no longer existed except in the old captain's memory. He said finally, still viewing something out in the darkness that only he could see, "It was a stormy spring night—a lifetime ago. In the spring, as you well know, being a Louisiana belle, the Mississippi becomes a wild animal; a giant, writhing, yellow beast, filled with the snowmelt of a thousand rivulets, pushing at her banks as if it were a cage, clawing up the levees to escape it. Our home was on a plot of land not far from here—Baton Rouge. We shall be there in the morning—and a storm was raging, swept up from the Gulf, feeding the animal and whipping her into a frenzy.

"I was a pilot back then. We had just taken on a supply of firewood and were crossing over to the east bank of the river when I saw flames on the far shore. As I swung the boat about and drove her in for a closer look, I saw that the fire was coming from my home. The levee there had broken and the river had already poured through, and my home was underwater to the second floor. I suspect in their attempt to escape the rising water, someone in the house had upset a lamp and the whole second floor was in flames. I ordered the anchor dropped and a yawl put into the water, and manned it with the strongest backs aboard.

"Making it through the broken levee was like riding an avalanche in a sled, but we got past it all right, and we rowed toward the house through the driving rain. In the flashes of lightning I could see Cynthia and my two children, John and Alicia, up on the roof, clinging together at one of the chimneys. Hester, the children's nurse, was there as well."

Hamilton paused, still staring out into the black nothingness of the river.

"We had almost made it to the eaves of the house when the roof caved in and my family disappeared. Through the hole in the roof flames leaped up into that black, raining night. The fire had stolen all that I loved.

"We never did recover their bodies. The next year the Mississippi leaped her banks again and widened her channel. What was left of my home, that charred pyre, was swept away forever. Today its foundations lie somewhere far out in the middle of the river. I think about that night every time I steam over the place."

"It must have been dreadful, Captain."

Hamilton looked away from the river finally, back at her. "It was, but one learns to live with such memories, although it took me a very long time to put the incident behind me."

Odd, she thought, but she was suddenly in no hurry to leave this old man. One moment she wanted to flee from him, and now she was quite content to be at his side. Although her brain kept leaping back to the senator, calculating what her next move ought to be, she was comfortable to remain with this old man, in the quiet of the evening, with only the chuffing of the escape pipes over-head, and the powerful engines of the *Tempest Queen* thrumming away somewhere beneath her feet. She felt comfortably isolated from her anxiety, and tried to put her deadly mission out of mind—at least until later. "Have you a portrait of your daughter, Captain?"

"A portrait? No, Alicia was too young. I never had one commissioned. But I do have an old daguerreotype some-where. Would you like to see it?"

"Yes, I would." She surprised even herself.

Hamilton escorted her to one of the ladders, and with some bunching and gathering of her skirts, Gen made her way up it and through the small opening above onto the hurricane deck. As she waited for Hamilton, she looked about for Gill, but the Scotsman was nowhere to be seen. Then Hamilton was beside her again. They crossed the hurricane to another ladder, only five steps this time, and mounted the narrow walkway along the texas deck. Hamil-ton led her forward, past the ponderous black chimney that cut into the walkway and radiated heat as they slipped past it, and onto a cozy porch at the front of the texas.

Hamilton opened the door for her. His cabin was fairly large, with a neatly made bed against one wall, a cluttered desk against another, and a door in the back wall; where it led, Gen could only guess. Hamilton put his cap on the hook of a coat tree and at the desk he moved aside some papers. He took up a tarnished brass frame with the faded image of a woman behind its glass.

"This was my wife. Her name was Cynthia."

"She was very beautiful," Gen said, taking the frame from him. The old image was merely a ghost of what it had been some twenty-five or more years earlier, but there was no denying the classical lines of Captain Hamilton's wife's face: her strong chin and the soft curves of her cheeks. She had been quite young as well, no more than twenty, Gen reckoned.

Hamilton pulled open a drawer, rummaged around, then tried another. In the second drawer, Gen got a glimpse of a revolver among the papers, and all at once her thoughts were back on Douglas. Hamilton shut that drawer as well and opened the next one down.

"Ah, here we are," he said, removing an old, leather folder that at first looked like a wallet, but when he opened it, two images appeared. These were not nearly as faded as Cynthia's picture. They had been made with a more advanced photographic process, Gen could tell, and being kept in the bottom of a drawer, where light seldom reached, had helped preserved them. "That is Alicia and her younger brother John."

Even now, with more than a quarter of a century gone by, she heard the pride in Hamilton's voice. Gen set her reticule upon the desk and took the pictures from him. They were merely two children, and they looked very nearly like every other child she had seen at that age, guessing them to be around four or five. She did not see any resemblance between herself and Alicia and decided that if any did exist, it was only in the eye and memory of Captain Hamilton. She made the usual comments just the same, the kind any parent would want to hear, but by now her mood had changed. Her need of respite from her hectic thoughts had been met and, as her old partner Clarence Banning used to say, "It must be on with the caper."

"I see what you mean, Captain," she said.

He smiled, as if this affirmation had been somehow important to him, and after staring at the images another long moment, he returned them carefully to their place at the bottom of the drawer.

Gen said, "I am beginning to feel quite exhausted, Captain. I think I ought to be turning in for the night."

"Of course. I will walk you back."

They left his quarters.

"Will we be stopping anywhere before Baton Rouge, Captain?" she asked casually, as if only making small talk.

"Only briefly to take on fuel, at Plaquemine. In half an hour or so."

They had turned the corner off the porch onto the narrow walkway, heading for the nearest ladder, when Gen stopped suddenly and said, "Oh, my, I have forgotten my reticule."

"I will fetch it for you."

"Nonsense, Captain Hamilton. I am the one who forgot it, and I will go back for it." She turned quickly, slipped once again past the warm chimney, and hurried back onto the porch.

When she returned a half a minute later, she had her bag in hand, a smile upon her face, and a lightness in her step that, she hoped, did not betray how much extra weight the bag had gained since she had taken it in with her.

CHAPTER TWENTY

When Allan Gill left Gen, he climbed to the hurricane deck and immediately crossed over to the opposite side of the boat and hurried down the ladder there. Once more upon the promenade—larboard side—he strolled forward. At the wide, curving staircase that descended to the main deck, Gill peeked around the starboard side and saw that Gen was presently occupied by Captain Hamilton.

"The captain should keep the lass from any mischief," he said to himself, and proceeded down the staircase to the main deck where his shabby duffel bag was stowed. As he walked, he whistled the tune to "Miss McLeod O'Raaset," and in his head he listened to the bonny pipes of his homeland playing the lively melody.

He found his bag where he had left it, rummaged though it for a small wooden box, and from the box extracted an alcohol lamp and a large iron spoon. Gill set the lamp up on a crate and removed the nickel-plated cap from its wick tube. A match flared in his fingers and in a moment he had a blue flame burning.

He adjusted the wick.

The tune in his head switched to "Bonnie Dundee," and so did the melody whistling from his lips.

From his pocket he removed a glass vial and worked the cork from its top. He sniffed, considered a moment, frowned, and sniffed again. Was that the odor of almonds he smelled? It was difficult to say for the smell of the coffee was stronger.

"We will see now, lass, just what it is ye are up to," he said softly as he poured the coffee into the spoon. He wrapped the handle in a rag and held it over the flame.

His whistling picked up the strains of "Bonnie Dundee" again.

The brown liquid began to sizzle in the spoon. He sniffed at it again and instantly pulled his head back. A small smile worked its way upon his face.

"Aye, I've got ye now, lass," he said, raising the spoon slightly so that the liquid in it continued to sizzle, but did not boil. With a piece of paper, Gill gently fanned the air away from himself, whistling louder until the liquid had completely evaporated.

He held the spoon toward the light of the burner. Among the brown powder that had been the coffee, he spied the yellow, metallic-looking flecks. Gill let the spoon cool, then wrapped it in a piece of cloth and shoved it into his pocket.

He blew out the alcohol flame, put the lamp back into its box, and went to find Captain Hamilton.

*   *   *

It was a fine fall night and the chill off the water was invigorating. After Captain Hamilton had escorted Gen to her stateroom, he had gone down to the main deck and spent a few moments at the side railing watching the black water and the lights of the *Natchez*. Captain Leathers's boat had pulled a mile ahead. Her lights danced upon the ebony surface of the Mississippi as they leaped across her choppy bow wave. Overhead, Hamilton could hear the voices of those few diehards who remained at the railing, but the passengers' enthusiasm had diminished now that the *Tempest Queen* was falling back, and had Hamilton been perfectly truthful with himself, he'd have to admit that his own enthusiasm had waned as well.

Nearby, Chief Mate Lansing was barking orders to the firemen, who were still tossing wood into the furnaces at a frantic pace. Hamilton stepped from the railing and made his way under the boiler deck where Lansing's crew was sweating in the fiery blasts of the furnaces.

"Evening, Captain," Lansing said, glancing over. The black backs of the men working at the woodpile glistened in the red fires of the furnaces.

"How is everything down here, Mr. Lansing?"

"Top notch, Captain."

"Good, good. We will be stopping at Plaquemine to take on wood. Hmm . . . why don't you have your boys keep the furnaces stoked while we are there."

Lansing grinned slyly. "You figuring on a quick start, Captain?"

Hamilton pursed his lips, deadpan. "We have allowed Mr. Leathers to work up a sweat. Now let's see if he can keep to the pace."

"Yes, sir, Captain," Lansing snapped smartly, clearly pleased with Hamilton's decision.

Hamilton turned to leave.

"Oh, Captain," Lansing said, stopping him.

"Yes?"

"I seem to have lost a man somewhere. You haven't seen Zachary lazing about the boat, have you?"

"Zachary is missing?"

"He is, and when I lay my hands on that no good nig—"

"No, I have not seen him, but I will keep my eye out for the man."

"You just shag him on down here if you do find that lazy son of perdition."

Hamilton sought out Seegar next and told his chief engineer that he intended to step up the race, and once out of the woodlot at Plaquemine he wanted him to boost the pressure and the revolutions.

"Keep an eye on those engines," Hamilton admonished the engineer, shouting above the din of the engine room as he left.

He made his way up to the pilothouse to inform Ab Grimes that once away from Plaquemine, and until they reached Baton Rouge in the morning, the race would be on in earnest.

She had made her decision, and at once felt better because of it—but was she doing the right thing? Mystie just didn't know. Running away had never been her way of handling problems.

She patted her eyes dry with a handkerchief, powdered her face, and then sat down upon the chair in her cabin with her reticule upon her lap to wait for the *Tempest Queen* to make her next landing.

She recognized Barnabas's rap upon the door when it sounded a few minutes later. A solid, confident knock. The disaster that now seemed so long ago had not shattered his self-assuredness in the least, even though it had devastated hers.

"Come in," she said.

The door opened and Barnabas stood there, grinning, with his hands on his hips. "Well, I fear the *Tempest Queen* has not the stomach for a good race. She has fallen miserably behind, Mystie."

She did not reply, but turned her gaze toward the window. The light inside the room prevented her from seeing out into the night. In the reflection of the dark glass, her unhappy face peered back at her.

He looked at her then, as if only now noticing her distress. "Is something the matter?" he asked.

Mystie took in a breath and said, "I am going ashore at the next landing, Barnabas." In the dark glass she saw him stiffen slightly. "I wish to leave the *Tempest Queen*."

"Leave? What on earth are you talking about, Mystie?"

She turned away from the window. Standing there, Barnabas Antone did cut a dashing figure in his dark gray sack coat and matching trousers with the fine, light gray pinstripe. But as she studied him, she was aware of a hardness developing about his eyes and face as his smile slowly melted away.

"I ask you again, Mystie, what are you talking about? Whatever has come over you? Is it still the accident? Is that what has caused you to behave so strangely?"

"No . . . well, perhaps partly. There are other things as well."

"What other things?" he demanded.

"Just other things!" she came back, growing irritated at his insistence. She did not have to explain her feelings to anyone if she did not want to—even to the man to whom she was engaged to be married.

A long silence filled the room. Then Antone said, "It is that fellow we met on the promenade earlier, isn't it, Mystie?"

"All right, if you must know. Yes. Yes, it is Clifton."

"Has he been bothering you?"

"Bothering me? No, it is nothing like that."

"Then why do you want to leave? I have purchased passage for us all the way to Alton. It would be foolish to disembark now and have to search for another boat making the trip. We were fortunate to have found this one. Every other packet that I inquired into would have forced us into innumerable transfers and delays."

How could she give him an answer? How could she tell him what she felt when she did not truly know, herself?

"If he has not bothered you, then obviously you have concocted some female fantasy in your head, Mystie. I have never claimed to understand women, except that I do know at times they can be most irrational. You are letting your emotions and your heart and some perceived romantic notions of some past suitor distort your thinking, Mystie. You are behaving childishly. We will not leave this boat until we do so in Alton, and that is my final word on the matter."

Her black eyes turned to flint. "How can you say that to me?"

"Face it, Mystie, you are acting irrationally."

"Irrationally!" Mystie's anger flared. "Perhaps I am. But regardless, when this boat puts in at her next landing, I am leaving. You may come with me or you may stay aboard. At this moment it makes no difference to me."

Antone's back went rigid and he considered her a moment, then said, "You are not thinking rationally. I will leave you now to reconsider. I will stop back before we put in. Perhaps then you will have come to your senses." He pulled the door open and left.

Mystie was shaking. She wanted to throw something, but *that* would have been foolish and senseless. Her wanting to leave the boat was not, however, and if Barnabas wanted to stay aboard, he was welcome to. She had fended for herself along the river before he had come into her life, and she could certainly do it again.

She steadied herself, the shaking ceased, and with renewed resolve, she returned to her chair to await the *Tempest Queen*'s next appointment with the shore.

Down the hallway, Zachary had been half dozing when Barnabas Antone had knocked upon Mystie's door. He stretched his long legs and stood, putting his back to the wall, and watched Antone enter her stateroom. He was hungry and thought about stealing down to the kitchen and trying to talk Maggie out of a slice of pie, but he decided against it. He'd been away from his post since the *Tempest Queen* had pulled away from New Orleans, and like as not, Mr. Lansing had begun to look for him.

He and Stewart had almost run into Lansing when they had sneaked past the furnaces and into the little cabin above the woodpile where the firemen slept. In a matter of minutes, the word had spread among the Negro workers that Stewart was there, and that Zachary would be away a mite longer. They would never tell Lansing though, for the bond they shared went beyond any loyalty that Lansing might demand.

But another member of the crew might see him, and for the time being, it was best to remain here, half hidden in a doorway, down at the end of a corridor where no one but maybe a passing chambermaid would see him.

Zachary wondered how late it was getting. Not very, he decided, for he could still hear the buzz of wide-awake passengers coming from the main cabin at the far end of the hall.

His thoughts were interrupted by the sudden opening of the door and Barnabas Antone stepping out. The man was scowling. Antone stood a moment at her closed door as if thinking, then wheeled about on his heel and strode angrily away.

Now, that was most mysterious. Zachary wished he knew what had happened in there—what had angered Mystie's beau. Suddenly, he was no longer sleepy or hungry but curious as he crouched back to his haunches to wait out the night and to keep his promise to Stewart.

Gen took a table across the main cabin from Senator Douglas, and when she set the reticule upon it, there came a muffled thump from the heavy revolver within it.

"Might I gets you somethin', ma'am?"

"Some tea will be fine," she told the white-coated waiter. He went off toward the kitchen and Gen's view went back toward Douglas. The man looked disgustingly healthy. There was little doubt in her mind that either his coffee had been removed and changed while they had been out on the promenade watching the *Natchez,* or those crystals that Robert had given her in the brown-paper packet were not poison at all.

Was Robert setting her up for a fall? This new suspicion drew her pretty face into an ugly scowl. No, he would never. He loved her.

The waiter returned with her tea.

"How long before we reach Plaquemine—to take on wood?" she asked him.

"Oh, I don't know, ma'am. I ain't had me a good look at de river lately. But I might guess it won't be but a few more minutes. I can go find out, if you want me to."

"No, that will not be necessary. Thank you."

The waiter went off to another table and Gen put together the rough outlines of her next move. She would wait until the boat made the landing, and then, when everyone went out to watch the men bringing the wood aboard, as this usually was an entertaining diversion when a boat pulled into a woodlot, she would shoot the senator and in the confusion escape into the night.

Plaquemine was a large enough town for her to easily get lost in, and afterward, she would make her way back to Carleton Manor. Luckily, she had been cautious enough not to use her real name. The plan settled upon, she felt a little better.

It was a crude way to deal with the problem, but it had now become necessary. She had run out of options and patience, and the longer she remained aboard the *Tempest Queen,* the more she felt as if her every move was being watched, her every plan foiled at the last moment. That was ridiculous, of course. No one knew her true reason for being aboard.

Gen sipped her tea. It did nothing to settle her nerves, and when the waiter came by again, she ordered whiskey, drank it down at once, and requested a second. The waiter dutifully brought it over. Although he did not question her, Gen could see that he was curious as to the outcome of so much drink.

Well, he could wonder about it until hell froze over, she decided, as a warm easiness expanded within her, giving her confidence. Actually, it wouldn't take nearly that long. In a few more minutes there would be no need for anyone to wonder any longer.

"She will have to stop for wood as well, sooner or later," Hamilton said to Ab Grimes as the pilot peered over the

elm into the night. Gip Dementor was lounging on the high
ench. He had come up a few minutes before to take over
he helm, as Grimes's shift was about over.

Gip said, "We can catch up to her with no problem,
Captain," and he nodded his head at the stern lamps of the
Natchez, now almost a mile ahead of them. "But I'm
wondering why this change of heart? When I first signed
nto the *Tempest Queen,* you would no sooner put her in a
ace than you would put a torch to her."

Grimes looked over, too, and although he said nothing,
Hamilton saw that the same question was running around
nside his head, as well.

Hamilton knew the answer. He had known it since he first
greed to the race, even though he did not like to admit it to
imself then. He answered, "Hmm . . . I suppose the time
as finally come."

Grimes looked over with immediate interest. "Time?"

"Yes, Mr. Grimes. Time. It comes for all of us—even-
ually."

"Just what are you trying to say?" Grimes asked, sud-
enly suspicious.

"I have decided that this will be my last season on the
iver. After this trip to Alton and then back to Baton Rouge,
am going to put the *Tempest Queen* on the block, sell her,
nd retire."

"Retire! Captain, what ever will you do with yourself?
The river is in your blood. Why, you could no more leave
he river than a catfish could breathe air."

"I am afraid so, Mr. Grimes."

Ab Grimes was momentarily speechless, which was a
are condition for the riverboat pilot.

"In other words, Captain, you are having yourself one last
ling. You are throwing your hat into the wind and watching
o see how far she is carried," Dementor said.

Hamilton looked over and grinned. "Not at all. I am fa
too old to go chasing hats in the wind, Mr. Dementor."

"Then what?"

"This is my little gift to a fine crew who has put up with
the foibles and sometimes severe nature of their captain."

For a moment, Gip Dementor was speechless as well
Then a knock on the pilothouse broke the silence. Hamilton
opened it and a shabbily dressed man stepped in.

"Yes?" Hamilton asked.

"Captain Hamilton? I must talk with ye."

The man had a look of intense urgency upon his face, and
although Hamilton had seen him aboard that afternoon
he could not call forth the name. That irritated him, for h
always made it a practice to study the passenger list and
treat each of them as if they were guests in his home. But
this time the senator's arrival had so fully occupied him tha
he had not had time to check it.

"What is it you wish to speak to me about, Mr. . . . ?"

"Er . . . 'tis Gill, Captain. Allan Gill . . . and I mus
talk with ye immediately, and alone."

"Alone? Hmm. Will my cabin do?"

"That will be fine, Captain."

Hamilton turned back to his two pilots. "I would appre
ciate it if you keep to yourselves what was said here
tonight."

"Sure thing, Captain," Grimes said. Gip nodded his head

Hamilton gestured at the door. "Shall we go, Mr. Gill?"

Gill stepped back out into the chill night air with
Hamilton right behind him.

CHAPTER
TWENTY-ONE

Captain Hamilton shut the door to his cabin and went to his desk, motioning Allan Gill to the chair near his bed. The close quarters of the crew cabins did not afford much extra room for guests, and even though Hamilton had the most spacious cabin on the texas, it was still tight. There were, indeed, much larger staterooms below for the passengers, Hamilton thought wryly as he sat at his cluttered desk. Senator Douglas and his wife occupied one of them.

"Well, Mr. Gill, what is so important that it requires my attention—alone?" Hamilton asked, raising a quizzical brow.

Gill chose to remain standing, and although his impassive face might have belonged to a man without the least care in

the world, his slight, impatient shifting from foot to foo
clearly told another story.

"Captain, I think we have us a wee bit of a problem
aboard your fine boat. Aye, and I think if ye don't d
something soon, that problem will be surely blow up in ou
faces."

"*We* have a problem?" Hamilton's view narrowed. "Per
haps you can be a bit more lucid on the matter, Mr. Gill.'

"All right, Captain. I will lay it before ye plain. Ye hav
a passenger aboard the *Tempest Queen* who is attempting t
assassinate the senator."

Hamilton's mild amusement was suddenly transforme
into an intense interest, and he came forward in his chai
"Senator Douglas? Are you certain, Mr. Gill?"

"Aye. I am now, Captain. It has taken me a while to ge
the proof that I needed, and up until now, all I have gotte
was what might be called circumstantial evidence. But jus
a wee bit ago, I finally got what I needed."

Hamilton was reluctant to accept such vile politica
scheming of this breed could happen aboard the *Tempes
Queen*. "Come, now, Mr. Gill. Surely you don't believe tha
Senator Douglas's life is in peril aboard my boat. Wh
would want to do such a thing . . . and more importantly
why? And what is this evidence you speak about?" Hamil
ton had grown impatient. He did not want to believe thi
man, but the intense lines cut deep into Gill's face could no
be easily ignored, and his accusation was ominous.

Gill extracted an item from his pocket that appeared a
first to be a rolled-up rag. When he unfurled it, Hamilto
saw that it contained an iron spoon, battered and blackened
and looking nearly as dilapidated as the coat pocket it ha
come from. "Take a close look at what is in the bowl, an
be careful not to touch it."

With some suspicion and a little resentment at this man'

wild claims, Hamilton took the spoon, turned it toward the light from an oil lamp in a gimbal on the wall, and held it out at arm's length.

"Do ye see those fine yellow flecks, Captain?"

Hamilton could not. Frowning, he pulled open his desk drawer and retrieved a pair of spectacles, hooked the arms over his ears, and looked once more at the spoon. This time he clearly saw the light brown residue clinging to it, but nothing more.

"I see no yellow flecks, Mr. Gill."

Gill frowned impatiently. "Well, they are there, Captain, I can assure ye. Ye just don't know what to look for. But never mind. Smell it. Smell the spoon and tell me what ye think is there."

Hamilton had had about enough of this. Who did this bedraggled fellow think he was, making preposterous claims, showing him a spoon that meant nothing? "See here, now, this has gone far enough."

"Smell the spoon, Captain." Gill's sharp command gave Captain Hamilton pause. Deepening his grimace, he sniffed at the spoon. "It smells only of coffee."

"Yea, yeah, of course ye smell coffee, because that is what it was mixed in. Smell it again, closer this time, and ignore the coffee. Use your nose as God intended it to be used, Captain! There is something else there that you are completely missing."

Hamilton was on the verge of tossing the fellow out upon his ear, but he refrained, willing to give him the benefit of the doubt one moment longer. He sniffed at the spoon again, and smelled coffee again. Concentrating, he told his brain to ignore the coffee, and when he tried again, he caught the faint odor of something else, easily masked by the strong coffee smell.

"There *is* something here."

"Aye, I knew ye would discover it, once ye tried. Now ye tell me, what is that odor?"

"I am not sure." He tried it again, concentrating. "I smells a little like a fruit . . . no, not fruit, perhaps a nut Yes, that is it."

"Good. Now tell me, what kind of nut, Captain?"

"I don't know."

"Then I will tell ye. Almonds."

Hamilton tried it again. "Yes, that is it. Almonds."

"And what smells of almonds, Captain—bitter almonds to be precise?"

"I have no idea."

"Then I will tell ye that, too. It is arsenic."

"Arsenic! Are you certain?"

"Positive. I took this sample from the senator's coffee cup while ye were all out watching that other boat pulling ahead of ye. Fortunately, I was able to switch cups before the senator returned, but I will not always be nearby to foil the assassin's attempts."

"This assassin you keep mentioning. Who is he?"

"He, Captain? It is not a he, but a she. She is going by the name of Genevieve Summers, but her real name is St James."

"Impossible!" Hamilton stood angrily. "How dare you bring that vile accusation against such a fine woman. Why I ought to have you tossed off my boat at the next landing."

"That fine woman, as ye say, is involved in a plot of murder; an intrigue of some sort. I have only now begun to fit the pieces together. It is a scheme, however, that will end in the death of Senator Douglas, I fear, unless we do something to stop her. Her husband, Robert St. James, has been buying up beef on the Texas frontier. And he was a secret delegate to a separatist rally in Charleston only last month."

"There is nothing illegal in that. Everyone knows South Carolina is threatening secession if Lincoln is elected. And buying beef is not illegal, either. Besides, the woman is not married."

"Ah, but she is married, and less than a year ago. She and her husband are a fine pair. He is Robert St. James of Carleton Manor, noted for his shrewd and ruthless business ventures. And that "fine woman," before her marriage to St. James, was a swindler and a capper to more than a few gamblers along this grand river. I wonder how many men have lost their shirts, as well as their purses, because of the lady's lovely face standing innocently by, watching over his shoulder, and all the while telegraphing his cards to her gambler friend across the table from him."

Hamilton was about to proclaim that idea as preposterous, but before he could speak, a dim memory sparked to life—an event that had happened more than a year and a half ago, about the time both Dexter McKay and young Stewart had come aboard. He remembered a card game on the wharf boat at Napoleon in which he had been cheated. The gambler had fallen before Dexter McKay's revolver by the time it was all over, but now, thinking back on it, he did seem to recall the woman there. She had claimed to be looking for her uncle or brother or some such relative. Hamilton could not remember the details, but now he did remember her lovely face—a face very much like Genevieve's. After the gambler, Banning, had been killed, she had mysteriously disappeared. And her name had been . . . His brows knitted together in concentration. Her name had been . . . *Genevieve de Winter!*

"Good Lord!"

"Captain?"

"I think you just might be right. I wondered what it was about that woman that had caught my eye—other than her beauty, I mean. I believe I had a run-in with her not two years ago, and she was working with a gambler at that time. And if I am not mistaken, she also tried to kill one of my passengers, Mr. McKay!"

"There, that sounds about right for the lass."

Hamilton's eyes fixed upon Gill's face. "Just who are you, anyway? And why are you following this Genevieve Summers . . . St. James . . . de Winter . . . or whatever she calls herself?"

"Ah, now, here I must make the grand confession. I have told ye a wee bit o' a lie, Captain Hamilton."

"Why am I not surprised?"

Allan Gill grinned. "My name is not Gill at all, ye see. It is Pinkerton. Allan Pinkerton."

"Allan Pinkerton?" Hamilton had to think a moment. "The detective?"

"Aye, the very same. I have been hired by a powerful man in the senate whom I am not at liberty to name, to keep an eye on our lady friend . . . and Senator Douglas, for the rumor is, there would be an attempt upon his life by either Robert St. James or his wife."

"But why? What could be gained by such an assassination?"

"Much. I have given this careful thought, Captain, and I think I have the answer. But that must wait. Now the time is short, and we must apprehend the lady before she can do any damage."

"Yes, of course."

At that moment the *Tempest Queen*'s steam whistle shrilled.

Allan Pinkerton glanced at Captain Hamilton. "That whistle. It means something to you. I can see it on your face. What was it for, Captain?"

"We are about to put in at Plaquemine for wood.

Genevieve had asked me when our next stop would be. Could she be planning something now?"

"Aye, that would be my guess."

"Then we should find her quickly and warn the senator as well." Hamilton tore the spectacles from the bridge of his nose and put them back in the drawer.

His hand stopped and he stared at the open drawer. In an instant he yanked it fully open and then, knowing immediately the truth, he turned to Pinkerton.

"What is the matter, Captain?" the detective said at Hamilton's sudden distress.

"I fear the matter had just become more immediate, Mr. Pinkerton. Less than an hour ago, Genevieve St. James was here, in my cabin. And now I see that my revolver is missing."

"Plaquemine, of course."

Mystie watched the familiar lights along the far shore as the *Tempest Queen* made the crossing. Over the muffled splash of the paddle wheel that turned just below her, Mystie heard the peal of the bronze bell up on the hurricane deck, its mellow voice drifting far out over the water, its three, clear taps calling the leadsmen to their posts. In a moment, the distant voices of the leadsmen reached her: "M-a-r-k three . . . M-a-r-k three . . . Quarter-less-three . . ."

Mystie remembered now that Captain Hamilton always used the woodlot at Plaquemine whenever he came up from New Orleans. That would be perfect, she thought. In Plaquemine she had friends where she could spend the night. Tomorrow, she would find a boat heading upriver, and perhaps she could work her way to Illinois. In any case, it would give her breathing room. Her brain was a swirling confusion at the moment. How could she have grown so close to Barnabas without seeing that overbearing side of him?

Perhaps some women would not mind it—perhaps most women—but not she.

She stepped back inside her cabin, collected her few belongings, and put them into her bag. Setting the hat just right upon her head, she went out into the hallway. Barnabas was not there, and neither was Clifton. That was a relief, but as she walked toward the side door that opened onto the promenade, a persistent tug at her heart seemed to slow her steps.

Outside, a crowd had gathered at the railing, watching the shore draw nearer. The lights of the woodlot reflected along the edges of huge columns of cut timber, a dozen of them, taller than a man, marching back toward a small hut where the woodcutter was standing in a wedge of light cast from the open doorway.

Mystie took a quick glance at the crowd. There was the famous senator and his wife, and the governor as well. She saw Barnabas among the many people peering out at that lonely woodlot surrounded by the blackness of night. His back was to her, and he did not notice her departure. In the distance, the lights of Plaquemine, perhaps a quarter of a mile still upriver, flickered through the trees.

She turned abruptly away from the crowd and strode toward the stairs at the front of the promenade.

"Miss Mystie!"

She stopped and turned back.

Zachary came hurrying up behind her, dodging the people there. "Miss Mystie, where are yo' goin'?"

"Oh, Zachary, it's you." She gave him a bleak smile and said, "I am leaving the boat. I've decided to stay at Plaquemine. I have friends here."

"Why, Miss Mystie? What about yo'r beau?"

"He is staying with the boat," she said, and in spite of her efforts, her voice cracked just a bit.

"But, Mr. Cliff, him has got some tings to say to yo'. Yo' can't leave de boat now."

"I am sorry, but I have to."

"How will Mr. Cliff find yo'?"

"It is better that he stops trying," she said, struggling with her emotions. Why did she feel this way? Clifton had passed out of her life long ago. She put her hand gently upon Zachary's arm. "Now, I really must go. Tell Clifton good-bye for me."

Mystie turned away. Barnabas Antone appeared suddenly in front of her, barring the way to the stairs.

"Tell *Clifton* good-bye for me?" Barnabas said resentfully. There was a slight slur in his words that told her he had been drinking. He peered down at her, his eyes lost in the shadows cast by a lamp behind him. "What about me, the man to whom you are engaged? Were you going to leave without telling *me* good-bye?"

"Barnabas," she said, her voice weighted with sadness. "We have already discussed this. I told you then that I was leaving."

"And I told you that you could not."

Mystie stiffened. "Yes, you did. How could you insist on something like that? We are not yet married, and even if we were, for you to flatly tell me what I can or cannot do is brazen and thoughtless. I am not your slave to order around."

Barnabas winced, and his anger disappeared. "No, of course not, Mystie, I am sorry. How did we ever come to this?"

"I don't know, Barnabas. But lately, since the accident, I have seen a different side to you. One you have kept hidden from me."

"No, I have kept nothing hidden from you, Mystie. I am in love with you. It must be the stress of the last week. The accident has weighed heavily upon me. Can you ever forgive me?"

Mystie's heart was torn. Was she overreacting to the stress as well? Could Clifton's sudden appearance have clouded her thinking toward this man? In all his dealings, Barnabas had showed himself to be true and honorable. If he had been anything less, surely she would have seen it before this.

Suddenly, she needed to be away from there, to flee from all the confusion. Instead, she felt herself being drawn into his strong arms. She pulled away, but not forcefully, and he held her.

She wanted to cry, but resisted. She should be away from him; somewhere where his closeness and her emotions did not muddle her thoughts so. She disengaged herself from his embrace and said, "I am leaving, Barnabas."

His face hardened. "Still, you are leaving? You are acting like a child."

Her anger flared again, hotter than before. "A child? Perhaps, but I know my own mind, and no insults you can fling at me will change it!"

The boat had put into the pier and already the crew was leaping off her guards and tramping down the landing stages, on their way to the woodpile that lay in long, shadowy rows upon the shore. She wheeled away from him, only vaguely aware that Zachary was no longer standing there. Some time during their argument, he had left.

From behind her, Barnabas's words burned like a fire-brand. "If you leave me now, Mystie, don't think I will take you back later."

She paused momentarily, shaking with anger, but did not

look back at him, did not answer. With renewed determination, she started once more for the stairway.

Zachary slipped away unnoticed, and once at the head of the stairs, he dashed down them and hit the main deck with his long legs pumping. Heedless of the chief mate standing there, directing the workmen to their tasks of bringing the wood aboard, Zachary flew past him and plunged up the ladder to the railless catwalk around the little cabin above the dwindled woodpile, and burst through the door.

All the hands were down helping load the wood, and the room was empty except for the lone, sleeping form upon a sagging cot—one of a dozen sagging cots packed end to end in the small cabin, with only a narrow space between the rows to walk down.

"Mr. Cliff! Mr. Cliff!" He shook Stewart awake.

Clifton came out of his sleep, groggy, disoriented at first, then he saw Zachary's face hovering above him and he sat up at once.

"Zachary! What is the matter?" Clifton's grogginess was instantly replaced with concern when he looked into Zachary's distraught face. "What is it?"

"It am Miss Mystie. She am got herself worked up in de worst way. She am gettin' off dis boat now! Yo' need to git yo'r wits together, Mr. Cliff, and dat cotton outta yo'r head, and git up dere lickety-split and try to stop her."

In a heartbeat Clifton was up and out the door, and Zachary was right on his heels.

Chief Mate Lansing was barking commands to his men when Zachary and Clifton sped past him. Zachary thought he saw the man's mouth fall open, and he knew he had heard a sputter in Lansing's finely tuned vocal chords, but he had no time for delay; Clifton had already wheeled around to the stairs, using the polished knot atop the baluster as a pivot point, and was flying up them.

CHAPTER
TWENTY-TWO

In a shadow in the bend of the promenade, Genevieve St. James waited. The *Tempest Queen* had slowed, and Gen's attention was divided between the shadowy woodlot on shore with its long, dark pier stretching out into the black water, and the promenade forward of her position where passengers had begun to gather at the railing.

The steamer's starboard paddle wheel stopped turning, and the big boat pivoted in midstream, then drove on into the landing with both wheels chopping the water. Gen watched Senator Douglas and his wife, accompanied by Sheridan and the governor, make their way to the railing.

Perfect.

She swallowed hard, and in her mind's eye reviewed the

thing she must do. She'd keep the revolver hidden until the very last moment, when she was right up beside the man. Afterward, in the confusion that would follow the shot and the senator's death, she would dash down the stairs and across the landing stage to the pier.

What about the crew down on the pier? Would they bar her way off the boat?

No! No wishy-washy thinking, now. It is going to all work out. Think this through rationally.

The workmen below would be busy hauling up the wood; they would not know what had happened. She would simply tell them there was a madman up there with a gun. In their rush to apprehend him, they would effectively slow her pursuers, giving her a few extra minutes to flee from the boat. Once ashore, she'd make her way into Plaquemine and lay low for awhile. Then, when the hounds were finally off her trail, she'd return to the safe confines of Carleton Manor, and she and Robert would wait and watch the course the country would take. If Robert's predictions were correct, Lincoln would be the next president and . . .

The shrill blast from the *Tempest Queen*'s steam whistle pulled her thoughts back to the present. The riverboat nudged against the docking fenders, and her hawsers strained as they pulled her to a gentle stop. Almost at once, two dozen crew members leaped from the guards, across the moving water to the pier while others manhandled the landing stages into place.

This was it. The time had come. Gen drew in a long, calming breath, let it out in a single, sharp blast, and reached into her bag. The heavy revolver came far enough out into the wavering lamplight for her to see that each cylinder had a cap properly in place. She thrust it back, took another deep breath, and with her hand still inside the bag, still tightly wrapped around the grip of Captain Hamilton's Colt, Gen started forward, toward the place where the senator was standing.

One deck above, Captain Hamilton and Allan Pinkerton dashed across the hurricane deck. As Hamilton put a foot to the ladder, the *Tempest Queen*'s shrill docking blast brought him up short.

"We haven't a moment to lose, I fear," Pinkerton said.

"I daresay, I hope you are wrong, Mr. Pinkerton."

"Aye, and I, too."

The two men hurried down the ladder. Hamilton, reaching the promenade first, spied the senator, standing near the railing halfway along the deck. He didn't immediately see Gen, and a wave of relief swept over him. Pinkerton, landing a moment later, did not break pace, but strode immediately toward the gathering of passengers at the railing.

Suddenly two men shot past them. One of the men was Zachary, Hamilton realized after a startled moment. It was the truant fireman that Lansing had been looking for—and the other man was . . . Clifton Stewart! Hamilton was promptly confused. Had he not left Stewart back in New Orleans? What, then, was the man doing aboard his boat now?

But Hamilton had no time to solve that puzzle, for almost immediately a woman in the crowd screamed, there was a sudden movement, and then a gunshot rang out, and all at once people were scattering like chickens before a speeding carriage.

Even as he came around the promenade, Clifton Stewart saw Mystie Waters wheel away from Barnabas. She was coming straight at him, although apparently her view had been clouded by something—an argument—and she had not yet noticed him. But he could see her distress in the tightness of her face, around her determined eyes, at the corners of her clenched lips.

Clifton rushed to embrace her. He passed Captain Hamilton on the deck at that moment as well, but it no longer mattered. The only person who meant anything to him was walking his way, and she, in her anxiety, was blinded to him.

"Mystie!"

She stopped abruptly.

"Clifton," she said, seeing him now.

"Zachary told me you were leav—" At that moment a movement drew his eyes from her. A woman not ten feet in front of him was raising a revolver. Stewart stood stunned while his brain registered the impossible. The revolver was being pointed at Senator Douglas!

Could no one see her?

Then a woman in the crowd cried out.

Instantly, Stewart threw Mystie aside and, diving forward, he grasped the revolver about the cylinder at the moment it fired.

A blinding orange flame stabbed out into the crowd. His hand seemed to explode with the revolver and a searing paint that was as sharp as a knife's edge cut into his palm. Then the momentum of his leap carried them both over and they crashed together upon the deck.

For a few crazy moments, Stewart thought they were to be trampled beneath the scrambling feet. He wrestled the revolver from her. It came free with little struggle. The fall had stunned her and she lay there gasping. Someone began pulling at him, dragging him back to his feet.

"Are ye all right?" a voice asked.

"Yes . . . yes, I think so." Stewart unfolded his hand from the bloodied revolver and winced. The exploding gunpowder and searing gas escaping from the cylinder had ripped a deep gash into his palm, but his hand still seemed to work properly. He flexed his fingers. "Yes, I seem to be all right," he repeated.

The whole event had taken less than ten seconds, and only now did Stewart begin to realize all that had occurred. The man who had helped him up was now helping the woman to her feet. A few paces away, a shaking and blanched Senator Douglas was staring at her with a frozen look of fear etched into his dimpled face and folded chin.

Stewart wondered where the bullet had gone. The revolver had been pointed at the senator, but beyond that, it had been more or less pointed at himself and Mystie.

Mystie!

He wheeled about and did not at once see his beloved. But there was Captain Hamilton, and two or three other people on their knees, bent over a body stretched out upon the deck.

"Oh, no!" Stewart pushed through the crowd and bent over the body.

Hamilton glanced up at him. "Mr. Stewart," he said briefly, and although it was a plain statement, there carried with it the underlying question: *What is happening on my boat?*

A fist reached up through his throat and clenched down hard as Clifton fell involuntarily to his knees. "How bad is it?" he asked softly.

Hamilton frowned and shook his head. "I am afraid there is little we can do."

Clifton took up the limp hand, looked at the closed eyelids. Where there had once been strength, he felt only soft, warm flesh.

"Can—can you hear me?"

He thought he detected a quickening of breath, then the eyelids fluttered and, as if with great effort, they opened and two lumps of coal stared up at him a moment. The hand within his own gained some strength.

"I . . . I's kin hear yo' jes' fine, Mr. Cliff." He coughed. "I ain't gone yet."

"Oh, Zachary," Clifton groaned, and his eyes filled. His friend's name caught in his throat. "Why did it have to be you?"

"What . . . what happened?"

"You've been shot."

Zachary managed a smile somehow. "Shee-oot, Mr. Cliff, I already know'd dat."

"Now, don't talk—"

"Why not? I hears what de capt'n say. He say I am dyin'. Am gonna have no more time to talk but right now." Zachary winced. "Who . . . who pulled de trigger?"

"It was some woman. She was trying to kill the senator, I think."

"Did yo' git her?"

"I did."

Zachary coughed, bringing up blood this time, and his eyelids closed in a series of small spasms. "Dat is all right den." His breathing ceased. For a long moment, a heavy silence weighed down upon them all. Then, with a sudden gasp, his breathing resumed, ragged and uneven, and his eyes opened again. His voice failing, he managed to say, "Now, Mr. Cliff. No need to shed no tears fo' ol' Zachary— no need to worry 'bout me—" Zachary drew in another painful breath. "Where I am headin' de livin' am easy, and dere will be angels singin' at me all de day long—" Another fit of coughing broke off his words. The cough halted abruptly and Zachary's hand grew limp beneath Stewart's fingers.

He stared at his friend, waiting for a breath, a twitch . . . for a sign. But the life had gone out of him. The sense of death was so overwhelming that Stewart imagined Zachary's spirit hovering over them, and when a hand pressed upon his shoulder, he turned with a start.

"He's dead," Stewart said, and patted his eyes dry with the sleeve of his shirt.

Mystie gazed down at him, her wide, dark eyes both compassionate and confused. "You really cared for him, Cliff. I can see that."

"He was my friend."

She hesitated before speaking next. "Did you ever feel friendship toward all the slaves on your father's plantation?"

"That was a long time ago," he said sharply. "I told you. Things are different. I am different."

"Yes, I see that."

Stewart didn't need his past to be dragged up and paraded in front of him—not now, not in his grief. He looked back at the body of his friend.

"I am sorry, Clifton." She studied him, then said, "I think you remind me of someone."

Stewart stood. "And who might that be?" he said, his eyes averted.

"My father. I have often wondered how he felt when he bought my mother and me from his father—bought us like a man buys cattle—and left his home to take us north to a free state. I think his grief must have been something like what you are feeling now."

Stewart could only listen in silence. He had nothing to say. He had changed since he had come aboard the *Tempest Queen*. He was a different man now, and he knew he could never go back to plantation life, even if his father would have him.

She seemed to know when enough had been said. She put an arm around him and remained at his side.

"Captain, I got the lassie, right enough," Allan Pinkerton said, bringing Genevieve St. James over. He had a firm grasp upon her wrist, and the crowd of people gathering there precluded any chance of her escape. "It is too bad, though, that we didn't prevent this tragedy."

Captain Hamilton stood and said, "What are you going to do with her now?"

Pinkerton frowned. "In truth, Captain, I have no authority to hold her. But you, being captain of this boat, you do, at least until we take her ashore." He handed the revolver back to Hamilton.

"Then what?"

Until now, Governor Moore had been standing silently near Senator Douglas. He said, "I will see to it she is prosecuted to the fullest extent of the law once we land at Baton Rouge!"

Gen laughed. "And what charges could you prosecute me on? Attempting to murder Senator Douglas? The man is unharmed! And besides, I'm a woman. Where will you find a jury willing to put a woman in prison? You won't, not in Baton Rouge—not anywhere in the South. My husband has powerful friends and I will be free in a week."

"Then you will be tried for the murder of Zachary," Stewart said.

Gen laughed again, and now the soft, prolonged syllables that had so marked her Southern speech were blatantly absent, replaced with hard, ice-brittle confidence. "He was only a nigger slave. No jury in the South would even consider such a charge unless it was brought against me by his owner. Even then, all I would be liable for was the cost of replacing him."

"Zachary was a free man," Stewart said. "And you can be tried for murdering a free man, even if his skin was black."

Gen smiled, her confidence unscathed. "Really? Well, we shall see."

"Enough of this," Hamilton barked. "Take that woman away from here." He searched the crowd for a face, and when he had found it, he said, "Mr. Lansing, see to it that Mrs. St. James is securely locked in one of the empty staterooms, and post a guard outside its window."

When she had been taken away, Hamilton enlisted the

help of the crew and they carried Zachary's body down to the main deck.

The crowd slowly broke up.

The senator came over and reached for Stewart's hand. Stewart glanced at the blood streaming down his palm and extended his left for the senator to shake. It was a heartfelt grasp, and Douglas said, "Sir, I give you my most humble thanks for your timely intervention in this matter."

"I could have done no less, sir."

"She is right, you know," Douglas said.

"About what?"

"No jury is going to convict her—at least, not in the South. Well, no use brooding over the injustices of this world. It is up to men like us to change them. Again, my thanks." The senator, surrounded by his wife, Sheridan, and the governor, left. A chambermaid came by with a bucket and mop and began working at the blood pooled thick and black upon the deck.

Stewart remained, staring out at the shadowy wood yard below, where men struggled under the weight of four-foot lengths of cordwood piled upon their "shoulder bones," as Zachary would have described it, carrying them aboard like so many busy black ants. Mystie stood beside him and neither spoke.

Farther down the promenade a dozen paces, Barnabas Antone came from the doorway and paused in the flickering lamplight there.

Antone struck a match and put it to a cigar. A puff of gray smoke flew off on the chill breeze, and he strode over. "Mystie, it is time to go." He took her arm.

She twisted it from his grasp. "No, Barnabas. I am not going with you."

"I have had about enough of this childish behavior." He reached again for Mystie, but Stewart's hand intervened and caught Antone by the arm, squeezing down. A year and a half of working side by side with the black firemen, hauling freight and heaving cordwood, made itself known now in his viselike grip.

Antone winced, and tried unsuccessfully to break the grip.

Stewart said evenly, "The lady does not wish to leave with you, sir."

"The lady is engaged to be married to me," Antone hissed through his clenched teeth.

The men's eyes locked. Stewart was aware of Antone's fist bunching at his side, and he was about to preempt this shipless captain's strike when from behind them, Captain Hamilton cleared his throat.

"Don't you two think we have had enough violence aboard the *Tempest Queen* for one night, gentlemen?"

"Mr. Antone was just about to leave, Captain," Stewart said, his eyes steadfastly locked upon Antone's face.

Antone glanced at Mystie. "If this is what you want out of life, a ne'er-do-well deckhand who will never be able to afford anything better than a backwater shack or a ten-foot berth on some steamer, then you are welcome to him." Antone tried to free himself again from Clifton Stewart's grasp and found he was still not able to.

Stewart held him a moment longer, then smiled easily and said, "You have insulted the lady enough for one night. You may go now. Good evening, sir." He released the captain's sleeve.

Barnabas Antone gave Mystie a final long, hard stare, then stormed about and stomped through one of the doorways to the main cabin. When he had gone, Clifton Stewart turned to Captain Hamilton, prepared for the wrath he figured was about to arise from that quarter.

"I must say, Mr. Stewart, I am surprised to find you still

upon my bo—" He stopped in midsentence, for at that moment his eyes happened upon the young lady standing at Stewart's side.

"Mystie? Mystie Waters?"

"Captain Hamilton," she said. "It has been a long time since that night at Natchez-Under-the-Hill."

His view shifted between her and Stewart. "Well, I can't say I am too surprised. But I had no idea you were aboard."

"I boarded with Captain Antone, at New Orleans."

"Of course." He glanced at Stewart, and all at once he seemed to understand. "And that would explain why you are here as well."

Stewart was not of a mind to tell the whole story—at least not right now, but he felt the captain deserved a brief explanation. "I thought Mystie had died in the explosion of the *Guiding Star,* Captain. That is why I . . . I made easy with the whiskey, sir."

Mystie gave his arm an encouraging squeeze.

"Later, when you put me off the boat, I learned that Mystie had survived the disaster. Zachary told me. He came and found me only moments before the *Tempest Queen* pulled away from the landing."

"Hmm." Hamilton pulled thoughtfully at his short, white beard. "Well, once again, you have served this boat admirably. I knew it was uncharacteristic for you to shirk your duties, and I didn't understand the reasons then, but I think I understand them now."

The steam whistle called to the shore, and the crew down on the pier began scurrying back aboard. Hamilton glanced up at the ceiling, as if he could see through wood, and said, "We are about to put back into the stream. I have a few things to tend to up in the pilothouse. Mr. Stewart, if you are free in the morning, I'd like to talk to you up in my cabin."

"I'll be there, sir."

"Good. And now, go find Dr. Reuben and have him see to that hand."

Stewart glanced at his right palm. In all the excitement, he had almost forgotten it, but now a reminder of the wound came back in sharp, stabbing pains, and his fist no longer wanted to close. "It is not serious."

"Have it tended to, just the same." Hamilton tipped his hat to Mystie. "It is indeed a pleasure to see you again, Miss Waters. Are you to stay with us to Cairo?"

She glanced at Stewart and her grip tightened upon his arm. "Yes, Captain, I think I will remain aboard."

The captain smiled. "Good. I look forward to catching up on what you have been up to." There was something cryptic in Captain Hamilton's tone that Stewart didn't understand, but Mystie obviously did.

The captain departed, taking the nearest ladder up to the hurricane deck, and disappeared through the hatch there.

Stewart said to Mystie, "Zachary told me you were going to leave the boat at Plaquemine. What changed your mind?"

"I don't know. I was confused then, but right now I feel as if everything is about to work itself out." She shivered suddenly.

"You are chilled. Let me take you inside."

Mystie nodded.

They started along the promenade as the *Tempest Queen*'s steam whistle sounded its parting blast and her huge paddle wheels resumed their revolutions, backing the big packet from the pier. The great bronze bell upon her hurricane deck pealed into the night, its sonorous notes drifting far out over the black water, summoning the leadsmen to their job, and from somewhere overhead the watchman shouted instructions.

"Starboard lead there! Larboard lead to your place!"

In a moment, the deep Negro voices sang out the depth of

the river, their calls relayed by the word-passers to the pilot-house.

"Quarter less . . . Mark twain! Quarter twain! Half twain . . ."

Everything about the night seemed right; the familiar sights and sounds of a riverboat, the chuffing escape pipes and splashing wheels, the pilot pulling his bell cords above, and the soft, tinkling response from the engine room far below. The smell of oil and steam, the bustle of sweating, singing firemen, the passengers in their gay traveling clothes—it was perfect. But what was most perfect about the evening was that once again, Mystie was at his side. Stewart vowed he would never again leave her, and if the South drove them out because of the tinge of Negro blood in her veins, then he would, as her father had before him, move to the North.

If only Zachary could be here now.

He put that sad thought out of his head. Zachary *was* there. He would always be there so long as he remained in Clifton's memory.

"Come, let's find Dr. Reuben," Mystie said, heading him toward the door.

Wat I say, Mr. Cliff. Dat lady is plum fetched wid yo'.

"Huh?" Stewart stopped abruptly and looked around.

"What is it, Clifton?" Mystie asked.

"Oh, nothing, I reckon. It is just that I thought I heard something."

"What?"

"I'm not sure, but it is gone now."

"You're tired, Clifton, that's all. Come, let's get that hand taken care of." She took him inside.

CHAPTER TWENTY-THREE

With the morning mist lifting from the Mississippi River, the *Tempest Queen* steamed into her berth at Baton Rouge and was made fast. Captain Hamilton sent a boy into town to fetch the sheriff, and then took a turn around his boat, greeting the passengers who were making an early departure. He strolled down to the stateroom where Genevieve St. James was being kept.

"How is the prisoner?"

"We haven't heard a peep from the lady all night," one of the guards said. Hamilton could imagine Gen smoldering in her anger, and he grinned at the thought. He was vaguely embarrassed that he had been so easily taken in by her charms, but then everyone had—everyone, that is, but Allan Pinkerton.

Hamilton had no sooner thought of the detective when Pinkerton turned a corner, singing a tune as he came up the promenade, smiling.

> *He was a braw gallant*
> *And he play'd at the glove*
> *And the bonny Earl o Murry*
> *He was the Queen's love.*

"Aye! Captain Hamilton. 'Tis a bonny morning."

"It will do, Mr. Pinkerton. The fog is cold. It makes my bones ache."

"But we have got the lass under lock and key and the senator is safe in his bed. And that makes up for all the achy-cold, does it not?"

"Hmm. There is something to be said for that. Tell me, Mr. Pinkerton, what put you on to the lady in the first place?"

Pinkerton thought a moment, his lips puckered and a forefinger pressed against them. "Well, I have a client who happens to be in the Senate o' the United States. A man who, out of respect for his wishes, must remain anonymous. He had information, though, that Mr. St. James was up to no good, and that he feared an attempt on Senator Douglas's life."

"But why? What could assassinating Senator Douglas have accomplished?"

"I think I have that figured out. You see, our Mr. St. James was a-talking big to some o' his friends at the separatist rally in Charleston. There had been some drink and jolly-making that evening, and he was overheard bragging that he was buying up herds of cows in the wilds o' Texas, and that once the South cut a run from the rest o' the country, there would be a war on, for sure. Well, if that happened, his cows would suddenly become valuable merchandise to a new country whose main output is cotton and sugarcane. A man canna' eat cotton, and not much cane, either. Ah, but beef, now there would be a commodity that would fetch a handsome price by a new nation fighting a war for independence."

"I still don't see how Douglas figures into it."

"Well, it is plain enough, you see. Mr. Douglas is Mr. Lincoln's closest competition. They are running neck to neck, and no man can call which way the voting will go. Mr. Lincoln is a stubborn man, but Mr. Douglas is known for his peace-making ways, and conciliatory views on slavery. If he were to be elected, why, that might postpone secession for years, maybe forever. In that case, Mr. St James's cattle would be worth no more than he paid for them.

"On the other hand, if Douglas were taken out of the race, Lincoln would win handily. Already, South Carolina has declared that she will secede if that was to happen. And once South Carolina bolts, it would be only a matter of weeks or months before the rest of the Southern states follow.

"Mr. Robert St. James was merely hedging his bets, ye see. He was going to guarantee the start of a war just so his investments would quadruple!"

"Hmm. Most intriguing, indeed, and most brutal. To put a nation at war, to slaughter thousands of her fine sons—all in the name of money."

"Aye. But I suspect those motives are behind every war, if you peer deep enough into the matter." Pinkerton looked past Hamilton and down at the wharf below, where steve-dores and deckhands were already moving freight. "Ah, there comes the constable now, methinks."

Hamilton glanced down as Thad Johnson came along the lane past stacks of crates, hogsheads of sugar, and the last of the season's baled cotton. He looked sleepy, as if the boy that Hamilton had sent into town had roused him from bed.

"Let's get the lady down there," Hamilton said, motioning to the men guarding the door to unlock it.

Genevieve St. James stepped out in the morning light with a defiant pout upon her face, and it appeared as if she had not slept much that night.

"This is a waste of time," she said. "I shall be free in two days."

"Perhaps," Hamilton said, taking her by the arm and starting her along the promenade, "But since you are aboard my boat, you will be turned over to the authorities."

Down the river, the *Natchez,* with her red chimneys billowing clouds of sooty smoke, suddenly appeared through the thinning mist. Hamilton paused a moment as Captain Leathers's fine vessel swung into full view. A thin smile spread across Hamilton's stern face.

Below, on the main deck and the wharf, the crew threw up a cheer and waved their caps at the approaching boat.

Gen was momentarily confused. "But when did you ever catch up with her, and how could you pass her by?"

"We passed her around three this morning, Mrs. St. James. One thing all steamers have in common is, they all have to stop to take on wood. The *Natchez* is a dandy boat, Mrs. St. James, but she is no match for the *Tempest Queen*."

"Is any boat upon this grand old river a match for your *Tempest Queen,* Captain Hamilton? I dunna think so," Pinkerton added.

Hamilton took Gen down to the main deck, picking up Governor Moore and James Sheridan along the way.

They arrived at the landing stage a moment before Captain Barnabas Antone came across the deck.

"Leaving us, Captain?" Hamilton asked.

Barnabas hesitated, a foot upon the plank. "Yes, I . . . I have some business to tend to in Baton Rouge. I will catch another boat later."

Antone hurried down the landing stage, shoving past Thad Johnson, who at that moment was coming up it. Thad turned aside to let the young captain stomp off, and then the sheriff stepped aboard.

"Captain Hamilton, good to see you again." He smiled at Gen, and shook the governor's hand as if they had been long-lost friends. "The boy said you had some trouble aboard. Something that requires my attention?" Thad raised a questioning eyebrow and twisted the end of his walrus mustache. He had been in such a hurry that he had forgotten his hat, and small beads of perspiration pricked his bald pate. "Since when does river business beyond parish limits involve me?"

The governor said, "In this matter, I have taken it upon myself to intervene. This woman has made an attempt upon Senator Douglas's life, and you will hold her in your jail until a jury can decide her fate."

Thad peered at Gen, clearly skeptical that such a lovely woman could be the recipient of such a serious charge.

"She tried to kill Senator Douglas? The Senator Douglas who is runnin' for president?"

"The very one," Sheridan said. "I am Senator Douglas's secretary, and I will sign whatever papers are necessary to press charges."

"Well . . . " he hesitated, "well, all right then, I reckon." He glanced at Moore. "If that's what you want me to do, Governor, let's take her down to the jail."

"You're making a big mistake," Gen said. "My husband knows people. If you value your job . . ."

"Just get moving," the governor said.

Gen shot him a poisonous look. "You will all pay for this!"

Thad started her onto the gangplank. She mounted it with an angry stomp and made for the wharf. On the opposite end of the plank, a dapper gentleman beneath a tall beaver hat and wearing a fawn frock coat over a checked vest, girdled about by a heavy gold chain, had just started aboard. The two met in the middle, and both came immediately to a halt, staring at each other.

"You!" Gen said. The fiery blush of her cheeks drained to white.

The man was momentarily shocked, but he recovered immediately and leaned casually upon a polished walking cane with a silver horse head grip. "Well, well, if it isn't Miss Genevieve de Winter." He grinned and glanced at the sheriff. "What has she been up to this time, hm? Er, perhaps an extra deuce up her sleeve?"

Thad Johnson said, "Oh, it is you, Mr. McKay. You know this woman?"

"Indeed. We met a good while ago, upon a wharf boat at Napoleon." McKay smiled at Gen.

Genevieve said, "I thought you were dead!"

"No, no." He rubbed his arm and said, "But I still carry a most unattractive scar where your henchman's bullet hit me."

"Dammit," she hissed. "Can nothing go right? Damn you all!" She pushed past him, onto the wharf, with Thad Johnson, the governor, and James Sheridan crushed in close about her.

A thin smile moved across Dexter McKay's face as he stepped aboard the *Tempest Queen*. He removed a cigar from a silver case and lit it with a match from a silver match safe, then sending a ribbon of smoke skyward, to be swept along in the brisk morning breeze, he said, "Good morning, Captain Hamilton."

"You are in fine spirits," Hamilton said, but the black crescents under the gambler's eyes and the lines of strain upon his face did not escape him. McKay had obviously not slept in days, and probably had eaten little during that time.

His properly trimmed beard appeared a bit ragged, and the hair that protruded beneath the tall hat was tangled. "No doubt your long awaited card game with the famous Devol went well?"

"The man is a stunning cardsman. I have never met any better. In fact, I would venture to say that George Devol is the best there is upon the river."

"The best?" Hamilton frowned and lifted an eyebrow. "Then I take it you . . . lost?"

"Lost?" McKay was wounded. "Captain, really. I suppose I ought to rephrase that. Devol is certainly the *second*-best cardsman upon the river." McKay reached into his coat pocket and came out holding a shiny, gold Jürgensen watch with a massive gold chain, two feet long, dangling a gold ace-of-diamonds playing card charm from it, set with a two-carat diamond in the center. "I did allow the poor chap to retain his shirt." McKay grinned.

Hamilton shook his head. "Mr. McKay, I apologize for any doubt I may have cast. Welcome back aboard."

"Thank you, Captain."

Hamilton stretched out a hand, but before he knew what the gambler was doing, McKay had dropped the heavy watch into it.

"Here, here, what is this?"

McKay shrugged nonchalantly. "That is my room and board upon the *Tempest Queen* for the next month."

"But this must be worth a fortune."

"A fortune? No, I don't think so. Two or three thousand dollars is all—that is, if you could find a buyer."

"No, really, I cannot possibly take it."

"Certainly you can. I already have one." He dangled his own heavy gold Jürgensen by its gold chain. "Besides, if you don't take it, it will find its way back onto the table sooner or later, and frankly, Captain Hamilton, that watch would look much more handsome upon your vest than across the belly of some two-bit gambler who happened— by pure luck, of course—to have had a better string of cards in his hand than I."

Hamilton hesitated. "Well, if you insist."

"I insist! Retire that silver piece you carry and put a real watch in your pocket."

Still unsure, Hamilton opened the lid, gazed at the gold and enameled face, then shut it and placed the watch inside the blue pocket of his jacket. "Thank you, Mr. McKay."

Hamilton remembered his manners and introduced the detective, Allan Pinkerton. The two men shook hands and Pinkerton said, "Well, my work is finished here, and thank goodness for that, too."

"Will you be disembarking here, in Baton Rouge?" Hamilton asked.

"Nay, nay. There is the matter of my fee, which I must now collect from my client. I will be with you as far as Vicksburg, Captain Hamilton." Pinkerton doffed his shabby hat to the two men and left. As he strolled along the deck, the words of a song drifted back to them:

> Will ye gang to the Hielands, Leezie Lindsay,
> Will ye gang to the Hielands wi me?
> Will ye gang to the Hielands, Leezie Lindsay,
> My bride and my darling to be?

Then he turned a corner and was gone.

"So, that is the famous detective."

"An odd sort, but a gentleman, nonetheless."

Dexter McKay hitched a thumb over his shoulder at the wharf. "Now, tell me about her. What did Genevieve de Winter do aboard the *Tempest Queen* to earn her such a

rand send-off? If I am not mistaken, that was Governor
Moore with her."

"It was, and it is a long story, Mr. McKay. I will tell you
ll about it later, but right now, I have an appointment I must
eep."

"Very well. I will just retire to my room and freshen up
efore breakfast," Dexter McKay said, and with his walking
tick tapping the deck in time to his step, he made his way
round to the wide stairway and up it to the promenade
where his stateroom was located.

Hamilton had only just arrived in his cabin when the
nock came at his door. He pulled it open and said, "Come
n, Mr. Stewart," and as the young man stepped through,
Hamilton got a glimpse of Mystie Waters waiting on the
eck near the bronze bell, beyond the porch.

"You wished to see me, sir," Stewart said.

Hamilton heard hesitation in Stewart's voice. "Sit down,"
he captain said, indicating the only chair in his quarters
ther than the one by the deck, into which the Captain
ettled with a puff.

"You all right, Captain?"

Hamilton smiled. "I am splendid. It is just that at my age,
verything becomes a chore . . . even sitting down." He
onsidered Clifton Stewart a moment as he pulled upon his
lose-cropped beard. "So, tell me, what are your plans?"

"Plans, sir?"

"Yes, plans. It is not exactly hidden knowledge that your
whole reason for remaining aboard the *Tempest Queen* was
o find Mystie again. Now that you have achieved that goal,
 should think you will be returning to your father's plantation
nd reconciling your differences with your father."

"I do not think that is possible. As you know, Captain,

Mystie is a mulatto. He would never agree to have her in hi
home as anything other than one of his slaves."

"Hmm. Of course, you knew this all along."

"I did, sir. But it makes no difference to me. I love
Mystie."

"Perhaps, but if word of her heritage should become
common knowledge, you will be run out of the South. You
would be lucky to escape tar and feathering. Of course, with
her light complexion, the truth might never come out."

"It is not something I would hide, sir," Stewart said with the
resolve that was so characteristic of the man. "I love Mystie
and would be proud to call her my wife." The dogged
determination that had so impressed Hamilton once he had
gotten to know the young man was back.

"No, I suspect you would not. And that brings me back to
my original question. What are your plans?"

"I haven't any. I was sort of hoping I might have my job
back, sir. I cannot return home, and indeed, even if I could
I would not."

Hamilton nodded his head as if he understood. "You
could not love your wife on the one hand, and see her people
enslaved."

"Mystie's father had to purchase her and her mother from
his father and take them to Illinois. If moving to the North
is what I must do, then I shall."

"And if it should come to that, what are you going to do
to support yourself?"

"Again, I do not know. I hope it will not come to that, sir."

"Perhaps it won't," Hamilton said thoughtfully. "Of
course, I will give you your position back, and you are
welcome to work aboard the *Tempest Queen* so long as I am
master of her."

Stewart came forward in his chair. "So long as you are
master? It sounds as though that might not be for long."

"In truth, I am planning to put her on the block shortly."

"You have spoken of this before. You cannot seriously be thinking of selling the *Tempest Queen*, Captain Hamilton. She is a part of you."

"Oh, but it is true. I have been considering this for well over a year. The time has come to turn her over to a younger man, I'm afraid."

"Then you do not yet have a buyer?"

"No, not yet."

Stewart leaned back in the chair, and his expression told Hamilton that the news had caught him off guard. "To be perfectly candid with you, Mr. Stewart, I think you would make a splendid boat master. I would sell the *Tempest Queen* to you."

"Me!" Stewart stammered. "But I have no money."

"True, but you have a name that is respected in these parts. Any banker would loan you the money—perhaps even your father would."

"My father?"

"You have not spoken with him since your disagreement. Perhaps the time has come to try and patch the breach between you two." Hamilton nodded at the closed door. "Beyond this stands your future wife, if I have not missed my guess. It would be to your benefit if you could reconcile with your family—yours and hers."

"I . . . I don't know. I shall have to give this all some careful thought, Captain."

"Of course. I do not intend to do anything until we come back down to Baton Rouge. Think about it."

"Well, well, who is this I see?" Dexter McKay paused by the bell with his walking stick over his shoulder. "If it isn't Mystie Waters!"

She looked at him with wide, black eyes. Her jet hair was

tied up in a bun and hidden under the bonnet she wore. For a second her face registered confusion, then recognition struck a spark in her eyes. "It is Mr. McKay!"

Dexter threw back his head and laughed. "And a more surprised look I have not had the pleasure of seeing since the constable hauled Genevieve de Winter off this boat. No doubt, Mr. Stewart is not far off."

"Clifton is in with the captain." Mystie pointed at the closed door of Hamilton's cabin.

"Well, then I shall wait here with you until the captain is free. You look well, Mystie."

"I feel perfect," she replied, smiling. "Are you . . . working here now?"

"Work! My dear lady, please. I have had a hard three days at the gaming table. None of this disturbing talk of work, now."

She laughed. They both heard the door open. Clifton Stewart came down the steps and across to them.

"Mr. McKay!" Stewart pumped Dexter's hand. "I see you two have met again."

"Yes, we have," McKay said. "And according to the talk I have been hearing, I missed a dandy of a trip."

"Not one that I would care to repeat," Stewart said, "Except it ended up all right. I found Mystie."

"We will have to talk later," McKay said, and glanced at Mystie. "But for now, I will leave you two, for I see by the anxious look upon Mr. Stewart's face that he has something urgent to say."

"Good-bye, Mr. McKay," Mystie said.

McKay walked off, and before he had gone three paces, he heard Mystie say, "Oh, look Clifton. Isn't that a *Regulus calendula?*"

"Why, it certainly is," Stewart answered, and there was

no hiding the ring of excitement in his voice. "Well, that is certainly a sign that winter is here."

"I shall have to start my winter checklist . . ."

McKay grinned as he stepped up to the porch and rapped upon Captain Hamilton's door with the grip of his stick.

"Come in."

McKay stepped inside. "I see that Mr. Stewart and Miss Waters are back together."

"Yes, and both have stars in their eyes."

"And birds on their brains."

Hamilton laughed.

McKay said, "The word is all over the boat. Senator Douglas is aboard, huh? And Genevieve nearly did him in."

"Yes, yes, and the sad thing of it is, she managed to kill Zachary in the act."

McKay shook his head. "What is this country coming to?"

Hamilton glanced up sharply. "War! Mark my words, Mr. McKay, this country is coming to war. I feel it in the air like the electricity before a thunderstorm. The land resonates with the looming clash. It cannot be far off. What just happened aboard the *Tempest Queen* was only a vignette of the tension ripping this country apart."

McKay nodded his head, for there was no denying the signs. He looked out the window, past the porch, to the river beyond. "If war comes, it will split this country in half."

At his back, Hamilton said, "And when it does, you know where it will crack, don't you?"

McKay looked back at him.

"It is going to crack right down the center—right down this very river, and you and me, Mr. McKay, you and me and every other poor soul on the Mississippi are going to end up in the middle of it."

McKay saw the intense zeal that was upon Hamilton's

face, and he knew the old captain was right. He looked back out the window at the river. The Mississippi would divide the land, and her waters would run red with the blood of young men—men like Clifton Stewart and himself. It was not a pleasant thought, and Dexter McKay did not enjoy dwelling on unpleasant thoughts. He hitched his cane under his arm. Beyond the window, he watched Stewart and Mystie, hand in hand, walk away, out of his view.

"I hope you are wrong, Captain Hamilton."

Hamilton stood and snatched his hat from the coat tree. "I do, too, but I think all honesty would compel a prudent man to prepare for war."

McKay studied the flowing river beyond the *Tempest Queen*'s hog chains, cables, and spars. It was a gratifying view. He imagined the river ablaze with the weapons of destruction, her waters bearing the drab gunboats of war instead of the gaily painted vessels of commerce. It was a most disturbing thought, but Hamilton was right. He felt the rising tension as well.

"Have you had breakfast Mr. McKay?"

"Not yet."

"Well, I am hungry." Hamilton pulled the door open. "Are you coming?"

McKay drew in a breath and the vision of powerful men-of-war bounding across the water with their cannons booming melted away. Perhaps the country would find a way to avoid it all, but somehow, McKay didn't think so.

The thought depressed him as he and Hamilton went down to the main cabin to breakfast and to the beginning of another day.